Nocturne
Wayman's Sky

C000165603

Andrew Dutton

LEAF BY LEAF

Published by Leaf by Leaf
an imprint of Cinnamon Press
Meirion House
Tanygrisiau
Blaenau Ffestiniog
Gwynedd, LL41 3SU
www.cinnamonpress.com

British Library Cataloguing in Publication Data. A CIP record for this book can be obtained from the British Library.

Desgined and typeset in Garamond by Cinnamon Press. Cover design by Adam Craig © Adam Craig.

Cinnamon Press is represented by Inpress and by the Books Council of Wales.

To my parents, for their love and support.

Dad, we wish you were here to share this.

Nocturne

Wayman's Sky

The Fall Of Evening

The Fall of Evening

'Faced with the stars, we are but dull-eyed worms that can hardly see at all.'

Who said that, eh? Eh? Eh???

Fizzmonger

'I don't *mind* the Moon,' importantly mused Wayman, 'but I tend to disregard it. It's mined-out; it's of no interest to me. Moonlight may be balm for lovers but it drowns out the *real* sky. When the Moon is full, the lovers can have it all to themselves; that's when I rest my eyes and get a full night's sleep. The stars, now, they're not for lovers. Lovers are too selfish; their vision is too limited, too narrow. They can have the Moon if they want, I suppose, but they should leave the good stars alone.'

Evelyn Lawton

'Clear eyes and clear skies.'

Those were the only gifts he said he wanted from life. He loved the fall of the evening; he would will the sun downwards, waiting-out its reluctance to let go, he would watch the line sketched across the sky, the divide between the dying light and the gaining evening. He would wait patiently, faithfully, as the stars became visible, flittering and struggling to take hold. He would savour the coming darkness and glory in the failing of the light.

Fizzmonger

I read somewhere that people fear the dark because they have had it dinned in them that darkness is the blanket of evil. Wayman was different: it was a blanket all right, but a comfort-blanket in which he loved to be wrapped. Most people check weather forecasts to find the sun and dodge the rain, but Wayman didn't much care for daytime weather; what he craved was a starry sky from sunset to dawn.

This is the nocturne, the nightlife of Alfred Wayman; there he was, every night, immune to cold, with the wonder-filled expression of the looker-up. You could have called that expression religious awe, but for the fact that he would have filleted you for saying it. With the stars, he said, he lived with beauty—and that made him far more an artist than a preacher. The preacher's concept of heaven, of the heavens, he said, was pure folly.

Old Wash-Hands

If he were of a religious bent, he would have been of the sort that would sweep aside all robed, cassocked middlemen and demand a direct line to what lies above. And on his arrival at the golden throne, he would be the one who cried 'move over, off my chair, there!'

Sabina Faslane

He could tell you the names of the stars, where to find the planets in any night's sky, the position, the rise and set of any object. He had the heavens mapped behind his eyes. To be shut away without sight of sky—that would have been the worst punishment for him, had he ever stirred himself sufficiently to commit a crime.

His measure of wasted time was to count up—through cloudy nights, illness, pressing business of various sorts and Moon-interference—the number of times he had failed to look aloft.

10

Fizzmonger

He was all height and bulk and unfinished edges; simply all-over awkward. The light never fell on him in any way that was flattering or helpful to the plier of the brush. Light didn't suit him, no.

Dressed habitually in a rough tweed jacket, an always open-collared check shirt and rather worn, stained trousers, Wayman always looked like the archetypal teacher, which is precisely right, filling his daylight hours with work and holding out for nightfall. Did he never sleep, I once asked him; how did he cope? 'I save my dreaming for the daytime,' was his only reply. He spun me a tale of being unable to remember what he had said in class, implying that he subjected his pupils to an unending stream of somnambulist unconsciousness, yet his students always seemed to do just as well as those of the teachers whose eyes saw a room filled with people, rather than whatever sleep-starved distortions appeared to Wayman.

In spite of his size, he drove a Mini; he made for a ludicrous sight in the driving seat, knees practically jammed against the roof, his body spread across two seats, looking like a man-in-a-can, the human equivalent of a ship in a bottle, the question forever being: however did he get *in* there?

Sabina Faslane

He once announced, with orotund self-mockery, 'My only mistress is Urania!' I begged him not to let anyone else overhear that one. What they would have made of it is too easy to guess.

There were rumours about him, of course there were. A nasty one persisted over years and was never choked off by disproof or scuttled by its own rank implausibility. Wayman was in any case the most sexless creature you could meet; as far as I could see he just was not interested. He was otherworldly.

Even his age was a puzzle, outside of generalised guesswork; he had that kind of face, the born-middle-aged kind. Those possessed of imagination could reverse-engineer his lined and pitted features, take them backwards through how-many-years of assumed time, stripping away the process of growing and coarsening, relieving that face of lines and lumps, accumulated ballast and scarring, to find their way to a small, lumpen child of predominantly saturnine countenance and intelligent but troubled eyes, but even those imagineers could not truly say how many years had been shed in the process, as the ever-old are always ageless in their way. Nor could anything but the superficiality of how he once may have looked be guessed; there could be no prizes or acclaim for divining that this face, from an early age, looked up to the stars and showed all the reverence of which it was capable, so much was easy. Everything else about him remained unknown: his family, background, upbringing, history so far and life to come, the shocks and kicks that would shape him—all this remained as obscure and unknowable as if the man had lived thousands of years ago and all that endured was disconnected bones, fragments and theories. Nobody tries to play remember-when with Wayman; they simply meet with a blank wall. If you want to give him a past then you can infer one all you like with the bare materials available, but you will be indulging in blind guesswork, dressing his life with your own insupportable assumptions.

Sabina Faslane

His pronunciations of some of the names of the planets and constellations were peculiar, funny: 'Joobiter,' 'Sat-earn,' 'The Orryon.' One of his favourite constellations was 'Boots.' I noticed that he never even attempted 'Ophiuchus.' I shouldn't snigger. It was, as nearly as he could come to such an alien state, rather cute.

Old Wash-Hands

I am ever suspicious of people who make idols, whether graven images or invisible, but fixed and dangerous ideas. Oh I had my eye on Mr Wayman from the very beginning. I can smell fanaticism and apostasy on a man.

Evelyn Lawton

Nobody knew anything about him, it was as if he had no past, none whatsoever. He never spoke of it. The only past that Alfred had was what we had given him, I mean the time that he spent with Bernard and me, our shared moments. He came to us as an unknown and remained an unknown to many; in many ways, even to us.

When you have no past, people quickly club together and knit one for you, all charitably gratis; it may not fit and you may not be so thankful, but that's all you're getting, and if you have nothing better to offer then that's what you're going to be stuck with.

That's what happened to Alfred: a wild tangle of conflicting tales sprang up about him, some of which may have contained and concealed a little of the truth but likelier did not: the question is, was the real man ever portrayed in any way? Did he care whether he was or not? His concealment of his past led to the tossed-off speculation that he must have something to hide, which then became a tourist, a real trekker of a rumour and subsequently brought to rest, parking and locking itself into a state of accepted, solid 'fact.' People just don't like it when there's no story—in the way nature supposedly abhors a vacuum.

We do this all the time, chattering, gossiping, tacking dubious and downright false stories where they don't belong, wantonly stapling dis-mis-information on to people's files, so to speak. It's just that with Alfred there was such a large hole to fill, a challenge, a real job of work.

Some conceal their names, first and middle names usually, out of an embarrassment that occasionally represents mere good taste. To do that is hard enough, but to cover up a whole past, a life, that takes a mighty effort. Alfred must have been in secret, silent, perpetual fear of turning a corner and colliding with some former acquaintance possessed of a long memory and no tact, someone overflowing with easy, loose-lipped recall.

Jilly Holdenbridge
I don't think I ever met anyone more frightening. Intense. I remember one lesson when he decided to debunk the notion that the Romans came over here to "civilise" us all. To do this, he seized hold of Glyn Capstone, this harmless, colourless boy who was doing his best to avoid being seen by the teacher or any of us, stood him up in front of everyone and declaimed, shaking the boy with each word, 'The Romans didn't come here and say "you-will-be-

14

civilised!"—No! They came here and said, "You-will-be-Roman! Or die!".'

'You understand the difference, I take it?' he asked casually, dropping the pale, limp youth back in his seat without even glancing at him again. That lesson took place thirty years ago. I suppose you could at the least say that it went in, and stayed.

Evelyn Lawton
'What qualities go to make a schoolteacher? The wisdom of Solomon, the patience of Job, the character of a saint, the knowledge of a doctor, a midwife and a sea-lawyer. These, combined with skill and determination and the hide of a newspaper reporter, add up to the most difficult and rewarding profession.'

I think we can safely discount the patience; the saintliness too, at least in its traditional sense. The rest is a pretty good fit, although I could name someone who was far better. But then I'm hardly an unbiased witness, I suppose.

Fizzmonger
The power of darkness: it meant something different to Wayman, something very different from the traditional intent. There was not a scrap of evil to it, no fear, not for him. It was a power wholly of the good and if the power of darkness was to be exalted, then so much the better for the welfare of the world. The day, the sun, what did they bring? Toil and sunburn; 'When did anyone ever suffer nightburn then, eh? Eh?'

It was my first proper holiday with my first proper boyfriend and we had booked to go as far from our parents as possible, so far that a missed step would send us tumbling off the sharp edge of the south coast and nobody would hear the splash. We were in a farm cottage, which stood alone and remote at the end of a long, curving, unlit track hemmed in by tall, drowsing trees, which awoke and hissed, *pssst,* in suspicious whispers at the hint of a breeze. We had been out for a meal in the nearest town, a good half-hour walk away, and were still only halfway down that lightless track long after the late summer sun had guttered and failed, the trees closed and began to mutter rather than whisper, and ill-prepared, torchless, we clasped hands even tighter, no longer in that couple-ish way we had been enjoying, but more as lost children playing out a fairy story —the nastier, un-bowdlerised ones. We stuck to the path, straying and panicking into thickets a couple of times and, ominously, blaming one another as our alarm grew.

We turned a sharp curve and to whoosh-breaths of relief saw the ghostly outline of the little cottage in front of us, nestled in the clearing we had last seen in bright sunshine. I heard the cottage keys jingle in his hand, while with the other he was pulling me, *pulling me,* towards safety. I broke from his grip; I stopped in the middle of that clearing. The trees still loomed and blocked out all but the cap of the sky.

'Come on,' he breathed, still sounding tense and urgent.

'No. Look.' my voice was no louder than his, as if I was trying not to scare off some exotic creature I had spotted lurking in the gloom. But it was what I could see in the clearing-above, the cat-black zenith, which had seized my attention. I could see my old friends, the summer stars, losing their place and slipping towards the horizon, but as my eyes adjusted in the growing darkness I could see that there were more stars, even in that hemmed-in patch of sky, than I had seen in my life; they were scattered, spilled, dusted across the unsullied blackness, revealed to me now they were no longer dazzled away by intruding lights. It was about midnight and I made a swift calculation that I had just a few brief, fragile hours to stand and let this sky wheel above me, revealing all this newness, this beauty, this treasure-store, usually hidden within and behind the familiar face of the sky.

'Come *on!*' He tugged at me, hurt me.

'No!' I hurt myself, pulling away.

'C'mon!' This time I dodged him in the dark.

'No: the stars!' I tried to be gentle, not bossy; it was so hard.

Another grab and yank at my arm showed that he had not understood.

'Look! All those stars!'

'Yeah, very good!' He sounded as if he were speaking of a friend's terrible painting and I dug in against another grab. I thought he was annoyed because I was denying him some other pleasures of the dark, I was even willing to grant him some, providing we worked things so that I could have an uninterrupted view of the sky, but there was something wrong, he was becoming angry and his next 'Come *on!*' was filled with a child's fear, his lust overmastered by a still more powerful primal force and lacerated with cold claws.

'Let's go in, please!'

I thought that he was still stuck in the fairy-tale, fleeing the close, conspiring trees, but that was not it, not it at all.

'Well I'm going in alone, do what you want.' He moved away from me and my head turned instinctively upward once more, until I snapped round, shouting, 'No wait, don't turn on the...' but I had guessed his goal too late and blades of light lanced out of the open doorway and windows, turning the clearing into a Halloween show and, worse, destroying my hard-earned night eyes: how I didn't scream, cry and go inside and try to shred his face I do not know. He called me to him again, this time his voice deep and commanding. Ah, his self-confidence was returning, all with the flick of a switch. We didn't last long after that. I could never forgive Mr Afraid-Of-The-Dark.

Fizzmonger

Now, what else did he come out with—how about this —'In ancient times, people put their stories in to the sky, it's how they came to name the constellations. They put their expectations up there, their hopes, all the pettiest and nastiest ones, usually. No wonder people can't see the stars as they truly are: it's too bloody crowded up there.'

Charles Durant Tobol

I think it may be said with perfect assurance that I do not yearn to be his friend. I do not know him, not in the sense that I could sum up his life or scatter anecdotes in the manner of a best man or eulogist. But I know more about him than he would be comfortable with. I know people, I observe them, I paint them; you cannot paint people without knowing them. That's why when Wayman draws and paints, it's only the stars and planets. People? He knows nothing of them. He just teaches their children to look backwards.

One more thing, however: remember the old saying—*only the bad man lives alone?*

Fizzmonger

I can just imagine what he would say had he seen what I did today:

'Technology is turning us into a race of lookers-down, of lookers-inward. The first three people I saw today—and I nearly ran over two of 'em—were walking along paying no heed to anything beyond their inner space, eyes glued on the little oblong of information in their hands. To them there was no sunshine, no daylight, no people, and, apparently, no prospect of imminent death. I bet you any money at least one of 'em was looking up their bloody horoscope and, what's more, it didn't say, '*Look out behind you!*'

Evelyn Lawton

Some people spun him a family background that would—possibly—account for him: full of melodrama, an absentee father, a cold and loveless mother, a locked-room childhood which forced him, making virtue out of necessity, to exalt loneliness for its own sake. Add a broken heart somewhere along the way, perhaps a dusting of other tragedies, something that made a compulsion to be alone beneath the stars explicable, anything to attach a story to him, any story.

Fizzmonger

It was the loneliness, the solitude, the self-exile, that's what I could never understand: without the touch of flesh, all that time, how could he, did he, bear it? Loneliness is corrosive, whether chosen and volunteered or not.

Glyn Capstone

One time, Wayman seemed to me to sum up his entire personal philosophy, working with huge, maniacal strokes of chalk upon the big rolling blackboard:

'IF WE FAIL TO LEARN THE LESSONS OF HISTORY'

...he paused...

'WE WILL FIND OURSELVES IN DETENTION UNTIL HALF-PAST FIVE'

God I was frightened of him—perhaps in awe of him. But there was something about him. He was the first, the only, to really reach me. That it was too late by then wasn't really his fault.

Sabina Faslane

Wayman once said, 'The dullest life can be set ablaze by starlight.'

I think he was talking about his own.

Old Wash-Hands

Galileo went blind after using that famous telescope of his. What if that is the decreed punishment for those who attempt to unseat the occupants of heaven? As people these days would put it, 'I'm just saying.'

Sabina Faslane

Every crank with an obsession fancies themselves a Galileo; persecuted as they try to usher in a new age. Wayman wasn't like that. He just wished people would break away from the old one. To remember Wayman, all you have to do is to watch the sky. But do it *properly*.

Glyn The Pin
Crusty old bastard. I mean, seriously.

The Stars As They Truly Are

Fizzmonger

'Ah!' pronounced Wayman as he swung open the door and we stepped outside, 'Now that *smells* like a night!'

I wondered how the hell he could smell anything; I didn't understand how completely still air could deliver a shocking blow as if from a crystal fist. I dabbed my nose, I felt some dampness around its tip, which I took to be blood. Wayman disregarded my sniffling and strode to his goal, his love, the darkness.

As I had expected Wayman to live perched on a hermit's crag, I was very little surprised to find that his description of living 'at the top of town' turned out to be some hybrid twixt a literalism and an arch joke. He meant that he lived where you could look down on the rest of the town, at the point at which you ran out of town altogether. It was near-exile; almost the perfect spot for one who wished to cultivate and commit to loneliness. Balanced on the top of a steep hill and, at its rear, after a small garden hemmed in by a knee-high dry stone wall, giving out on to flat, featureless grassland with open fields and moorland in the hilly distance, there was more than a touch of the lunatic preacher's wilderness about the vista; it was dark-skies territory of course, Wayman lived at such a height to be near the stars—nothing else. But still he complained of people—of what they brought; their pollution, their spillings, their leftover light. People, he groused, were excruciatingly talented at staining the sky.

I first saw the expanse at the back of his home in a midday light; filtered through a grimy cloud-deck it was flat, light, even and unremarkable, emphasising the colour-drained featurelessness of the interminable grasslands, the steppe that rolled and then finally fell off a cliff or spilled over the horizon, somewhere far away. There was a road across the flatness at a distance, hidden by a fold of land but undeniably there, making its presence felt whenever Wayman wanted pure, uninterrupted dark night. Cars would crawl along it, scraping the sides of the sky with their double-barrelled searchlights, bumping and dipping through the anonymous strip that cut through the emptiness. They sometimes cost Wayman his night-eyes and that got him mad. To him, these intruders and his nearest neighbours conspired to leak light, blasting the dark in any thoughtless way with porch-lights and open curtains, bonfires and barbecues, torchlight waving across the stars, even latterly those silly little light-sticks that sucked the sun's rays and then parcelled them out in irritating, parsimonious quanta throughout the night.

Wayman's house looked unlived-in (yes, I abused his hospitality and sneaked more than a few looks, I searched more than a few corners). The place had a look of neglect and decay such that it was easy to imagine another bad winter would see it shiver, crack, slide and tumble into shards and rubble. I parked on the base-camp slope of the cracked, weed-riddled driveway and struggled upwards, past the neglected garage; through its cracked panes I could see Wayman's infamous Mini, ill-fitting and swallowed by the shadowed space within. The house was much like the garage, held together by not much more than flaking paint and the simple habit of standing. The windows were just swirls of thick muck, fossilised remnants of the last half-hearted attempt to wave a cloth at them. Those windows, the front door too, were hung with lace curtains that had become moth-wings, ready to melt at a touch.

Within, it was plain that this was the lair of a night-creature, an outdoor one too, a dun and dull-white space bereft of shades of colour or any relief from the monotony, little acquainted with light. Yes, there was not much use in there for colour vision. Modernity intruded only in the form of a fridge and washing-machine, both hidden as if they were misunderstood things, looted from another age and concealed in this house of years-gone. Wayman lurked in the back room, which was just as drab but slightly better-kept than any other though still neglected, brown and comfortless, with books-books-books scattered around, some actually on shelves but mainly in wobbly stacks on chairs or on the floor, scattered teetering structures always with the smallest volumes at the bottom and the largest caught in mid-wobble at the top, or face-down on a smothered table, on the mantelpiece, in the grate and even the cold and unused fireplace. Anyone else would have begged to excuse the mess; with Wayman I knew that if I didn't like it, I could take a flying leap and, besides, what was I doing there nosing, eh?

His bed seemed unslept in: a rumour was that he never slept, that he taught during the day, went home and used up the last daylight by reading, to stare at the stars until the thieving dawn came again to take away his happiness.

I searched for anything that would speak of a past, something I could attach to the man and the years that made him; to frame him, forge him. Naturally, I looked for pictures; why would I not? Some hint of his heritage and family, or at least his taste in oils, watercolours or acrylics, concretes or abstracts, but there was nothing. No clues. *I need to know this man*, I told myself, *in order to paint him*. But things had gone far beyond that, even in the earliest days. I drew my observations, of many sorts, from many visits. What happened, developed rather, was strange, unintended; I had meant to study my subject, get to know him, see him in many lights, decide on how to render his face, yet somehow the meetings carried on into, what, some sort of apprenticeship, some attempt to pass on his passion, to persuade me from faces and to draw and paint something more important, eternal? I was not convinced and yet continued to visit, long after the portrait was gathering indifferent dust.

So we spent nights together in that wilderness-garden of his, pondering light, the most ancient of light. I wore a heavy coat, even on 'warm' nights I kept it handy, and tried to protect my feet from the seeping cold—once my feet and hands feel the chill as it leaches in, I am lost—I yearned for the flick of a switch and for instant heat, but was told firmly that such self-indulgence would upset the lens, distort the sky: Wayman said that the air shimmered quite enough without artificial aid, thank you very much— the stargazer must remain perished in order to pursue his little rituals, so it seems.

Sabina Faslane

'Miss, Miss, is it true Miss, that Mr Wayman's got one that's twelve inches?'

Heeheeheeheeheeeeheee!

Alfred had warned me about this sort of thing.

'Sir, sir, are you going to use your telescope tonight?'

'Probably.'

'Will you be looking at Mars?'

25

'Probably.'

'And looking up Uranus?'

'I rather think you will be looking at yours, stuck indefinitely in the detention room, if you try that tired old jape again, boy.'

Heeheeheeheeheeeeheee!

Alfred didn't take kindly to his stars being made a smutty joke.

Fizzmonger

The only thing that looked at all cared-for—not new, just cared-for—was the curious structure that dominated the garden. Brown, boring-looking and wooden, with a small door at one end and strange rails running a short distance from its front and back, it occurred to me that this thing was designed to split in two, for the halves to be pushed back, to reveal what was unlikely to be a collection of forks, rakes and hoes, given the certainty that the garden received little attention apart from the periodic, violent application of a blunt scythe. The other curiosity about this structure was that it sat directly where any sane man would have placed his garden-chairs, table and parasol, but these things, apart from the two unfortunate, ancient plastic chairs upon which we sat out there, had been abolished from the place, ousted by this cumbersome oddity.

'Run-off shed,' explained Wayman, gruffly and too briefly. Had he been any sort of a normal man I could have made a lame joke about it being the place he would 'run off' to when he and his missus had a tiff, but, well… it went unsaid.

'It's in there, my telescope. When you're fit to use it you'll see the stars, the good, proper stars, as they truly are:

no nonsense, no horror-scoping and *no* artist's bloody impressions.'

So that was why this old shed, although seasoned, was clean, neatly patched in places, kept sealed from the weather, varnished and... loved. I suffered a rush of childish wanna-wanna desire; I wanted to see within, I *had* to! It would have been like staring inside Wayman's heart.

'Things to learn first. Telescope later. I may even relent and show you the Moon. Even I admit it looks good through that.'

I would get my treat—but first I had to be good. How had I ever been drawn into this business?

Charles Durant Tobol
If it had been pure, proper misanthropy that motivated the man, I could at least grant him credit for that. But that wasn't it, not it at all. Besides, who says he was alone? That damn painter was always there, even after his job was long-since done; as for that little Missy Fastlane, her car was seen often enough heading in the direction of his eyrie. Some say it was parked outside his house at the onset of twilight and still there when another twilight came. Well, he had to have some way of keeping warm in the dark, did he not?

Sabina Faslane
I envied Alfred's equipment, I wanted to be taken in his shed, I would have liked to spend the night with him... you could keep them coming for ages, for ever. He wouldn't have laughed. Probably best not to.

Heeheeheeheeheeeheee!

He talked, but rarely of anything but the night sky. 'I'm not as day-blind as people say behind my back—yes, I know they call me The Daylight-Dodger. I don't just notice the stars, you know. Take tonight for instance. I notice the trees, even though they are losing shape, melting in the twilight, and soon to blend into one silhouette, but with the light that is left I can see that their limbs have filled out, their skeletal fingers are now dressed fresh with renewed leaves, there are geese in flying, jagged v-shapes overhead honking in triumph, returning heroes all, and there are the bats, silent and flittering, moving so quickly that their flights seem disjointed, discontinuous; they're accelerating particles, disappearing in and out of thin air.'

'Are you quoting from something?'

'If I borrow words, I will always say so. Always credit your sources.'

'So what are you saying?'

'I'm saying that it's not just by the rising of Spica that I know that it's Spring. My eyes are not always closed to the daylight.'

But I could sense his impatience: his enemy was not only rosy-fingered dawn but also crimson-taloned sunset as it hung on, shredding the curtain of the sky.

'Come on Wayman; it always comes to sunset, doesn't it, with you?'

He had the goodness to smile at that; thinly, but remarkably, the gentle jibe seemed to twitch at a nerve, he became a little defensive, as if suddenly challenged to prove that he was a whole man, not just a dweller in night's shades. But still he chafed silently against the persistence of the light.

He claimed to enjoy watching the trees bud and thrive after winter death, the swifts play sky-high games in summer, listening to the owls' cries as twilight came; he told a funny story of one long summer sundown, looking across that endless grassy expanse and seeing a woman walking a dog, trying desperately to control it as it broke from her and chased a bird which flew in curling, turning, wheeling corkscrew flight up and down close to the ground, daring and tempting the dog, which ran in its own furious, grounded curves and turns, forced to mimic the bird's spiral motions, barking furiously as the agile bird teased it, and, orbiting them both, running and lunging to clip a lead on the leaping, bouncing dog, the poor owner, panic and exhaustion showing on her face as she was constantly defeated and outpaced, run dizzy by dog and bird.

The thought of Wayman genial, patient, bathed in evening sun, bird-watching and adoring earthly nature, well, it was ridiculous. He was there to police the sun, to see it off, and that was all. These were all the excuses of a man who was watching, time-filling, waiting for the light to die so that there was only night and stars. In winter, of course, he did not have to stage his vigil; it was dark even before he had drawn the last lesson of the day to an end. It was a surprise he didn't just vanish with the sun and abandon his charges either to quiet study or open riot.

Pink-purple was one particular evening's stubborn sunset, forced down by the weight of Wayman's will for dark and night, but still staining the horizon rosy-bloody, out of spite. Waiting as ever to win the contest, Wayman held forth—as ever.

'We are losing touch with the sky, the stars. People are ill acquainted with the truth of the sky and so they fall prey to twaddle, to nonsense. It's remarkable that the less freedom a person has, the less they can see the stars. They are held back by tiredness from overwork, too drained even to step outside and away from the glare and look up, they are living too squashed-together in light-polluted shanties, they are made to work under artificial lights when the sun is down and they should be free.'

'The stars only live now in sayings; "ill-starred", "star-crossed", "lucky stars", our whole blasted language is infected with it. "The fault is not in our stars…" Why can't they leave the bloody things alone?'

He spoke as if he were the guardian of the whole damn sky.

I learned quickly how to blaspheme in his universe. When I told Wayman that his night sky looked empty and dull to me, *well:* he gave me a deadly, poignant look.

'I thought there would be more stars, brighter, filling the whole sky.'

'Hmph, what, whirling and blazing like Vincent's pinwheels? Typical of a painter.'

I truly thought there would be more of them and that they would burn more fiercely, yes, just like Van Gogh's spiral swirls. But there seemed to be so few; it took a good look once every month on a dark night and you've seen the lot, you're done. The same stars circle round us endlessly, they don't change. I had an idea that we drifted slowly though the heavens and that there was always something new to look at, an ever-changing backdrop to the Moon and the slithering planets, I thought that was what must be of such interest to the madmen squinting through their close-field lenses. But the stars don't change; they are just there, always there. I didn't treasure that; it didn't remotely

30

impress me. But instead of taking against me, he grew kind in his way and undertook to train my light-dazed eyes in the arts of the dark.

Old Wash-Hands

Those black-night vigils, I see them as an act of prostration before a pagan sky-god, an act of abject, fawning apostasy.

Fizzmonger

I continued to offend, however.

'And what about the colours, Wayman? That sky is so *dull.* White-on-black in the main, a little orange, a few puny reds, watery yellows, but mainly white-on-black, white-on-black, what about the *colours?*'

'It's an evolved universe, not your piddling paint-pot! And you can't set up a scaffold and "restore" to your peculiar tastes, it is what it is, astrophysics rules out there, not bloody colour theory!'

Wayman grumbled on, cursing painters and their ignorance, artists and their impressions, but he managed a small concession as his mood returned to relative benignity.

'There's one called the Garnet Star, I'll show you, it's the reddest of all the stars, like a little drop of blood on black velvet. There are beautiful double-stars, deep-red opposing emerald green, yellow offset by purple, *very well yes*, it's mainly oranges, reds, yellows, whites, but there are blues, greens, violets… you will see more clearly when you're fit to use the telescope.'

Charles Durant Tobol

Night is the enemy of colour and so it is the enemy of art. By the principle of my enemy's enemy, I should therefore ally with Night. But it already has an ally, a worshipper, who excludes that possibility. My enemy's enemy is not my friend.

Fizzmonger

What we had in common, that old stargazer and I, was light. He was concerned with its gathering (and the exclusion of certain undesirable sorts), I with its interpretation. We pursue a curious relationship with light. We can be its makers but are not its masters, and we never will be—the reverse, rather. If we do its bidding it will be good to us, but if we attempt to chase it, to outdo it, it will outpace us with silent contempt and make our efforts look foolish. If ever we manage to gain on it, to match its velocity point-to-point, it will punish us by robbing us of time, of causality; it will make everything we know turn in upon itself, collapse. Light is radiation and radiation kills, is that not so? Light cages us, contains us and dominates us. My peculiar involvement with light is not a violation of the rules, but could come close to offending. I have sought to catch it, trap it, freeze it, represent it and imply its passage in a still frame. I have attempted to paint its portrait. It is an integral part of every face I have painted (but of course) and it has been the heart-and-soul subject of every piece of work I have ever shaped.

Charles Durant Tobol

Wayman was, at least to some extent, an art-hater. Not that it compensated for his faults. He once railed to me (in what was, almost, an admission of owning, of being owned by, a personal past, for it was surely of his own experiences he spoke) against 'artists' impressions' of the stars and planets in books and the media, the overheated imaginings that portrayed ancient cities on the Moon, or burning Venus awash with pretty blue oceans and inviting, cooling forests, alien spacecraft saucering across our sky and thumbing their noses at Einstein, and, worst of all for Wayman, vistas of alluring darkness stuffed and studded with parti-coloured, brilliant, almost reachable waterfalls of stars that were so inimical to the truth, the dullness, of his monochromatic nights.

Fizzmonger

He may not really have been a daylight-dodger, but he was certainly a Moon-dodger. He knew her movements as intimately as anything that swam aloft, but he would respond with tactics of avoidance, minimal exposure to her dazzle.

I sat in that garden again on one of those many nights, clutching a very meagre drink and trying hard like a good student to learn the star-patterns, but my eyes kept being drawn away to the Western horizon, a neck-crick from where Wayman was pointing and lecturing; the crescent, earth-lit Moon was settling to the horizon like a coin rolling into a slot and I felt it drawing me, pulling me across the emptiness, to merge with its fading light.

'You're falling for it; the seductress,' snapped Wayman sharply and without sympathy; the teacher had spied the pupil whose attention was wandering. I was to learn more of his peculiar disdain for the Moon.

'That intruding attention-seeker! Miss Look-At-Me, drowning out all but the brightest stars when she is at full strength and an irritant when waxing or waning. It's the first and last thing most people will ever look at should they bother to raise their eyes aloft. The crescent Moon is pretty and happily not long-lived, it sinks away and the fools coo as they would cute-cute at a baby, pretty-pretty, ooooh. And they pay attention to nothing else. The Moon is a light-polluter, a blessed vandal!'

The Moon had eased its curved back into a bath of dun clouds; its glow was stifled for a short time, but then reborn, transforming that smothering mass into a diaphanous veil, shot with imperial purple and brilliant gold. It reminded me of Anna Keyes, fruitily nude but for her silk scarf around her willowy body, tempting me one night from work, tempting with blood-rushing success...

'You're falling for it again.' Wayman's cracked, dissatisfied voice called me from a warm bed, warm skin to touch, back to the cold and the growing dark. The clouds rallied and thickened and claimed the sinking Moon and Wayman was happy that one enemy was vanquished, but he kept a cautious eye on the horizon, watching for the advance of another.

'Do you know the collective name for clouds?'

I didn't. It was a teacher's question anyway, twisted cousin of the rhetorical.

'An annoyance. No; a blight.'

Sabina Faslane

'Are they still there, Miss?'

'Still there? What?'

'Still up there; in a line. Can you still see 'em?'

'Good gracious, that was *ages* ago. Weeks. Jupiter and Saturn may still be where they were—relatively—and Mars too, *sort of...* but Venus isn't visible any more, it sank behind the Sun a while back, and as for Mercury, it's well-named, it moves quickly, it broke the line first and fastest of all. And incidentally, you'll notice that the world didn't end.'

The girl simply shrugged. The planets weren't lined up anymore and the stupid world hadn't ended; I couldn't help the dig, they'd got a day off out of it and she wasn't interested any longer.

Given that they lived under it day and night, it was odd to me how people never understood the workings of the sky. Some thought that we were on an endless rocket-ride combined with a carousel, the stars constantly refreshing in an impatient whirl that almost left contrails through its dizzying speed, nothing ever the same from night to night; others assumed that the stars were locked, changeless, dead, or crawling sclerotically across a reluctant, resistant night. None had as much as asked about it, never mind looked for themselves, unbidden. I yearned to put her right, to put them *all* right, to talk about the sky, the true sky, the stars as they are. But... there was a curriculum, a job to do. I lured the child and the others back to History, as far as they were ever willing to come.

That had always been my problem, assuming that people should know what I took for granted. I had recognised this at an early age: I said recognised, not overcome.

Fizzmonger
There still fizzed within me some of that boy-child excitement as Wayman, ponderous and purposeful, unbolted and slid open that curious old shed of his and pushed its square-coconut halves back to the stops of their short rails. I was going to see the telescope, the famous telescope; I was to be brought closer to the heavens! But excitement was swallowed by surprise, the anticlimax of

disappointed expectations. Telescopes, I thought, were meant to be slender, elegant, simple; you look in one end and the far-travelled light meets your eyes as it comes in from the other. I had expected to see a larger version of the plastic toys I'd played with as a kid or the pay-slot magnifiers at the seaside. This thing, however, was, well... elegance and slenderness were scarcely features. Like its owner, it was huge, hulking, overbearing and almost-not-quite-totally ugly. It stood on a low, strong pillar set in concrete, was arranged with complicated sets of jutting arms, weights and what looked like a small electric motor. It did not look the least like an arrangement of skilfully-ground lenses to capture starlight and hurl it at the appreciative eye; in fact, along with its complicated driving and aiming mechanisms, its fat, round, dark mouth was better suited to spitting out ordinance and choking smoke, aimed as it was at some unseen enemy in the grassy wilderness beyond.

Sabina Faslane

My telescope, my first, beloved telescope; it's still with me, in a place of honour. I spent hours with it, bent over the eyepiece, making myself familiar with new sights, new stars. It was only a small thing, four-and-a-half inch mirror, (a white tube mounted on a light wooden tripod like an artist's easel, I could pick it up and move it around effortlessly, to my chagrin it didn't need to be housed in an observatory dome but stored in our spare room). I had just set it up one night and was training my eyes to track the fading of the twilight when I realised that for some reason I was not quite alone in the quiet back garden.

From the thick, unruly bushes, which formed a sort of no-man's land at the end of clashing suburban gardens, came suspicious swishing, cracking, snapping sounds: something was coming, a cat perhaps, or that damn fox that was driving my mother mad by crapping on the lawn in the dead of night, but no, whatever this was had no stealth, no grace; it was clumsy, blundering, loud and there was definitely more than one of it. A tramp, a burglar, one of those terrible strangers that my parents feared would snatch me away if I stood out there alone at night? It took the application of hard rational thought and a measure of stubbornness to quell the fear that rose inside my belly, but I have always sworn never to surrender to fear of the dark.

When the three figures emerged they were, for me, far worse a prospect than any night-stalker. It was Carla Bradley, older than me, who was at my school and a thugette, accompanied by her nominatively appropriate best mates Tessa Salt and Kerry Buttrey. We regarded one another with our usual mutual hatred, spiced with a little surprise.

'Well, fuck me; it's Swotty Goldilocks. Nice, eh?' This was her playground tone, the precursor to a push, a slap, a thump in the face, anything that took her nasty fancy. My instinct was retreat, to fall back to the house where my parents may see what was happening and bawl away the attackers, but my telescope, my telescope, I couldn't leave it! I had already taken a few steps backwards but I stopped by the telescope, ready to defend it, for had these vicious little gits worked out how precious and fragile it was, they would have delighted in doing whatever damage they could.

'Snotty Faslane's gonna get her head kicked in, in her own little pretty garden,' crooned Bradley, gesturing to Salt and Buttrey as she did, but her lieutenants hesitated, one a staggered second behind the other, as they spied my hand fall on the mirror-end of the telescope tube.

'Wassat?' spat Salt; I treasured the dawning of fear in her face. She, Buttrey and Bradley were faced with a short, fat tube surmounted by a sight and an open, dark mouth, pointing in their direction. Spot-frozen, nervous and twitchy, Buttrey looked to her leader for orders and assurance, but got neither.

'A gun! She's got a gun!' Buttrey's frightened voice came out as a cough, which broke down into a choke.

'A gun, a fuckin' gun! Fuckin' cannon!' Salt was infected with Buttery's panic and with athletic spins, swift and competitive as sprinters, they bolted for the wild patch they had come through. Bradley looked minded to tough it out, but within moments her face crumpled and I saw her too vanish into the gathering dark without even a last gift of a threat of what would happen 'next time.' I could hear all three as they crashed through the bushes, I could almost feel their skin scraped and their faces and eyes poked by the sharp springy twigs as they fled in terror towards whichever hedge they had originally hopped to begin this misadventure. I could hear them for quite some time after, they didn't spare the yelling and I must confess it was most enjoyable. But then silence regained, the night had fallen fully and it was mine again.

Fizzmonger

'I want you to understand something before you put your eye anywhere near that eyepiece.' Wayman had reassumed his classroom manner. 'Something that will help avoid unnecessary disappointment. Up to now, everything you have seen of the Sun, Moon and stars has either been your own naked eye observation or, at the other extreme, pictures in books or TV. You need to understand that such pictures are taken by the biggest and best telescopes or even by robots that have achieved the most exquisite images; furthermore, those images are sometimes overlaid, tweaked and improved by computers that do a paint-by-numbers job to make things look their best. Now that's not what you're going to see: this is a good telescope and I'm proud of it,' he paused, patting the solid base of the thing as if it was a pet, 'but it doesn't do close-ups and it doesn't do camera-tricks. What you may see can be impressive, but compared to what you may have seen before it may seem nothing at all. I'll show you the stars, the planets and some beautiful nebulae that look like spiders' webs patched across cracks in the universe, star clusters like swarming beehives or overflowing jewel-boxes, I'll even find you an alien galaxy or two to wonder at, but even then I warn you that a small-boyish part of you will still feel a bitter crash of disappointment that you're seeing no neatly-framed picture, no dazzlingly enhanced colours, that sometimes you'll only see what appears to be a blob, a smudge, a semi-luminescent patch that looks as if something's been spilt in the sky and then half rubbed away. If you know what that object is, how far away it is, how old its light is when it comes off the mirror and though the eyepiece to meet your gaze, then you'll retain your sense of wonder and be duly impressed, but if you forget all that in a mad rush of desire for an instant cosmic close-up then you're going to wind up feeling just a little bit sad.'

Clearly I was not to be allowed at the eyepiece without this final pep talk; I told myself that I felt perfectly relaxed about that, but then I suffered an involuntary twitch—*let me at it!* He showed me Sirius: he told me that it was the brightest star in the sky, then undermined its impressive status by adding that if all things were equal it would not be special at all, although when I put my eye to the lens that dent in its glory was utterly forgotten: I had never seen a star *blaze* before—it flickered and danced like a flame, a white-hot point as if it were the head of a blowtorch cutting through from the other side of the sky. It didn't twinkle, that makes it sound cute and loveable, not to mention far, far too slow, it burned wildly as if it was on the brink of spectacular self-annihilation, it seemed animated with an uncontainable energy, scarcely able to stay still in the sky. The telescope held firmly to its target, its motor grinding slowly and contentedly tracking the wild star's movement patiently and tenaciously as I remained gazing in awe for a far longer time than I would have credited, thinking of nothing but that light, of how I could not possibly describe it in words and finally wondering if I could ever capture and commit its brilliance to paper and paint. Wayman had worked his magic.

Charles Durant Tobol
Clouds blight his sky at every compass point, from horizon to zenith! Hide his stars, blind him!

Fizzmonger
'Do you have a favourite star, Wayman?'
'What on *earth* makes you believe that I would be so foolish?'
'Sorry.'

But then again I had noticed softness in his voice whenever he mentioned (and, I'm told, mispronounced) exotics such as Spica, Arcturus, Antares, Fomalhaut. I learned the names of the stars from him, over time, and not just the bright, dancing ones. For instance, there's a long chain of stars in the Spring sky, it strings across half the sky and yet is featureless, full of nothing, snaking along low-down, faint, barren; but it has one star, just one, that stands out. Its name is Alfard—oddly reminiscent of *Alfred*, don't you think?—and it translates as 'The Solitary One.'

The Sky Through Other Eyes

Charles Durant Tobol
Alfred Wayman is an awkward old bastard. Those are his own words, it's just reportage. Though no admirer of Wayman, I am no character assassin. You will note, however, that I do not appreciate Mr Wayman in the least, and I may dilate upon the reasons at a more opportune time. Still less do I appreciate artists and perhaps the reasons for that too will become apparent.

Sabina Faslane
Do astrology-buffs even *look* at the stars? I say no; it is not the stars these people are interested in, it's themselves. They are not looking upward, but the opposite, down at some chart or little scrap of fortune-paper and even then their gaze is misdirected—that is, inward. To them the stars are irrelevant, they may equally well be looking up football scores, racing results, logarithm tables, any old thing that they simply don't understand. They have borrowed the stars, shall we say misappropriated rather, deriving from them a slender skim of glamour and a superficiality of romance. They never open their eyes to look at the real sky, it would never even occur to them because they know they will never see their yearnings for riches and happy-ever-afters, not in that old, cold and indifferent sky. So they rely on those who claim to interpret the stars and give them meanings, the chancers and charlatans, the money-makers who, like their audience, could not be bothered facing the cold feet and cricked neck of the true stargazer, for they know that the faraway stars will offer them nothing. They

42

are all seeking affirmation of their own significance and from the true sky they will receive reminders of the opposite. They cannot face their smallness and so they cannot truly face the stars.

Glyn Capstone

I have never looked up at the stars. Never bothered. I had one encounter with the heavens and that was enough. What are the stars anyway except pinholes poked in black card, five-pointed pretty-things in picture books for kiddies?

Jilly Holdenbridge

'Twinkle-twinkle little star, how I...'

I did wonder, but never aloud. I didn't look up, except secretly; such things were not exactly unpermitted, but they were discouraged, shall we say. I did wonder what they were, how they shone, why they twinkled, how near or far they were, why they rose and set. But I didn't ask. Head down, arms tucked, move slowly, say nothing. It was all part of being Jilly the Shuffler. How ashamed of me my dad would have been.

Charles Durant Tobol

Wayman is a teacher, a colleague (but not one that, I remain at pains to point out, I would claim as a friend); one of those ageless pedagogues who've been at the chalk-face forever, the breed that never retires, never dies. History's his subject, but he's not a history teacher, he's *an historian*. Important distinction, you see. He's an old-fashioned (gentle)man also, and old-fashioned (gentle)men aren't truly defined by their day-jobs; such (gentle)men have hobbies and through these out-of-hours devotions they display their true hearts. Wayman watches the stars. I'm fairly certain he never sleeps, not when there is so much as a patch of clear sky after sundown. Not so much a hobby, then, as a life's passion. Or a consuming madness.

On the matter of love: he is unmarried, unpartnered too, I have no idea as to his taste, if he has any, or his romantic history, if he has one. That's a side issue, although his lack of romantic spirit is very much part of what I am mulling upon here. He is large in all dimensions, ungainly, rumpled, only his mother could love him, so he says, and I believe that he lost that comfort a long time since. He is an eccentric, though he refuses to label himself so. A self-appointed eccentric is a phoney, so he declares. Does a lot of declaring, Mr Wayman. Anyway: Alfred Wayman spends much of his time alone. Too much. It has eroded his social skills—if he ever possessed any. And he spends that empty time self-isolated under an open, dark sky.

On the night that now occupies my thoughts, we, a mismatched and half-reluctant (reluctance on my part anyway, I was pressed into the situation by well-meaning colleagues) gang of revellers, were in a restaurant in the centre of town, one of those modern palace-eateries with car showroom windows, brilliant white walls, black furniture, every angle a right angle, harsh lights that abolished all shade and shadow. Pictures on the walls, but of the sort that machines produce, machines or machine-people, things that filled space rather than attracted the eye. The noise was terrific, frightening layers of loudness, the clash of cutlery and plates, footfalls, chatter, shouts, laughter, all by and large drowning out bland machine-music manufactured to match the pictures. Conversation had to be held at the pitch of the lungs, there were no lulls in the din; one was compelled to add to it, or be consumed by it (I had hoped to hide away within this appalling soundscape, ignore what I half-heard, pretend not to hear what I could, shrug helplessly and pass the evening uneventfully, but I was to be robbed of this comfort). On the whole, I would describe the place as rather 'young' and trendy—and expensive too: everything in fact, which was bound to make an old relic such as Wayman look and feel out of place.

It was foul, cold and soaking-wet outside, not a chance of a crack in the clouds, and that was the sole reason for Wayman's presence; he was cut off from the stars and he had time. He never knew what to do without his stars. He was seated roughly opposite me, quite against my desires and flatly against my planning. Next to him was that preening creature, the portrait painter, whose commission (a joke that had got way out of hand, its savour all lost) he seemed to be pursuing with unseemly ardour, shadowing, observing his subject but also, as was his irritating old habit, chatting to, almost confiding in me, as if the employment of brush and easel made us brothers (I deny that brotherhood; why don't you bond with someone else and get yourself away from me?).

The evening had been sold to me as a staff-only do, but as it transpired it was an evening of unintended, chaotic and rather unfortunate companionship; someone somewhere had become a little confused about the arrangements (hadn't listened, more like) and wives, *partners*, friends and other odd attachments appeared at the table, one table became two, the seating-plan that I had sketched for myself (purposefully keeping myself away from Wayman and any acolytes of his) was swept aside by this jumbling tide and an uncomfortable, if instructive, little evening proceeded with all due awkwardness.

Considering they were add-ons, supernumeraries, many of the unwanted strangers were very aloof, not bothering with us and attending to their own little cliques (or is that claques?—the arrangement suited me well whatever the word) but two young women sitting to my left, beautiful and beautifully dressed I must concede, (but whose squaws or daughters or molls they were I cannot say and I was not told) attempted to overcome both the din and the social mix by being pleasant and chatty to the strangers who had been foisted on them. It was at this point I first noticed with unease that the portrait painter, seated beside me, was mentally framing their features with more than an artist's appreciation of beauty, and this rather obvious ogling persisted and irritated me as the two girls attempted to socialise, to create a getting-to-know-you spirit (that or they were just kind-hearted) and they struck up a conversation with Wayman. Why him? I'll never know. The painter was annoyed too.

Fizzmonger

Paintable they were, a very paintable pair, almost enough to revive my jaded taste for faces, and they did far more for my sense of skin tone, flesh, body. Thank your gods and lucky stars for poor taste and immodesty, that's my motto. And yet they homed in on the one man least equipped to appreciate them. Wayman was already soup-stained and rumpled. 'Not the ideal man for any young thing to make small-talk with,' as I said to Tobol, and was rewarded with a glare that seemed to wish a cold, cruel death on me. That man had grown yet sourer since last we'd met. I hadn't thought it possible.

Charles Durant Tobol

I was overcome with well-accustomed crawling dislike and could have slapped the man: the painter, I mean, (this time at least). I had wished him upon Wayman, but in doing so I had inflicted him on myself. The heavens abound with malign gods.

'Hi, my name's Amanda. This is Jancis,' spoke "a small, dark-haired beauty" (the painter's lascivious commentary) in an off-the-shoulder dress that revealed fine skin but slightly too knotty a neck. Her friend was "taller, weightier but still elegant". By "elegant" the painter meant "tasty", I knew, with disgust.

'Charmed,' responded Wayman affably enough, 'I am Alfred.'

'Are you Great?' ventured Jancis with a nervous giggle. I wondered if she had intended any double entendre, but I supposed not.

Hahahahahahahaha! they chortled, to carry the moment. Wayman, though looking a little pained, made some limping witticism about habitually burning cakes and everything seemed to be settling into a relaxed and easy pattern of painless chit-chat that I could lose among the general racket until, my social duty done, (lip-service paid, anyway) I could slip away respectably home.

Fizzmonger

'So tell me Alfred,' ventured Amanda cheerily, after a little more inconsequential chitchat, 'what is your sign?'

'Sign?' I saw Wayman tense; he became alert as an animal sensing a trap. The line of his back, the way he held his head, the set of his face, they all changed in an instant and the creases of his face became a refuge for all of the over-lit eatery's fugitive shadows.

'Your star sign,' explained Amanda brightly.

'I'm afraid I don't have one.' The tension filled Wayman's voice, put a quiver into it (though it seemed, to me, a perfectly innocuous enquiry—to any ordinary man).

'Of *course* you do, everyone's got a sign!' Amanda pressed on, perhaps unwisely. 'When were you born, what month?' That the young woman was chirpy and just a little patronising deepened Wayman's discomfiture.

'April,' he responded with heavy reluctance as if he had been through this conversation many times before (well of course he had) and only wearied patience held him back from some outburst. 'But I assure you I haven't got a "star sign." Truly.' Wayman's tone was almost pleading, but in the prevailing general noise the women missed the proffered hint.

'Early or late April?' pushed Jancis.

'Fairly late.' Wayman's voice took a downbeat and was almost swamped by the all-enveloping racket, but still I could hear it grate and grind.

'Then you're a Taurus!' Amanda spoke as if she had filled a yawning gap in the wretched man's knowledge.

'I really, truly am not,' Wayman spoke still pleadingly, but more firmly if still containing his growing frustration.

'Stubborn. Typical Taurus,' said Amanda to Jancis, intending Wayman to hear. His patience was sputtering and a tirade looming, though those unfortunates knew not.

Recalling the incident later, the portrait painter chuckled; an unpleasant, self-complacent sound. '*What's your sign?* It's a bit of fun, a cheap conversation-starter that doubles as a hackneyed old chat-up line. Women seem to use and respond to it, the most and the best; yes, it's definitely a woman thing. I've used the opportunity—and a handy if superficial acquired knowledge of astrology—to shape my own future quite nicely before now, starlighting my way into several perfumed beds with well-chosen words. How could they resist me when it was their destiny? But Wayman… well, I don't know if girls aren't his thing, if he hasn't the ability with the chat, or if he was just such a cantankerous old swine that he couldn't just smooth things over and forget what had been said, such a pedant that he couldn't be silent in the face of foolishness.' Certainly he was unable to contain himself any longer.

'Stubborn, intransigent, *bullish*. Yes, I've heard all that; heard it many, many sad and tedious times. As a Taurean I am not also supposed to be a fine dresser with the money to indulge my habits? And what about the dominance over women, eh? You weren't going to mention those other bits, were you?' Wayman brushed crumbs off his lapels as he spoke, accidentally smearing the soup stains further across his front. 'I could have assured him that he'd have no dominance over women, not on this night or probably on any other, but he'd not have listened.' (The painter, later, but of course.)

'No you weren't going to mention those little attributes, were you? Horrorscopers never do mention the inconvenient stuff. For instance, there are thirteen signs of the zodiac, not twelve. The misfit is ignored, of course; its name is long and tricky to pronounce, Sun, Moon and planets travel through it just as with the rest of the zodiac —it's *there* but it doesn't fit the myths, the lies, so it gets left out. That alone should scupper the entire absurd structure —but no. Some planets also wander inconveniently out of the zodiac altogether—what do horrorscopers say when Mars is not safely in the house of the Ram or whatever, but in the belly of the Whale? Nothing. It doesn't fit, so out it goes.' ('To me, you know,' observed the painter, 'Wayman's angry, wounded tone was nothing less than that of a misfit speaking up for all the other misfits.' No argument from me on that.)

The girls were clearly embarrassed: as the painter said, asking about someone's sign had always been a friendly opening gambit to a conversation with a stranger. They had clearly never before encountered one of the founding members of the awkward squad.

'You don't believe in astrology?' asked Jancis with gentle, smiling redundancy. She sounded as if she were mocking this foolish man; he knew it and was finally done with *politesse.*

'Astrology is utter nonsense. Tell me: if we stepped outside now—I mean if we were to look up at a clear sky— could you show me your "star sign" up there, or mine?'

'Well, no…'

'Could you point out any of them?'

'Well, no…'

'In fact you couldn't point out any constellation, bar a vague stab at "The Plough." Astrology believers never can, in my experience. How can you place such faith in something you can't even identify? Do you not even know that constellations are just imaginary pictures, drawn by

50

people? The stars within them are nowhere near one another, I mean that they are millions or billions of miles apart, we just see them the way they are because of line-of-sight, simple chance. How can they have any influence on us other than gravity—and you and I sitting here have more gravitational effect on one another than stars do upon any of us? How is this hogwash supposed to *work*?'

'It's more a spiritual thing for me,' said Amanda.

'Yeah, I'm more of a seeker after truth,' agreed Jancis.

Wayman's voice wasn't heard above the hubbub, but his mouth worked at, 'Oh, *fuck me*.'

'It does no harm, it's just another way of viewing things.' Amanda was more defensive than her friend, her voice rang with a slight, hurt whine; perhaps a little flame of anger burned too. Wayman, meanwhile, had adopted a peevish, lecturing tone.

'No harm? Let me give you two examples why it does harm. Who, would you say, was the most powerful man in the world?'

'Well… President of the USA?'

'Right answer.'—very much the teacher—'Now, the current President is…'

'Ronald Reagan?'

'Just so. He has ratcheted up the Cold War with the Soviet Union to the point where each is prepared to use nuclear weapons to stop the ambitions of the other. The whole world is truly in danger of being blown to smithereens, for the sake of two damnable political systems and their ridiculous dreams of empire. And yet it is not the politics that frightens me, it's the dratted mysticism. Reagan, you may know, is a "born again" religious type who believes the end of the world is coming, and coming *soon*: that his electorate has placed in his hands the means of delivering Armageddon must make perfect sense to him. But, worse than all of that, somewhat contrary to the instructions of his supposed Lord, Reagan is consulting an astrologer: he and his wife scarcely make a move without her advice. And what if the stars one day decide to send a message that it's time to press the button? Boom in fire we will all go— capitalist, communist, believer and unbeliever together—at the whim of a half-wit and his pet horrorscoper.'

'Perhaps she stops him doing it. Perhaps she's a force for good,' ventured Jancis, much to Wayman's exasperation.

'The point *is* that we are all at risk, every one of us, from crazy predictions with no grounding in reality, plucked from the air but not from the sky. The point is that it's *not* harmless, it's dangerous on a grand scale.'

Wayman saw that his argument had made no impression and he sighed. 'Very well, what about this then—the world was not at threat, only one person suffered and yet in many ways I hold it just as great a crime. I once worked with someone—let's called her Mary—who was a thoughtful, kind, clever and loving person, yes, she had a lot of love to give but she was forty years old and single, she was alone, alone, and her world was filled, poisoned, by that aloneness. She was heartsick for a man, a true lover, every moment of her every day was spent waiting for him, thinking of him, pining for him. I think she had seen her share of cads and chancers along the way and yet still her hope burned, but that hope blighted her life. And there was another blight too: every day she would be there, supposedly at her work but really there she was with a pile of tabloids and mind-meltingly vapid magazines, multiple damn horror-scope in front of her eyes, reading and re-reading them, seeking meaning out of their mutual contradictions, hoping they would tell her that today's the day, your luck will change, you will find him, you will find him. She even paid a series of greedy charlatans for "personal" readings, expensive and cruel postal rip-offs. She was obsessed with "her" stars and what they would bring: and by having her head filled with fakery and buncombe, she never looked around her, never saw anything for herself, she never saw the real world or the real stars and never met her man. Whoever introduced her to that horror-scoping foolishness was an enemy to her, and to humanity too.'

'That's very sad.' Amanda, *tch-tched* and wagged her head.

'Tragic is what I call it,' pronounced Wayman. 'Like people from time immemorial she put herself in the hands of the wretched fortune-tellers. It grieves me that people do it, *grieves* me.'

'She was looking for comfort, perhaps she found it,' Jancis argued chippily.

'She was the spirited one. Yes, I would have made her my target had it not been for...' (The painter suddenly remembered that the tale was not about himself and his lechery, but Wayman's apparent social ineptitude and so he resumed his recall, taking up the teacher's voice.)

'It is a measure of human vanity—"the stars are all about *me*." You are all surely looking for comfort; but do you not feel like puppets? Not the puppets of the stars, no-no, they are indifferent to you, indifferent to us all, I mean the puppets of the horrorscopers?'

'Don't you ever look for comfort? Not in anything? I think you live in a sad, empty world.' Jancis was now openly at war with this sceptical, cynical, ageing, ugly man.

'The empty world is yours dear lady, and it isn't even starlit: you can't see the good stars for the stinking fog. And your prophets and horrorscopers can make you only one prediction, one promise—"Tomorrow I shall lie to you".'

Fizzmonger

'You talk as if the stars belonged to you and you alone.' Amanda was by now even more warlike than her friend.

'Funnily enough I think I have said quite the opposite. The stars are for everyone and the sky is stateless, owned by no one; it is truly free. It should not be annexed by human vanity. My dear young lady, truly you can espouse any beliefs you wish, any at all, but kindly do not impose them on the good stars.'

Those would quite possibly have been the last even barely polite words exchanged between those parties that night, but at that moment some gallant lad finally interrupted the conversation, carried it off bodily in a quite other direction and rescued the poor, browbeaten girls. A charmer he: seeing off the threatening dragon, and before long Wayman had finished his meal and vanished. His share of the bill was found under his plate, although nobody saw him put it there and no one saw him leave; perhaps it would be more accurate to say that his departure went unnoticed. I didn't stay much longer; those girls were lovely but I was tainted with Wayman's proximity and they weren't for me, not that night. Perhaps one—or both even—went off into the night, in gratitude, with their rescuer. Lucky bastard.

Charles Durant Tobol

I wanted to tell the priapic jackanapes that he had an opinion of himself scarcely congruent with reality, indeed that he clearly couldn't tell the difference between his paintbrush and prick, and that those girls, for whatever best-concealed reasons, were far more interested in Wayman than in him, even when he began to subject them to his habitual, tedious rationalistic homilies. But my private thoughts had seized me and I reflected sadly upon the mistake I had made by summoning this face-stealer, this boastful body-collector. Where the astronomer had rued the influence of fortune-tellers, I had come that night to resent more than ever the swaggering, stifling tyranny of artists.

No Oil Painting

Fizzmonger

They have commissioned me to waste time and paint on this grotesque, this farrago of disproportion; why can't it be someone more deserving (and better for me), why can't it be she, the ripe-corn hair, the face both innocent and intense, that little space between her front teeth that brings the child to her smile, the gentle curl of that ever-present turtle-neck; I could spend paint on her most profitably. It would be quite like older, happier days. Happy days by a bend of water. Yes.

Charles Durant Tobol

A great man once wrote: 'At fifty, everyone has the face that he deserves.' You won't find that piece too easily, it's just a note made before he died (who knows what would have come next?), but it is a good starting point. For what Mr Alfred Wayman has done to deserve his face is a matter for the most intense speculation.

Fizzmonger

Wayman's face, that's what got me started again, it rekindled my interest and sent my hand returning to a brush, once I was reconciled to the fact that beauty was no longer my portion. Those curious, lopsided looks; I didn't know how anyone could look like that without being in pain. So many folds and creases, wrinkles under active construction, jowls —dewlaps. We are talking about a moon-face, a baggy full-moon face, craters and pits and blotches, shadows, folds, rills—mountain ranges too, all present and correct. Not a cheerful night-light that's all friendly bright yellow though; more the colour of a sunset sky when the dust and dirt swirls in the upper air like a stunt-flight of stinky demons. A face, a man, full of secret history, but devoid of anything else attractive; it should all have added up to ugliness and yet somehow did not—not entirely, anyway.

Glyn The Pin

Word is that the painter bloke is here to do a portrait of old Wayman. Good luck to the painter bloke and double good luck to Art. But at least Wayman shows up some colours, even if they're mixed-up and dead raim. I suppose if anyone tried to paint me they probably couldn't mix their paints into something seethrough enough to capture my nothingness. Or, more simply, there'd be an artist standing, looking straight through me, waving his arms like a madman and yelling 'Hoy! Where's my bloody sitter then, eh?'

Fizzmonger

There were no mirrors in that house of his, none. It would be facile to say that a man of his looks would avoid mirrors, that he had no use for them. He certainly did have a use for them, but only as components in elaborate traps that preyed upon starlight.

Charles Durant Tobol

In an early marque of my design, I half-ventured, but then choked off, the suggestion that given a template of my devising, everyone concerned could contribute to the portrait, if only a hesitant brush stroke here and there, to express their feelings, their truths about our subject—albeit cluelessness and question-marks, by and large. Come one, come all and play sweet add-a-line! At first I thought it would produce a dizzying, sickening embarrassment of conflicting styles, my dark, bare-coded stabs and slashes clashing with halos of optimistic light and hope from loyal, pretty Fastlane, misdirected, blotto blobbings from the inebriate brush-hand of the Head and indecisive dibs and dabs from Old Wash-Hands as he havered endlessly over whether to be a condemner or soul-saver, never quite getting round to either, waiting to see which way the tide of painted opinion was going, so determined to be a just person he is paralysed by his to-and-fro mania (I could use watercolours, he could dip his paws in the pot to slosh 'em off, shuck off responsibility; he'd like that).

Yes, it could have been funny, a tenth-rate, ticklish *commedia dell'arte*, but I reminded myself that I did not want *funny*, the picture itself would be a laughing-stock, a collage, something that is always a risible patchwork of me-too amateurism, the form via which the well-intentioned (but stupid) deceive dull, talentless children to believe they are capable of producing art—there dears, we all took part and everyone's a winner. I did not want it to be a passing joke. I wanted something more durable, darker.

Glyn Capstone

I wonder if the painting was some kind of attempt to recreate, remake Wayman, to see how he ticked—sniff out his secrets, maybe dig up that past he never spoke of? I saw the painting once—I mean before it became quite a thing and so hard to see. It was hanging up in the hall at a school reunion, standing out among the erect, crisp-clean academic Heads and Deputies in their glazed prison frames like a rotting cabbage in a rose display. I wonder where that painting is now; probably in a Chamber of Horrors somewhere. High-hued, flecks of the whole spectrum scattered here and there as if someone had taken a hammer to the rainbow—yet if you looked closely, and yet closer still, you could see how it held all the dark of night in it. Its subject would surely have approved. That is, if it was the right kind of darkness. I was never sure.

Fizzmonger

How to portray him? As a grand figure, gazing boldly aloft (with clear-eyed, steely determination, but of course) and with his hand resting on a stack of books (all read and some written by him, all crammed with the wisdom of the universe)? Or, with a globe perhaps; a sky-globe naturally. As Joseph Wright's Philosopher with his Orrery? What clothing? Boring old teacher-garb, his daily dull outfit, or robed as a grand truth-seeking Greek, or an even grander be-toga'd Roman (better not, given his views on their activities)? One of the Lunar Society (oops no, not the Moon)? Kepler then, complete with ruff, or bewigged Newton (*no* apple, thank you so much), untidy, tongue-poking, space-bending Einstein? Ah, that would be flattery and that is neither my style nor Wayman's; after all, he's no pioneer, no discoverer. What boundary-breaking knowledge or alien sphere bears his name? And it would be contrary, I rather think, to one of the unstated but overriding clauses of my commission.

Perhaps a little mischief would fit the bill—I could scatter some children in the background to rake up old rumours of a secret family, but surely, I could protest, they are merely symbols of his daily charges. Or perhaps a miniature of a woman tucked provocatively away somewhere (shall she have corn-blonde hair and a little tooth-gap?) or a cameo of the child who would become the crazy stargazer, a hint that the painter has stolen the keys to his past? A busy frame filled with clues, hints, stories, teases, guesses, the odd downright lie: ah, but all that would offend the spirit of my commission.

I'm told that the warts and all approach is the only one he would tolerate, but I understand that it is intended that I should also add warts wherever I *don't* find them. By god, that Tobol has become a force for evil; thank goodness his orbit is so small. And to think that he once showed such promise. *Tut.*

Charles Durant Tobol

It was my idea, my stroke, my strike, not the general, fuzzy-warm idea, but the cold detail; the picture, but not the big picture, could we say? It was my satiric, revengeful stab, and I claim it. I was even prepared for the others to whisper behind hands that it was some form of back-scratching artistic freemasonry, grubbing up work for a fellow-spirit, I didn't care. I suggested both the idea of the painting and name of the painter, but not for reasons a single one of them would suspect. I knew the man, I knew his work and I knew fine well what lurked within it. It was near perfect. With any luck both artist and sitter would have become infamous.

Sabina Faslane

I was surprised to be roped into the little ad-hoc deliberating committee. It certainly wasn't some well-meant attempt to remedy desperate gender-imbalance; such lily-livered delicacy was hardly in the best traditions of the school. I was levered in there to lend legitimacy and credibility to the gesture. 'You know him, you're his friend,' was quite sufficient to get me co-opted by people who had known him far longer. They sounded rather desperate and I felt sorry for them in a way. There were deeper currents lurking, but I knew nothing of them; fluff-headed little girlie, eh?

It had been suggested by the Head that we should contact Bernard Lawton if we wanted a truly expert opinion, everyone nodded wisely and she tottered off, only for Mr Tobol to advise that we ignore suggestions from 'that brandy-soaked pudding.' I was disappointed; I had yet to meet this legendary figure, I was curious, but our meeting was to be delayed. I wish to record that I am sad about that delay.

Fizzmonger

I can read a face; I can start with the face and close in, move deeper, I can come to know someone so uncomfortably well. There is so much that sits upon the surface, the face, hints and glimmers of what lies further down, and sometimes this requires additional investigation, some deeper mining. Crevices, cracks, crooked noses, crooked smiles, lopsided features, pits, depressions, blemishes, boils, warts (of course) and eyes all shades of bloodshot. A true painter does not have subjects; he has victims. When I paint you, I know you and stay with you. I spy out your secrets and paint them into my canvas, but you never notice, flattered as you are that your face will live forever. I could so easily make a little dirty profit as one of those tell-your-fortune shysters, for they are not reading anything but the face, digging especially for vulnerability, gullibility. I am after far more.

I don't just sign my work, I haunt it—I am in there with you whether you like it or not, lurking in some symbolic figure, or splayed like Holbein's anamorphic skull—though hidden, not advertised so. If you have sat for me, you have given yourself to me and never knew it. Portrait becomes portrayal becomes betrayal—that is how I work. Be careful.

Old Wash-Hands

The spirit, if not the stated aim, of the offering of this gift of appreciation was of course, 'Thanks For The Years. Now—In The Name Of God—Go!'—Wayman certainly was in need of a hint or two in that direction. They were helpless, the lot of them, floundering, amusing to observe from a prudent distance, until the little Art master played his ace. All they knew was that they desired to see him depart; dislodged with a gift, nudged to retirement with a little never-again flattery.

And much as I despised Tobol, I couldn't help but applaud, when I perceived it, the subtle, admirable malice of his 'helpful' suggestion. Mr Wayman, you've been framed (intended, intended).

Fizzmonger

'Funny what happened, eh? Eh? What happened with that picture—eh?'

'Yes Wayman. Funny. Very funny.'

By this time I had learned to be patient, very patient.

Personal Statements

Miss Fastlane

Sabina Faslane

Mr Wayman raped me; did you hear about that? He set up a completely fake meeting of some school society that didn't even exist and it was held in the evening so there was no one else about and he got me trapped in this room and it was upstairs so I couldn't get out of the window to jump and the windows were locked anyway and he shoved desks in front of the door and he knocked the lights out and then he grabbed me and then he raped me and then he let me go and then we both turned up to school the next day and we taught our classes and we said hello to one another and we sat and read newspapers and drank coffee with other teachers in the Staff Room and neither of us said a word about it but he had raped me. And no one would ever have known about this tremendous moment in history but that some brave investigative reporter of a youngster carved into a desk with the words 'WAYPIST WAYMAN' and pretty soon the word was out, everyone knew that Wayman had committed an horrendous crime and yet somehow the police never came and he was never in trouble, I never spoke a word, never even slapped his face for him, and he kept his job even though *everyone knew* what he had done.

Old Wash-Hands

This new creature, this *Ms*—she's a *Ms*, no doubt of it, indeed I'd make book on it, she is a *Ms* and she will insist upon being addressed as such and that she'll not hesitate to cause a scene over it; so much cannot be misunderstood (intended, intended). She will scold a man for being chivalrous too, *patronising*, she will call it, condescending, creepy, she will make him feel like a fool and a cad even for such a simple, kind gesture as holding a door open for her; whereas all he is being is a civilised, decent gentleman.

I believe in gentlemanliness, in manners: in order. I believe that manners distinguish us from the animal. I believe that this slew of new arrivals, this permanent wave (intended, intended) of feminised invaders will upset everything that we have ever worked for. They may not intend to, but that will be the result. Wayman once asked me to consider that somewhere there may be a possible world in which to open a door for a woman is to insult her, where to demonstrate the manly instinct to lead and to protect is to give the gravest offence. Relativist piffle-paffle. As I have ever said, the world would fall apart with people of his stamp in charge; indeed, that is precisely what is happening in these modern days—QED. Saints preserve us against the day that they should seize power.

Sabina Faslane

I find stories fascinating; sometimes even ugly and improbable ones have their peculiar attractions. More than just "sometimes". An historian has to spend time to unwind myths and stories from the facts, around which they grow like a deadly and unrelenting weed, the nasty, sex-obsessed, slanderous bits remaining much more attractive to the eye than the dull, boring old truth that was choking to death, strangulated in their grip. But I do require stories—and essays too, come to think of it; are you listening, schoolkind?—to make sense, to have a beginning, middle and end, and to contain some semblance of a... *point*. They should also aim at some semblance of truthfulness, even if that is achieved via allegory. I even prefer excuses for having done no homework to have a little narrative structure, some consistency; is it also too much to ask for a dash of originality from our tale-tellers?

Where the rape story got its start in life I don't know for sure; from what I know from others I think it was perhaps a reheated rumour over forty years in the maturing, involving quite another teacher, quite another victim, and almost certainly just as little truth or credibility. Alfred was a colleague and a daytime friend to me—by which I mean we had little social contact after hours and in any case he has no friends, not at night—he doesn't want them. You may have heard that too, but it is at least the truth, or something close to it.

One of the rape-story's problems, a fundamental and probably fatal one, was that Mr Wayman and I were never alone together, not for a moment, not at that time anyway, not at the school, not outside. One variant of the rumour was that he gave me a lift home and raped me in his car, but I think everyone knows about Wayman's car. No room for manoeuvre, you see. Even then, slim and willowy as I was (and proud of it at the time, but all such things pass, become past) I would not have fitted in there with him. Wayman didn't squeeze comfortably into that tin can solo; I think my point is made. That, of course, didn't trouble the storytellers and whisperers, the wood-cutters, the desk-markers, the guerrilla artists of schooldays. They told their tale and spoke plainly to the world, both of their prevailing, rather depressing ignorance but also of the random bits and scraps of their education that had stuck, too.

'RAPPER WAYMAN'—that one was cut deep and inked fully and boldly, the artist must have had some time on his hands for this work. 'WAMAN RAIPED SABINA'—this one done with as few pen-strokes as possible, not deep and not bold. A swift job performed under pressure, the danger of observation and apprehension perhaps. 'I wd rape Sabina and make her drop cubs too' was another contribution—how they loved the historical echoes of my name, the little dears. To add to the disturbing incongruity, rape-fantasies as woodcuts, the last scribe had added a little heart alongside my name. As driven, outspoken and most of all downright confused as their elders, our little fabulists and myth-makers of the desk-telegraph played with and reshaped history, making mud-pies with its primal ingredients of sex, force, oppression, possession, bastardy and legitimisation. Perhaps they were historians in the making.

They played with my surname too, adding a 't'—witty little sausages, eh? And don't imagine for an instant this was definitely the work of the kids—that may be an assumption too far. I wanted to attract attention to my teaching, but as a realist-idealist, I knew perfectly well that, with tiresome inevitability, from the moment I arrived an accretion of rumours, name-calling, tall tales and dirty talk would swirl around me; what I underestimated was its strength and toxicity. Let's not say potency.

The school, I knew, had been a boys' Grammar, long past its prime and long-accustomed to the flutter of moth wing-beats, and upon this hollowed-out demi-Eton had been foisted the comprehensive system, to the poisonous resentment of staff, boys, parents and certain local politicos. The Sixth Form, still clinging on to a starved, bony existence, was the first to go "co-educational" and then the first new intake would be mixed-sex, mixed-ability, with the boys-only elite flushed out slowly over the following years. It was planned to turn this wheezing anomaly into a sleek, efficient and modern High School.

The ancient elite, male culture of the school enduring a drawn-out demise, one in which the processes of decline and decay were accompanied by a loud and impenetrable denial that many mistook for continued virility. Yes there were problems with the old ways, but they were wholly surmountable and also—*also,* they were demonstrably—*demonstrably*—somebody else's fault. We used to play rugby here—now there are girls. We used to teach Latin here—now there are girls. This used to be a respected institution —now there are *girls.* That exam-failing thickoes of the male variety were being ushered through the gates was horror enough, but there were also *girls.* The school's ancient patriarchal soul was in deep, icy shock: nothing good could come of this; nothing good *would* come of this.

I arrived with the first wave of females. I thought—I *had* thought carefully about my appearance and considered that my woolly sweaters, while nicely feminine and definitely not of the old black-bat style of caped and be-suited schoolteacher, were also sufficiently modest and curve-concealing to prevent any stupidity, but in that I was indeed off-target by a country mile. I found out that my very first nickname was 'Sweaters,' which was quickly refined to 'Sweaterbusters,' and the woodcutters of the school's ancient desk-artists' guild rapidly rendered curvy, impossibly booby caricatures accompanied by witticism such as:

'SWEATERBUSTERS, SWEATERBUSTERS—MAKES ME SWEAT.'

I tried not to care, not to think about it. Another carving read 'just wait till summer'—and omitted any clothing at all, bar slight scratchings perhaps to indicate a bikini. 'Goldilocks—she's just right for me' ('me' scratched out—replaced with 'my cock', which lost in romanticism but displayed a sort of brutish honesty). Oh hell, their hormones were burning up, how in the world was I going to be able to teach them history? The advantages of the veil became suddenly clear.

I was also labelled Gaptooth—this was by some way the nearest they came to offering a compliment, but as a matter of fact subcultural opinion was divided as to whether the dinky little space between my two front teeth was attractively girlish and added to my smile, or infantilised me. As a matter of fact it had always divided opinion; 'I can't carry on going out with an eternal six year old!' declared one boyfriend in the throes of full retreat, one so rapid I never got to throw in my retort that I had managed the same feat for the previous three months, and yes, goodbye. I like my tooth-gap; I think it makes my smile brighter. Uniform perfection is overrated.

There had been female teachers in the olden, golden days, of course, but they were necessitous battleaxes or trainees hurled into the cage for their first blooding, to emerge red-faced, wet-eyed and beginning to plan their quickest exit towards the safe harbours of primary education, or better to clear off out of it altogether into marriage and the production of future occupants of the school's feral dens. Only a special sort of woman could fit in here: a cleaner (unseen, ignored) or lab assistant on the "Chemmy" labs, whose primary function, more or less consciously part of the job, was to serve as the first sexual fantasy for a certain kind of boy. For girls to sit in these hallowed halls and learn was a breaking of the rules, a violation enough, but for a female (who didn't fit the above categories) to presume to stand and teach—*well!*

Some of the woodcutters took the presence of a living, breathing female before them as the chance to indulge in informal life-classes. At least their anatomical detailing became a little more accurate. But the shock-wave among the teachers was on a different and more serious scale. Two or three resignations and a scattering of retirements followed the appointment of a headmistress. Someone told me that even the venerable Bernard Lawton had cited the influx of femininity as a factor in his decision to depart, although Alfred Wayman countered that that was "twaddle"—and we all know Mr Wayman's intolerance of twaddle. Many assumed me to be a domestic science teacher; I was pretty unimpressed and flatly unamused at the nonstop jokes and calls for "egg and chips". When they found out that I taught history, perhaps they thought I confined it to the history of kitchen sinks and cleaning cloths.

My confidence nearly took a great swan-dive not long after I joined the school. That down-falling confidence of mine, it is my Achilles heel, every time. I overheard conversations, of the sort artfully crafted to make one feel that one is an eavesdropper but which are perfectly well intended to be heard; discussions on the way academic standards were crashing, how the school was "going to the dogs": I shouldn't have been fooled for a minute, their game plan was plain. They talked of how things had reached a pretty pass "since they've introduced females... and other animals". Alfred helped resolve this little crisis of confidence—he had served for sufficiently long to know the identity of the chatterers and what festered beneath their chatter. It was muttered and mumbled around the Staff Room that unless I changed my state of undress, there would be unanswerable consequences. That meant "my fault", are you with me, do you understand? It meant a rape, a real rape, vicious and bloody, my fault for being "*sweaterbusters-sweaterbusters-makes-me-sweat*". The little trick of repetition turns it into poetry, see. It's a real touch, don't you think?

Charles Durant Tobol
Ah, the Painted Lady. Wayman's ward, or was she more? We shan't ever know, not from her, she's discreet, and that *is* a virtue, surely, in anyone's reckoning. But she was, shall we say, disruptive. Her kind cannot help but be so. To paint is to provoke, as I'm sure you know. It is also to deceive.

I was never against the girls or women coming to the school; anything that would advance the decay and ruin of the place was meat and drink to me. But Faslane became too much of a distraction for some of my colleagues, they became obsessed, obvious and frankly tedious.

'A woman like that is incapable of feeling love; not, at least, until her looks start to fade, tempering her vanity.'—Old Wash-Hands holding forth; his voice ever-thinner, his spine curving with gaining age and his head more and more bowed so that every passing day he increasingly resembled not so much a moral prophet (how he saw himself), but an angry tortoise, grown tetchy because it was not yet time to hibernate.

'Give me the pure, or none, says the poem!' he intoned, misunderstanding the poem in his desperate self-satisfaction.

What distracts men more than the lure of sex is the lure of *imagined* sex, the more ludicrously unavailable it is, the better. The imagined availability of Faslane, the fantasies they built around her—I include the insane notion that sexless, remote Wayman attacked her in any way—brought my colleagues to a fevered state, god knows what festered amongst the kids.

The war against women holds back the war against art, just as foolish indulgence of beauty makes art offensive.

The wickedness of 'these deluding tricks... all your artificial shows,' the old saurian assumed that these things are inherent in the face of a woman, like others he believed all the poetic spite was directed against the woman, where it should have been directed against the *paint*.

With oils, and paint, and drugs, that cost
More than the face is worth

Nature hates all needless arts, the poem goes on—but again it misses the point: all art is needless. *That* is the point, *my* point.

Sabina Faslane

I was a Grammar Girl myself; Swotty Faslane passed her exams and proceeded to a girls' school dominated by men. Oh, there was a Headmistress and plenty of female staff and yet... there was a particular teacher known to me as Stuffed Shirt; he taught English, always wore a black cape over a shiny suit, had ears like the handles of a milk-churn and longed to be Headmaster at Waveway Girls, so much that we all feared he nursed notions of murder in pursuit of his vain ambitions. He also had religious mania, no sense of humour and a tendency to treat the school rules as if hewn by ancient writers (or probably, more believably, their slaves) out of tablets of stone. He also went out of his way to add the word "please", tacked to the end of his sentences in a dead, redundant-afterthought fashion, whenever being particularly officious or nasty.

Free, gratis and entirely unrequested, he undertook our moral education. Unusually for him, he didn't employ earnest homily, lofty denunciation or recitation of the rules; he used more subversive tactics—to wit, a poem. We heard more of 'To A Painted Lady' than we did of almost any hymn.

What Nature did to view expose,
Don't you keep out of sight.
The novice youth may chance admire
Your dressings, paints and spells;
But we that are expert desire
Your sex for somewhat else

Stuffed Shirt made us chew over that poem time and again. What was dinned into me, courtesy of his gavel-beat renditions, was not that we were "the pure"—quite lovely enough without employing deceiving arts—but that to be a girl, a woman, was simply not good enough, that to attempt to improve on inadequate nature was at the very best a crime. Naturally, I resorted to the paint-box as quickly as I could, colouring and shading with growing daring, wilfully provoking his sarcasms and then his spite. It was then that I knew what he desired our sex for; not just to fit the scansion did 'expert' become more '-spurt' in his mouth.

74

He wanted to make-believe that he was our upright moral instructor preaching purity and abjuring painted preening, but there was a lascivious lip-smacking about his delivery which gave it away; he awaited and expected the coming of vain whorishness, for him that was all that girls could achieve. That drove me from the make-up as fast as you like and I became comfortable and content with my unadorned face. (Was that his intention? Was he a subtler preacher than I bargained for? Was I cleverly tricked, my own head-strength turned against me? Stuffed Shirt is long dead and I shall never have my answer.)

The "painted lady" business was revisited against me for a while at this school too, but that dirty little tag could not hold, as even the gossips' own near-inexhaustible disregard for the facts could not sustain the illusion. So instead they made a quick switch to hating me as unfeminine because I did *not* bother to paint up. Easily done, they discover a gigantic rip in their argument, but!—*there*—repaired, just-so, with a swift dose of magical thinking.

I refuse to stare out through a mask—I don't blame those who do, I'm simply stating my own case. Yes, yes, nature dealt me a more than fair hand and I can live without help, but, my old teacher's clever deception notwithstanding, by using make-up, painting and plastering, we give way to a male conceit, ultimately we surrender to their control.

Accuse me of exaggeration if you like (and this lot certainly would) but we are slowly gear-grinding backwards, the old male attitudes are gradually returning to the surface with a renewed respectability, a sheen provided by fake intellectualism, religion and the age-old fear of women bearing the apple of knowledge. I always found that a

75

contemptible story. To revert to vacuity and renewed subservience, to expect to be… I was going to say *to expect to be raped*, but perhaps we're not there quite yet—but not to know much difference between passion and obligation, to expect to have diminishing power, diminishing choice. But, I suppose, I'm just an hysterical woman.

Jilly Holdenbridge

I think I was waking up, by this time, coming to my realisation. There's no doubt that the move to the new school and being taught by Faslane, Miss, had a part in that. I was making my way, but as ever with a slow, foot-dragging, shuffling sort of progress; the changes helped to speed things on. Light was coming, dawning slowly, gradually, within me.

I heard plenty claim—later, not when he was noisily, terrifyingly there—that they were 'inspired' by Mr Wayman, but not me. I was too much in fear of him, too overawed, far too afraid of doing something to provoke that strange, irrational temper of his. I couldn't learn from him, I was always too nervous, waiting for the next outburst. I didn't think that I could learn from anyone, I felt so guilty if ever I did. But it changed when Faslane, Miss, she came along. I was changing already, but she helped.

Sabina Faslane

When they learned I was pregnant, the widely expressed opinion was: '*Tch*. Well, she would, wouldn't she, here comes time off for her and more work for us. She gets to do nothing and is paid for it. *Tch*. But at least she won't be back. What do you mean she's already set a date—you mean to get married to the father? Oh, to return to the

76

chalk-face! Good god, what presumption!' No one exactly claimed it was Wayman's baby, but somehow the storytellers managed to collapse the timeline between the 'rape' and the bump's first acknowledged appearance, and it became possible to all that Sweaterbusters was about to give birth to a carbon-copy of that ugly, strange, awkward man.

Glyn The Pin
History just lies there dead. It isn't going anywhere, is it? You have to go to it and if you do it's like visiting a graveside. You always know where to find it.

Dead things aren't supposed to change, but history does. That's what I learned, before I learned to close my ears to things that wouldn't do me any good.

Jilly Holdenbridge
I thought, was taught, all the way up the schooldays ladder, that there was history on the one side and, well, just lies on the other: yes or no, true or false. Then I encountered Faslane, Miss, though she wasn't a Miss for much longer after that, Mrs Westenra she became, a name the others couldn't make much out of anyway, pisstake-wise, so they hung to Fastlane. I hung to Miss. She talked not of this-happened that-happened, instead it was historiography, competing theories and goodness knows what: all in all, she turned everything I'd ever been taught inside out, from then on I knew that there were a million-million ill-fitting tale-tellings trying to fit in one hole called history, called truth.

Sabina Faslane

Am I—do I delude myself that I am—the defender of history, just as Alfred is the defender and guardian of the sky?

I loathe false history, but it's everywhere. I consider it my main job to stamp out falsehood, the falsehood that creeps in if we slacken our vigilance for one moment. When gaps arise, people plug them with speculation, conjecture, the blatant insertion of fiction, the falsification of history in order to flatter some leader, to lend credibility to some dubious narrative, rearranging the facts so that orders to kill are the fault neither of those who gave the orders nor of those who carried them out.

Historians are unlucky. Geographers don't have this much bother with flat-Earthers, physicists don't have constant harassment from gravity-deniers, mathematicians have it positively cushy. I suppose that biologists are still harassed by Darwin-haters, but I still say that history takes the most serious wound.

Jilly Holdenbridge

There was the Indian Mutiny. It was simple, so simple, it did not need to be disturbed. Britain had an empire and it owned India, which was a fact, a fact of history. Some Indians decided they didn't like the arrangement and tried to fight the empire. They rose up, they killed some women and kids in truly disgusting ways and then they were beaten, as people who do dirty things like that should be, right defeated wrong, light overcame dark and the empire went on—for a while, anyway. But Faslane, Miss, she got me really confused and angry, she came out with this stuff about how it wasn't really a mutiny as such as it wasn't just the army, and they didn't do some of the stuff history said they'd done and that some of the atrocities, such as stuffing kiddies into cannons and that sort of inhuman filth, was the work of the empire and not the Indians at all.

But the empire was us, *us*! We didn't, we don't, do things like that. I wanted, needed, orderly things at that time. History had to run in straight lines and it was either true or not. She was supposed to tell me about the *true* history, not wash it in mud and slush. Plus the lesson wasn't about the Indian Mutiny, we were supposed to be doing Napoleon and she'd done one of her asides, she'd heard Dumbcluck Parsons saying something stupid and she'd decided to talk to him instead of letting him wallow in his pig-ignorance; she'd gone off on a tangent, it wasn't even the proper, timetabled lesson. I was furious with Faslane, Miss, it was a betrayal, it broke her spell for me, for a short time anyway. She'd smashed up history and things no longer ran on their ancient, unbending lines.

Sabina Faslane

I have tried to shape myself into the woman I want to be, to shape myself and also beat out, un-buckle, the damage and distortion inflicted by others. In this way I've become, well, a bit of a stickler for truth in everyday dealings, after I have been caricatured as a temptress, sex-siren, painted whore, a slag, a child, a lost soul. And if it is so hard to keep order, to maintain the truth of one's own story, what hope is there for history, filled with worms, fictions, fabulations, poisons and wilful obscurity?

Glyn the Pin

I worked it out. History is like a recipe—you decide what you want in advance and then no matter what's there in store (in the pantry, Auntypoos would say), you take only the bits you want, combine them in the way you want, whizz it in the blender maybe, cook it up and present it as perfection and truth, *this is what was.*

Sabina Faslane

Mr Wayman is going to marry me, did you hear about that? Whether as the triumph of some icky romanticism or the just punishment-restitution for his crime of rape I don't know. I assume that the marriage-tale and the rape-tale did not have the same author, though I can't be sure; I'm just not close enough to the storytellers to find out. For me, it is the marriage-tale that is somehow more unbelievable and far sadder than its ugly cousin. I wonder why this is so. Is it that it is a puny effort to inject some hope and love, some honour and justice even, however desperately conceived, into a vile situation? Does a story of true love, I wonder, seem less credible than something that hurts and befouls? The marriage-tale certainly garnered a far smaller audience than the rape-tale: isn't that… sad?

Old Wash-Hands

Old Wash-Hands

I don't believe I ever saw old Alfie Wayman jealous but once. Left to myself I would have pronounced him merely envious, but all others employ the precise usage 'jealous' and so perforce I must bow to the vox of the pop, as I must not outrage my cardinal, guiding principle. Bernard Lawton, though, the man who made Wayman envious-jealous, he did not 'give a toss' what the majority believed; he would say bluntly what he thought and that was that. Wayman was another couldn't-give-a-tosser (sorry old man, unfortunate phrase; ah but no—it is intended, intended) about what he said. That shared characteristic was the root of the jealousy. It was all to do with Lawton's retirement speech.

Most people in this place drift towards retirement, that or they crawl, exhausted, emptied, drained. Some grow quiet and absorbed within themselves, day-counting and flicking at a mental abacus, calculating pension pots and lifespan-left, contemplating eternity and quietly fearing a survival made up of drawn-out illness and creeping, taloned poverty. For myself, I'm a crawler; meaning that I am proceeding to my goal, but belly-flat and sinuous, keeping out of the line of fire in a war that is forever about us. There will be no bravery recognition for me; I am not one for posthumous rewards. Besides, it is not my fight.

A retirement is a moment of mourning (bye-bye, missing you already, for God's sake don't embarrass us by coming back) and it should be dignified, sombre, quietly hypocritical, filled with dentured smiles and sad, stoic resignation (intended, intended) but the occasional awkward old dog won't lie down and be quiet; Lawton was one such, Wayman—will be—another, but Lawton was the elder, he was the one who had the chance to do it first, Wayman was demoted to being his batman and bag-carrier, and I suppose it would take a super-human not to resent that accident of seniority just a little.

Lawton was a rarity; an unextinguished idealist and enthusiast who departed the school possessed of the same fire and drive he exuded as a pink-cheeked newcomer back in a lost era, one that he swears was not really any better (nor worse) than the melee of today. He saw generations of fools come and go, some behind classroom desks, more behind office-desks and far more still on the green and the red benches of the politics that toys with our lives and work whether we wish it to or not. We referred to him as Professor Lawton, we in the Staff Room that is. Saints alone know what the bedlamic masses, the papuliferous populace of this scholastic scrapheap, called him: I kept myself well clear of that morass.

The "Professor" label was well-meant, indeed it was offered in honest tribute; we all concurred that a teacher of his calibre should have been researching and teaching at a decent if provincial-ish university, not hiding his light in the clapped-out pedant-lair of a province of a province. But Lawton had some self-harming penchant for standing before the slack-jawed and the indolent with the intent of rescuing them, a precious few at least, from the morass of ignorance in which they revelled and rolled. Now: that labour of love on behalf of the profoundly ungrateful demonstrated the self-sacrifice and self-harm that is the stamp of the true missionary, and to his credit over the

82

years, he certainly persuaded many an atrophied brain to catch afire and thrive. Rumour has it Mr Wayman was one such—back some way in time. Privately, I called them the Head and Deputy-Head of History. From that you may calculate how many History teachers there were in the school. And you may gauge a number of other things too.

The Head knew that trouble was coming: the speech was made in closed session, like Khrushchev's (yes indeed, I can do history too), no outsiders, no press, for God's sake no press. Her valedictory speech was an artful work of pious fraud, cobbled from hastily canvassed and shallow good-chap reminiscences: she plainly expected a *quid pro quo* from Lawton; go peacefully, old man (not 'go in peace,' she wanted rather more than that).

She had only been in post for three months: she knew Lawton was trouble, but had no real idea of what she was dealing with, and had either been poorly advised or elsewise someone fancied a little entertainment and had misled her with a sly, sporting grin. Lawton stood: those who knew him could see his head was trembling, a side-to-side motion portending the gravest danger; any member of any class of his from time immemorial could have told the poor Head what was coming; indeed, anyone blest with the least dash of sense. This night was not going to end without an accumulation of rhetorical casualties. But if she was afraid Lawton was going to expound upon the somewhat truthful rumour that the contents of her ever-present cup of coffee had origins more French (by which I mean Napoleonic) than Brazilian, her fears were groundless. Lawton was a gentleman; he would never have used such information, no matter how well founded, never. *Ad hominem* was not his style. Chiefly, anyway. I will grant him that much.

'May I begin by offering thanks to the Head for her... *kind* words. As a retiree—Is that really a word? Let us do away with it—and as an historian, I am in so many ways a man of the past. All I can do is look backwards. Studying history has taught me not to measure anything by my own span, "looking back" was always over centuries, millennia, as far as we can go, it gives one a healthy disdain for the significance of individual human lifespans. The past is full of lessons—good grief of course it is, that's why and how I've earned my corn for the last four decades—and people are forever saying that they will "learn the lessons of the past". How few of them really do can be demonstrated by the Ooslem bird flight that we call "progress". Material progress is made, I grant you, but progress as people? Progress of the mind? This is where my doubts take a frosty, cold hold upon my heart.'

There was a preacher's tone in the air, a pulpit atmosphere. I was always uncomfortable around evangelists (odd, I know, given my subject area). I recall my own schooldays, things were so much more comfortable then, but never trouble or controversy-free, and from the beginning I found the path of no-dissent to be the smoothest, even though from time to time I had to swallow some very bitter offerings and suppress the desire to gag. My two colleagues, however, kindled the zealot's fire. Of the two men, Wayman was perhaps the more dangerous, more possessed of that terrible missionary drive and dreary indefatigability of the true crusader. No sooner had he laid his chalk-stick to rest at the end of the working day than he headed home in that ludicrous car to spring-clean his optics and wait the fall of night. Him and his stars: least said, the better. God help the colleague who might venture to talk about, even to have the damn newspaper open at, the horoscope column. Lawton would at least shake off his black cape and relax with his good lady, though I've no doubt his domestic conversation was both charming and erudite, and the television, if they ever possessed one, remained firmly off.

You could not call Lawton any kind of Trades Union "millie", the accusation wouldn't stick to his old-school (intended, intended) hide. He was grown and mature aeons before the unions overplayed their hand and committed public hara-kiri at the feet of their hated political enemy. Lawton was more, what can we say, hardcore awkward-squad, a member even before the team-name was invented. More Groucho Marx than Karl—'whatever it is I'm against it'—he was no rooted, rigid opponent of change, nor one of those swivel-eyed fanatics who believes that "change" consists of smashing something up and waiting for someone else to arouse its phoenix spirit ("creative destruction" is the phrase, I for one have never seen it work). Wayman perhaps would be a millie but that his head is lost in those clouds. No, not the clouds, the clear sky. His fanaticism is spoken for. These men have no doubts. Not one shadow.

'I became a teacher not through naïve idealism but the perfectly realistic determination that I could, with hard work and, I knew, little reward, make my small contribution towards making each successive generation perhaps just that tiny bit less appalling than its predecessors. I did so by slipping them knowledge that was dangerous—I mean dangerous to the machine-world that the system has been, by and large, shaping them to fit. Knowledge such as: *life is not a blasted competition; achievement is not measured on a count of broken skulls and bodies used as stepping-stones.* If just one or two left here with that scintilla of subversion tucked away within the folds of their growing brains, I counted that as a success; I had sent out some little stars to shine brightly in the darkness.'

I am a creature of instinct and when, for instance, a storm is coming, my instinct is to seek shelter and where possible close the door, firmly. So whenever Wayman or his mentor started to darken like thunderheads, you can guess my tracks. No matter how mighty the storm, the world is more or less intact afterwards, albeit that one finds the occasional unsheltered unfortunate has been struck by lightning. I never nursed the wish for that to be me; living to fight another day is more my line.

'Had I been honest—by which I mean cynical—a "realist", if you really must cast it that way—I would have sat them down, one and all, year after year and said: "I shall tell you what you are. You are the beaten, the defeated. It was stamped upon you on the day of your birth, when the weight of inevitability was chained to your ankles. You are going to be encouraged, exhorted even, to 'achieve' here at school, to 'do well,' to strive to beat the rest: but the truth is that strive as you might, you will achieve at best primacy among pygmies, and by comparison with the real pack-leaders you may as well have switched off on day one of your so-called education and dreamed of sweet sugar-plums, or whatever takes your fancy. Because they have it all, those boys and girls out there, whose daddies and mummies pre-ordered their success, and whose own successes and eminence were not ordained by nature but purchased, ordered up, like the groceries. It is, it was, all for nothing, my cubs, the whole bally lot of it".'

Paints a bleak landscape, Mr Lawton, does he not? One that is seized and held in perpetuity by a well dug-in, well-established enemy with everything in their favour; money, power and very probably the will of God, whether suborned or not. So is he going to give in, our rhetorician, our little Cicero? Naturally not. He doesn't know when he is beaten and by George he is proud of it. It is super-hero time, boys and girls, watch him fly and watch Wayman sulk, earthbound, envious.

I am no advocate of equivocation, two-minds, dither or fudge. I am that which Lawton scorns (the word only, he and I do not need to agree on definitions) for I am a realist. Just as well as any scientist, any historian for that matter, I listen (so much more so than do others), I study, I weigh the evidence and then I decide. It is a moral process as much as an intellectual one, but a process it is, and a rational, quantifiable and justifiable one. Those who shrill their passions to the empty air shall not dub me a coward, pronouncing volubly before their brain has shown a flicker of electrical fire. I am decisive, but I am also considered and careful. It is no sin to withhold approval for the foolishness of others, but it is a foolishness all of its own to stand against it when no power can prevail. If you wish, by the bye, for the portrait of a boggler, an equivocator, then I invite you to survey our glorious leader: so eager is she to please all, to mollify the modernisers but also to succour the crusted ancients, that nothing ever gets done.

'Energised, inspired and downright arrogant as I was when I first stepped before a blackboard, I longed to hear a mighty voice boom out across the land, "Gradgrind is gone!" and, what's more, "Bernard Lawton bloody well killed him stone dead!" But, no such luck. The old fact-fiend has merely been… replaced. Updated. *Monetised.* This school used to have a spirit of independence, it was somewhere creative thought was cherished, now it has a management-board that spouts, parrot-fashion, all of the streams of comedy catchphrases and acronyms that the Department cares to vomit forth. There seems little point in us having any localised "management," we may as well take on the Orwellian touch and set up speakers and screens so that Whitehall's diktat can be delivered direct, one may say intravenously.

'We are being required—is that compelled?—to pervert all principle to teach an "island story" full of progress, glory and unending achievement, an over-inflated balloon of a national narrative, in which our country is always right, never wrong, never defeated, never even the least tiny bit mistaken. This is inimical to the understanding of history: history is *not* just something that happened to the English, with occasional happy consequences for Johnny Foreigner.

'What is teaching? We must decide. Is it an exercise in head stuffing, a manufactory process with a defined and undeviating end, an algorithm? In such a world, an exam-pass is the gate through which the successful shuffle towards a one-size-fits-all fate, while the failures meander, awaiting further instructions. Or is education the shaping of a whole person, to be equipped for all life, not just daily productivity and order taking? If we shape our children gingerbread-style for roles demanded purely by the immediate needs of the here and now, what happens when the progress before which we have abased ourselves declares those roles obsolete and our inflexible producing becomes pointless, our products themselves without a use, a purpose, superseded, redundant, "progressed" out of existence... have we not then failed?

'We need to teach the value of the feeling of knowing something, I mean by that *understanding* it, not the facile need to show off a superficial command of disconnected gobbets of "fact" or glib tags trotted out in a dead tongue, but to communicate and demonstrate that warmest feeling, true and lasting comprehension that aches to be shared. Another thing that troubles me among the hornet-swarm of un-settled scores that I foresee in clouds until the grave claims me is that concept of progress. Time was, it meant advancement in science, understanding, invention and exploration, pushing at horizons and making life better, either because life itself was easier or more explicable—preferably both. Nowadays, "progress" has been redefined, narrowed down to parsing measurements of economic growth, of production, of consumption, of my tiny-minded ability to sell to you rubbish that you really don't want, and your cunning talent in returning the dirty-palmed favour. An historian is in a unique place to detect backwards motion—as he is perpetually looking backwards, he suddenly thinks he's going forwards, he becomes... queasy.'

As I said: the preacher's tone. It always made me wish to flee, but as always I was obliged to remain to be bombarded. There was one teacher, a relic, a trace of my long-lost childhood and yes, she too had a dash of the gleam-eyed Ranter—very much a Lawton-Wayman creature in her unknowing way. When she taught us about the Bible, she came alive, hideous-goblin alive. They had a fine way, at that little school that I recall so well and chiefly fondly, of working Bible-stories into everyday lessons. We children would have been in favour of a perpetual Christmas—now there was a story we could understand and relate to—but this one, she was more a chops-smacking raconteur of tales of sin and wickedness, betrayal and blood-money, nails and thorns. She revelled in the company of devils and demons, ah but they were there to be battled and vanquished, but her prime, profoundest interest (by interest I mean obsession, I mean hate, I mean with relish) was a man. None other than the Procurator of Judea, Mr Clean-Paws, the Roman, Pontius Pilate. His actions were, for her, the crux (intended, intended) of the greatest story she knew. Pick up your texts and join me, Matthew 27:24 (*King James* version please, for God's sake—intended, intended).

Confident that with your fine education you have the words engraved upon your heart, I shall epitomise: the mob is baying and the Roman, minded to acquit, is at a loss, his wisdom received as no more than juridical wriggling, he is locked in a hopeless struggle. Exhausted by the unteachable, he calls for water, and, by washing his hands before the witnessing masses, admonishes their injustice, informing them that the problem is now theirs with a terse 'See ye to it.'

The missionary, on reading out the passage, spat: 'You see now? See what he did? You see it? That man, that wicked man; more wicked yet than the traitor Judas!' She held that the old hand-washer, the procurator, the authority in the land, knew that her Lord was innocent, but that he gave way not even to some devil-sent temptation but simply to his own spineless nature, he feared to stand against the howling demands of the crowd, but instead chose to absolve himself and make a coward's offering of an innocent man. Pilate's brand of moral evil delivered her

Lord to his death and she cursed that Roman ahead of all the bestiary of villains in history or literature.

Lawton nurtured, zoo-kept, his own peculiar bestiary. 'That the current Secretary of State for Education emerged, made entire, from a mould, rubber-faced and rubber-brained, pre-shaped in every feature and with a misprinted circuit for a mind, is a sad fact, but it has little bearing on the further sad facts on which I must dilate. He is merely the latest in a line of gobbledegook-spouting mannequins who have "managed" the schools system to near-destruction. We are surviving, barely, a man who wishes to marketise and monetise—more nasty little nonwords that wear their ugliness face-forward and proud—who has talked up empty phrases such as "localism" and "parent power" whilst cramming power into his own possession like a hamster filling its elastic cheeks—who has talked of shedding from the school day "soft" subjects—take a bow, a final one, PE, law, art, drama, *history* and other notoriously unmonetisable disciplines—and to turn our little back-gardens of Academe into rump-schools that take the kids that the pay-schools don't want because they will spoil their spotless reputations, cost them coin with which they do not wish to part.

'Our political lord and master has gone so far as to refer to the teaching profession as an obstruction, "the fat monopoly," even comparing us to a giant ball of grease currently blocking the drains of Central London; an interesting comparison, most revealing in its own way. We block progress—the progress of sewage, if one follows his claims over-literally, *pedantically*.

'But the enemies of promise are not just exhaling dry dust and meaningless management-speak in Whitehall, they are *here* too. The same mynah-bird phrases have percolated inside this little village schoolhouse, inside staff meetings and training days, we have been drip-fed the notion that an attempt to offer an all-round liberal education is to block progress, that we as a profession are behind the times, we are "the fat monopoly", with its lumpen face set against "the future", whatever that may mean.

'That politicians spout nonsense is axiomatic; the more important the politician the greater the vacuity. What appals me is the slavish repetition of their silly pronouncements closer to home. The current catchphrase, the language of the hour, is echoed, nay parroted, as it careens down from ministerial to pastoral levels. Competition, then, has been set loose on us—competition for children's heads (forget their souls, a dubious concept anyway, if they exist then they are pre-sold), a money-mania so blatant that soon we will not just be branding the school and the classrooms with corporate logos, but the kids themselves will be compelled to sport ad-space on their foreheads and sell each other trivial trash to afford their lunch. We are heading for a "future" in which schools are failure-factories, churning out industrial components of indifferent manufacture, components which will be used—as in employed—or not as the needs of modern business go, used and dispensed with, with no concern for those little cogs and gears themselves, as they will have no worth outside of their immediate utility and the manner in which they can be persuaded to part with their pay, such as it is. And those cogs and gears, they are shaped with the needs of the current, foreseeable market in mind, not even the market of tomorrow or the market-to-come. Unplanned obsolescence dogs their pitiful careers and dictates their fate. We were once told that we were heading for a machine-future and so we are, but it is a vending-machine future at best. So this is the appalling, tragic message for the average, the ordinary, the ones whose parents cannot buy them a better model of life: accept that you are beaten, allow the mediocre but moneyed to rise high, buoyed by their vapidity.

'In the battle between the teacher and the technocrat there can only be one winner. I am sorry to be deserting the field, but soon enough I should have to be carried on the back of a younger warrior, probably, sadly, in the heat of full flight: I shall soon be a burden, not a fighter. So perforce I must be a quitter. But I don't depart wholly in despair: the fight is not at an end. Younger and better fighters, I hope, are there to turn the tide of battle. If a fat monopoly can prevent the coming of this vision of the future from a man of the past, then praise be to that fat monopoly.'

And so the sermon rolled like a boulder towards a ponderous conclusion. Lord preserve us from world-savers —they are nothing (save One) but trouble. This one was not quite finished, however.

But—my thoughts return to that other vehement exposition—it seemed, still seems to me, that the man Pilate just wanted to avoid a whole lot of unnecessary fuss; any other decision would have provoked a riot, which would have had to be suppressed before too much damage was done; time, men and resources put at risk or wasted. Sat among uncomprehending youngsters, all aware and afraid of her tone but few grasping her meaning and vaguely fearing her anger was directed their way, that she was somehow digging out and condemning their own petty

93

villainies, I comprehended more, if only just a little, than did the rest of the class. I remained silent but I was not stupid; had Pilate not acted as he did, I reasoned, how could the holy purpose (that which she clutched to her scrawny breast like an amulet and preached at the drop of a hat and the top of her voice) have been achieved? If Procurator Pilate had behaved like a jurisprude (intended, intended) there would have been no Golgotha, no Passion, no Resurrection. How much greater a villainy would *that* have been? The question was formed, perfectly in my mind, but my hand never went up. Of course. There would no doubt have been an answer, a retort, but not one that carried me toward enlightenment or contained any thought at all, and besides more than just a storm-flash or two would have accompanied it, is it not so? As I said, I was not stupid in my silence.

Matthew and Luke, do you know, regard him, Pilate, as innocent: Matthew believes Pilate only gave way to the unrelenting pressure of the Jewish leaders who believed that He had blasphemed by claiming a special place for himself before God. These leaders aimed to unsettle the Roman, to whom such charges could, of course, mean nothing, by telling him that Jesus claimed to be King of the Jews; no Roman could ignore the empire-threatening implications of *that* claim. But still Pilate remained unmoved; he saw that no Roman law had been broken and was moved towards amnesty. The washing of his hands, by the way, is a story exclusive to the Gospel of Matthew. It was his way of abjuring murder, of refusing to condone something that he possessed the sagacity to realise that he could not stop.

'What *is* a "monetiser"? If we are in the business of minting new, appalling wordlets, let me identify it as the price-tag, the pound-sign, now attached to every school exercise, that is the intended *point* of every one of those exercises, from the coulombs and joules of the sciences to the crafted words of literature to the dates and doings of history, ancient and modern. Truth is now weighed in cash.'

'What is truth?' asked Pilate the philosopher, faced with his dilemma. Worthy of Socrates, and it parries Lawton admirably. Now understand please, I do not make an icon of the old hand-washer; I know better than to offer up to false idols (after all, I know my trade), but I do consider Pilate's to be the representative of a neglected but noble corner of the nature of humanity; to wit, the capacity to admit when a situation is beyond one's control, not to go headlong, self-destructive, against an irresistible force. Pilate and I, we represent the true soul of the common man. The others, the Lawtons, the Waymans, the fierce priestess of my childhood schoolroom, they are the distortions, the stray rays. To my mind, crusaders have a habit of charging in, laying about them and then loudly claiming victory and holy vindication before retreating, bloodied, disorderly and tatty, with their Jerusalems afire and peopled with the new, involuntary dead. The occasional realist raises his shield, blocks his view of the shining city and admits it is time to go home, but most of them press on purposefully and blindly, taking no account of the lessons of history (intended, intended).

I espouse and uphold a philosophy, a gentle scheme of thought which, if taken up widely, could bring boon and benefit to one and all, and harm to none. Unlike others I do not prate, preach or rant about my convictions, I believe that example followed by emulation is best; I set an example of thought and behaviour I hope will seep into my listeners, draw gradually through their souls, so that they feel its blessings mounting gradually within and correct their behaviour, leading to the spread of the good gentleness, the treasuring of true justice, the protection of the weak (and, may I add, the meek—intended, intended) and in doing so I shall make sure that an historic wrong is righted.

Vox populi, vox dei—that is more than a phrase, it encapsulates an essential truth. Sometimes, what appears to be the will of the mob is better described as the wisdom of the many, through which one may descry the true plan of God: in such circumstances, it is the correct thing to withdraw with dignity, trusting not the mob but the pure, just and universal mind that animates them, unbeknowing though they be. Wise is the man who can tell when his calls for earthly justice stand in the way of a greater plan, strong is he who, having realised this, can step away and allow the greater scheme to prevail, even though he be smeared throughout eternity with the reputation of a traitor, or a coward.

Sometimes I plead his cause, Pilate, to my classes. Not openly, certainly not in the manner of the fire-priestess, for that would not do—not to mention that it would buck the curriculum and probably undermine the ethos of the dear old school. Still, I find ways and means in the course of moral and ethical discourse (if one can call it that, if that can be had amongst unformed, callow tadpole minds). Did you know that Peter effectively absolves Pilate of blame in the Acts? That even Dante is half-hearted about the procurator's punishment—that is if he can be seen to be mentioning him at all—bathing his palms in the Acheron, if present in the land of hopelessness at all? I care not if they understand. I suppose they simply think (intended, intended) that I am musing to myself. I suppose I am. But a lesson whose meaning is buried is a lesson nonetheless. Not every moral has to be floodlit and fanfared.

I was there; I watched and I listened as the old man spoke. I agreed with some parts of his oration and very much not with others: but to take sides, applaud or throw rotten eggs? No fear. I stuck with my philosophy; the brave may claim the favours, in the very short term. My kind and I do not want them. I didn't, in any case, consider Lawton's behaviour courageous. He was not orating to a fired-up crowd that hung on his every word, it's true; but he did not care, he sought to sway nobody. He just wished to have his say and be gone, what happened after that was scarcely his business. This was his Parthian Shot: the great crusader was washing his hands of us all (intended, intended). He used an opportunity, a safe opportunity it may be said, to deliver himself of his scorn; after all what were they going to do to him, what *could* they do? Safety breeds a false and showboating bravery.

Whatever his intentions, all Lawton stirred was sludge— a faint tremor in the dull apathy of those in the room, he addressed the exhausted faces of what was just another branch of the species of the beaten. Only Wayman was electrified and he was alone, if loud, when he applauded and cheered. There were one or two expressions of interest, but I could detect the majority-mood and was not minded to oppose it. Not me. Old jealous Wayman, now perhaps he was the one who showed the true courage (or call it foolhardiness) to have *hear-heared* his man so openly, for he forewarned the powers that be of what was to fall from his lips in the vaguely-dated future when he himself would step up to claim his pension and make his parting speech.

If Pontius Pilate is the patron saint of moral cowards and backsliders, so be it; I always saw the right and good in his actions. For me, he was the 'just person' in that ancient story, he knew that he could not win and had the largeness of soul to admit it, in public too. Pilate was guiltless, and he was also in the right, and I wager he never ended up on the wrong end of a vengeful sword, or a fork of lightning. That is my answer, unspoken as ever, to those who praise the 'moral courage' of the likes of Bernard Lawton.

'The current government is making a fetish out of "academic rigour" but, owing to their appalling stupidity, we are beset not by "rigour" but "rigidity", so set, immovable, it is brittle and will break. Into pieces.'

The aim, the point, of life is to be a good man (I maintain that *man* is the correct form and I will not accept lectures; Miss Faslane please take note) and resist the follies of men, especially when they gather and the mind of the one joins with those of others and they commune, they share their rage and illogic until it becomes magnified, exalted and the reason residing in those minds is somehow shed. To recognise this process, to resist it and try to restore that lost reason is the function of a good man, but there is no good in him sacrificing himself to the mob-instinct when it is loosed untrammelled and unstoppable, he is in all ways wise to step aside and having done this remains in all ways a good man. And where better for this man to be placed but within a school, where he may attempt to nurture his gentle philosophy in the brutish

98

breasts of the bedlamic masses, to offer precious wisdom to their as-yet unformed minds, a grain of hope far better, far more precious than Lawton's nuggets of "forbidden" knowledge or Wayman's baseball-bat approach to teaching.

Indeed: moral education is what is required and part of the point of a good moral education is to reach the point where one may calculate when one is outnumbered, outplayed. Lawton was wrong; our youngsters are not beaten from the off, but they have certainly never been taught to realise when the game is no longer worth the candle. The brightest of them (intended, intended) came to the correct conclusion long before the dull remainder did, and it was the ones who recognised when the limit was reached and who settled for their lot at that point who did best out of life, I can guarantee you that, time after time, generation after generation. Those who kicked against the pricks fared, of course, the worst of all. Tub-thumpers such as Lawton and Wayman encouraged this wrong-headedness, preached them to their doom by encouraging them to exceed their own tipping-point. Once you are aware that you are in a cage, why gnash and gnaw against the bars and seek impossibilities such as escape?

Once you have encountered your limits you are far better committing your energies to the task of exploring and defining the fullness of your boundaries, finding your place amongst the space allotted you. Those who reach this realisation are the ones to find and claim the prime spots and to settle well. Bar-chewers are left with bloody mouths and angry minds and also the least promising places. This fuels their indignation, but it does not make them *right*. One does not have to see these things as any kind of justice (Pilate saw no justice in what went on before him, after all), one needs only to recognise the inevitable. If you must, then, behave like fools, see ye to it. It is nothing to do with me.

Glyn The Pin

Glyn The Pin

I have a gift, a talent, if you'd call it that, which I reckon I wouldn't. Perhaps I would if I knew more about it, how to tap into it, control it, then maybe I could use it to some sort of purpose, maybe bottle and sell it; it would be popular, sure. But as things are, as they always have been, it knows me and it uses me, not the other way round. If I could just control it, I don't even want to understand it, just turn it off and on when I want, then it would be amazing, I could do so much, go pretty much anywhere I wanted, take whatever I wanted and no one would ever know it was me. Yes, go anywhere, do anything, touch anything (or anyone). No one would know.

I really can't stand people when they treat me as if I don't exist, like I just don't figure with them. It gets my goat, I lose it and that's got me into trouble quite a bit over the years. The least people can do is acknowledge that you're there; there's no call for them to go pretending that there's just a blankspace. But they do it and they do it often. They turn me into empty air. I get see-throughed, blankspaced, so often I just can't cope with it.

Glyn Capstone

Teachers used to do it to me; other kids too. Then it was the dole office, then bosses, people in the pub, on the street, friends of my snooty ex, supposed friends of mine —all sorts, in fact. They judged me, the lot of them, and my sentence was invisibility.

It goes way back in kiddyhood, for me. I'm not trying to be an amateur head-examiner; I just know it's true. I've a pretty good memory. Lots of my childhood is hidden by clouds, but some bits come out clear and true, even now. It's not my fault that they're the bad bits, the bits that got me mad and keep me mad. I was a happy kid, a pretty one too; I still have the photos to prove it. Here's one of me, age three, moppetish golden curls (that hair proved none too long-lasting, but that's a separate complaint) and what my aunty called a roguish smile. She meant it as rib-nudge praise. She still had a bit of time for me then.

I'm not afraid to point the blame; I think this thing started somehow with Auntypoos. She had an infantile, jackdaw personality, the tendency to swoop down on the brightest-shining thing and make it wholly hers for a day, an hour, a year or more, but eventually to get bored with whatever she had previously clasped to her heart, now lying broken or neglected, out of sight and definitely out of mind. That was the way in which she had rescued her dead sister's little baby, the way she cooed and wept over him and ruffled his growing curls, then realised he was a bit of a drag and a tie and learnt to bend her vision around him, to incorporate him into one of her plentifully broad blind-spots. She kept me in a state, alive and yet nonexistent, that others gradually learned to accept. The birth of a blankspace: there you have it.

I couldn't have been much older than I was in that colour-drained snap when it happened, the first blanking I can remember. I was on my own, a bit bored, quite a bit bored as it happened; it was just-me that day though that was not uncommon. I was in this garden I didn't know, I think it was the friend's, yes, the aunt had met the friend by

102

then, and I was kicking stones, pulling at things that trailed and chasing birds, anyway for a while the aunt and the friend must have gone indoors and I was alone and the thought came to pull myself up on the fence; it was way above my head height and I wanted to see inside the next garden, where I could hear the voices of children playing. I was strong and determined and bored so I climbed easily and got good hand and footholds so I could see the other garden.

Glyn The Pin

There were three or four kids there but only one near enough to call to; he was tiny, wimpy-weedy, specky and all sort of sapped-white like he had no blood—if anyone was a born blankspace, there he was. I let choices pop up in my mind: talk to him, ignore him, climb over to play with him or maybe hit him. But I was super fed-up from being left on my own, and anyway I realised that I knew this boy faintly, we'd been shoved together by our keepers some time before while they gave us the ignore and just yattered: we'd played with buckets and spades in a sandpit where the sand was blackish-orange and full of dead leaves and other vile bits, but still okay for patting down in the little buckets and coming out castle-shaped, because the bottoms of the buckets had tower-shapes for corners. Yeah, I remembered that day's play and it was okay, so, I thought deck the idea of hitting him, try being nice, good way to pass the time, so from me it was a matey 'Hey!' but his white face didn't even twitch; he looked at me like you'd look at mist.

'Hey! It's me! Remember me?'

He was such a little snot, he'd probably learned all his manners for teacher and church and for in front of grownups, but there in that garden he forgot them quick enough and didn't even bother to spare me any embarrassment, didn't even try to remember me, didn't even care.

'Me!' I kept the smile going, but that feeling was on the up in me, the feeling that was to become familiar; I made one last grab for recognition.

'It's me, Glyn, Glyn Capstone, you know, Glyn the Pin! We played in the sandpit and…'

No good. He didn't even have me in his eyes any longer. He saw nothing but the emptiest of air. I smashed a renewed desire to jump the fence and lamp him. I gave up, dropped back down and let the fence swallow both him and my red humiliation.

Glyn Capstone

Perhaps people only see me if they are looking through a filter. I exist in a different, shifted, wavelength of light. You need special equipment, high-tech, sci-fi detectors. There are only a few who can spot my occasional slips out of the shadows. I could've been some kind of spy, a secret agent, something really impressive, if only I could've been the master of this thing. But it had me beaten, all ways up, right from the start. I get spotted occasionally, but then, so do ghosts.

The phenomenon, once begun, happened time and again, thick and fast: me, blotted out, flipped into nonexistence. I had plenty of time to test my power, this gift, and found out quickly that a power or a gift was what it just wasn't. If I wanted to get attention I'd be blankspaced, but if I craved invisibility to spare my blushes or get away with something bad, people's eyes would fall on me as if I was floodlit, standing flat-foot guilty in an inescapable circle of accusing brightness and without a single shadow to dart into. From light-ray resistant to pinned down and dazzled. That's always been the extent of my lucklessness, the way things work, consistently—and against me. I'm not so much the Invisible Man, I'm more, what, a flickering bulb? That'll do; it's appropriate, you'll see. Even my friends, best mates sometimes, could blankspace me, turn me into emptiness. I am the, what, Subluminal Man: struggling against being a nullity, battling forever, vainly with voracious obscurity.

Glyn The Pin

Alright, I admit I was rushing; I was late for school and I knew I was not so see-through that I could get away with claiming I had been there at Registration the whole time. My teacher, second year primary, was Mrs Hailibury; she blankspaced me most of the time, but she was hard to fool. Hard? Impossible. As impossible to fool as she was to please. I had to get there in time, prove I was present and only then could I blend with the background. In my hurry I made it down from the aunt's house to the main road and I was going at a good clip, playing bumper cars and dodgems with the slow-motion shoppers and the office workers stalking the bus, not one of them saw me but I didn't care. But what's that horrible saying about don't-care being made to care? I realised I wasn't the only straggler; there across the big road was a foursome of kids from my year, two girls two boys, and alright-alright, I admit I wanted to join that gang, not just then but ever since I'd started school—but—you know without needing to be told what had come of that little ambition. They never even saw me, not even enough to make a thing out of ignoring me.

I do stupid all too easily—so, so stupid. I chase after things I can't have, can and will never have. This time I did some real, sprinting chasing, my stupidity gave me foot-wings and I ran after the four so fast I nearly left my breath behind.

Glyn Capstone

Perhaps I thought if I mixed in with them I'd be in less trouble if I was late for school, I could dilute my guilt somehow; that was how the stupidity took complete possession. I sped up, I waved my arms, I yelled 'Hoy! Hoy! Hoy!' though I'd never yelled 'Hoy' at anyone ever, so there it was, so over-stupid, so mad for just one at-me glance had I become. And the knot of school-goers I was pursuing? They didn't flinch, didn't turn and peer, neither slowed to let me catch up nor sped up to leave me trailing. They were just like the adults in the street; they were not even ignoring me, not even trying. I'd dropped off everyone's radar again and this time it prickled my skin like a shower of hot needles.

Even the car seemed to nudge me gently aside as if I were nothing but a swirl of wind, and yet the impact made me coldly aware I *was* there, touchable if not seeable, I was sent into a sequence of crazy back-flips, a spiral I thought would never end, not until I hit a wall, a lamp-post or another oncoming car perhaps, and got turned into blood-mush. I don't remember landing, but the pain came clearly enough and remained with me, throbbing, scraping and insistent. My vision was in a whirl, as if I were still doing my somersaults, but I quickly realised that amongst other things I had been whirled and twirled and spun into visibility, by misadventure. People were gathering around me, the passers-by who only seconds before had been passing me by very effectively, the driver of the car standing over me looking both concerned and scared, I thought I even caught a glimpse of the four kids I'd been chasing, craning over the small crowd, but maybe that was my hope, my fancy. I was lifted, put in the car, taken home and presented to the aunt, who flittered and gibbered for a short time before the friend came round and calmed her, and in calming her triggered the aunt's forgetting me all over again. I was taken to hospital but after a long wait, one I could tell had started to annoy the aunt and for which she was silently assigning the blame to me, it was established that I just had cuts and bruises, that I needed to be put to bed and allowed to sleep and put there I was, out of sight and very much out of mind once more before much more time could go by.

I got some stares and gasps when I went back to school and I got asked what happened and if I was okay, but there was a sense of duty-done when they had asked and minds and eyes slid off me yet again. My hopes were raised a little later, when the Head, who loved to raise his voice and point his finger, took up the cause of Road Safety in one bass-boom school-assembly homily to the children, all gathered around cross-legged to hear his wisdom mixed with the daily prayers and hymns. The Head was tall, solid, intimidating and always reminded me in stature of a policeman, his granite looks, grave air of authority, the way he towered over us and the way his head seemed unnaturally long, tapering away carved and helmet-like. He should have taken up directing traffic to keep us safe: it would probably have worked better than booming lectures, all in all.

We were commanded to Walk And Never To Run, told that Dashing Is Dangerous, that we were to Look Left, Look Right, Look Right Again And Then Cross, and if we didn't then there would be Serious Consequences. Yes, he Talked Like That. You could always tell when he was going to get to the good bit of his talks when he boomed still more, coming out with a sky-cracking tone that he should probably have saved until he knew for sure that the end of the world was near; everyone would've taken him seriously, no one would've laughed. To be fair, no one was laughing that day either; we all knew that this was the voice he used when he Named The Guilty: condemnation had previously been heaped upon absentees, litter-droppers, people who came to school with colds instead of Staying Home To Sweat It Out—but this time it was to be Children Who Dashed Across The Road.

Glyn The Pin

'Just last week we had a Boy Who Almost Lost His Life At Our Very Gates! Ran out into the road Without Looking didn't you, Thomas Pettington? Indeed!'

I knew the Head was exaggerating; I was there, saw it happen, though maybe, probably, nobody saw me. I was at the school gate when Pettington, someone who was almost as near a nobody as I was, came haring past me as if Ginger Jarrot and his mob were after him (they were already gone, I'd seen them too, part of making sure I could go home a different way from them, knowing that I couldn't rely on invisibility, that was part of my security routine) and straight into the road, eyes dead ahead, as if trying to blankspace the cars out of his way. You can do that to people but not cars, as he found out, running head-on with the side of a grey Ford as it crawled by and boinging back to the pavement with a pop-eyed-amazed look on his face. But there's no way that Pettington Almost Lost His Life, the car was going dead slow, he was going quicker than it, he'd probably hit a trampoline harder in his time, but got a nicer bounce out of it.

One thing more about that little incident; Pettington was carrying this toy car, a die-cast Corgi he'd been showing off all day just to get jealous looks, and as he rebounded off the 1:1 scale car, his model flipped through the air and landed neat as you like in my hand. I could never really catch properly, but this fell dolly to me, plopped into my palm as if it had been just handed, and for one moment I thought if only I could rely on my power, use it, and just vanish into blankness with this little prize as my secret. But I couldn't. I mean I couldn't rely on the power. The moment I decided to steal that toy I'd have been stabbed with light rays, revealed, caught: Shown Up, the Head would have called it. So I stayed honest and unremarked.

'And there was a recent Incident That Was Even Worse!' intoned the Head, his eyes bulging as his voice boomed, 'One girl from this school was seen—Running On The Road Deliberately—Playing "Chicken!"' At this, a really ugly girl, we called her Freak Face, suddenly got even freakier in the face though it was a hard thing for her to do as it was already twisted, wonky and dead spotty, and though she reckoned she was as hard as any boy she went all teary when the Head looked right down at her, 'Is That Not So, Janice Hownall?' That was Freak-Face finished.

Glyn Capstone

Now at this point I should've been terrified; surely the Head was going to turn his granite-statue body round to blaze his eyes at me, 'And who was knocked flying by a car because he Ran Across A Road Without Looking, Glyn Capstone?' Yet I was waiting for it, to hear my name called louder than I had ever heard it called, to have not just his angry attention but the curious, mocking, maybe even some sympathetic gazes of everyone in that room, teacher and schoolkid alike; waiting for it, anticipating, yes I was looking forward to it. But the fire in his eyes died, the boom crept out of his voice, he lost his anger and the lecture was over before I could get a mention. Next thing he was congratulating some stupid school sports team and I was cocooned in anonymity while Pettington and Hownall stole the spotlight.

Glyn The Pin

It works opposite-ways too, like this. I was drifting, stargazing falling dust, old Mrs Hailibury was talking, she was getting one of her sick-making favourites to stand up and show off his stupid fiddle—violin he'd call it, the snoot. His name was Rosin. Nickname, I didn't know the real one. He spoke nicey-nice, sat up, paid attention and never stargazed dust. He made plink-plink-plunk noises with his fingers on the fiddle strings and then he tucked this yellow duster under his chin, which made him look really stupid, and then he started sawing. Now I'm not saying the tune was bad; it was a bit slow, bit sad, bit dull, I should've guessed it was something like a hymn, but the basic thing far as I'm concerned is that it was nothing to do with me. I wasn't going to stop the teacher or Rosin or the music, I just wasn't interested or part of it and I just wanted to go back to my dust-beam starfall.

'So,' said Mrs Hailibury loudly, even before the tune had stopped, just like a DJ on the radio who can't wait to start on yabbering, 'who can tell me what tune that was?'

I couldn't tell her, but I didn't mind if everyone else wanted to play guessing-games.

'Can *you* tell me—Glyn Capstone?'

I went rigid with shock. I was *visible*. And visibly, I thrashed like I was ditched in deep water; don't-know-don't-care would've been a true answer but Hailibury didn't want true did she, she wanted *right*.

'I Was Born Under A Wandering Star?' I burned as I said it, it was the closest thing I could think of, it sounded a *bit* right, but I knew it wasn't going to be right enough.

'*Feh*,' said Hailibury, that and no more; at last her eyes emptied and her gaze left me, I was gone again, to my relief. I didn't care then and I don't care now but that tune was 'Amazing Grace' and I can't hear it now without unwanted remembering; it intrudes on me, invades peace like all bad memories. I would've waited outside after school and done Rosin one to get back at him, but for the fact that he grabbed my elbow after he'd put up his fiddle and said, 'Those songs do sound alike. The rest of the class didn't know the answer either.' Rosin now, he only noticed me because he wanted to avoid a hitting.

Glyn Capstone

I met my opposite, my flipside. I should have hated him, but one of the few lessons to which I bothered listening taught me about magnets, opposite poles. Alan Brotherton came into my class in the last term before we were all due to take the big exam that everyone was scared about. He had a sly look, handsome-sly but still sly, and he always had an idea that would be a "good grin" or a "good doss", and we would "neverever get caught". The fact was, though, *he* never got caught, but as he slid out of sight there I was, trailing, noticed and nabbed every time. But when he wanted attention, there it was sitting begging. He had timing and style and every other hateful quality. Greeny, our teacher, a kind, gentle and easy-smiling man who sometimes forgot to forget about me, was going on about colours and said that soldiers dressed in khaki.

'Does anyone know what khaki is?' he asked.

'Yes, you start your engine with it!' chirruped Alan Brotherton; the whole room blew up laughing, the whole room his, teacher too, and he milked the laugh by miming driving, bouncing up and down on his seat, but instead of being told to calm down or stop now, like I would have been (had anyone ever paid enough attention to listen to a joke from me) he kept it going, kept getting laughs and admiring gazes, then he even managed to calm down and stop before the joke was done to death, restored order all on his own and was even more admired for that; he did it so right he was admired for the rest of the day and much longer, and he didn't try to follow it up or outdo it and he was admired for that too, damn him.

Glyn The Pin

I got mates with Alan Brotherton, which was good, well sort of, as ever with me, it had bad bits, bad for me. In my head, I called him "light fingers". I know that usually means something else, but my meaning was that he made light, produced it from his fingers, as if he spun with it like a spider with silk. He got attention, Alan, and he got it when he wanted it, but not when he was up to no good; he wasn't one for getting caught and looking stupid. People always looked at him when he was doing something good, or clever, or funny. He didn't just make the light, but attracted it, brought it to himself and then bounced it off to the eyes that he wanted to be seen by.

He had light inside him I was sure. He could always do things when I couldn't: the incident with the battery and the bulb showed me that. I took a half-ruined birthday present to school one day, an electricity kit that let you build circuits and light tiny bulbs with wires from batteries; well, that was the idea, but all I did was lose the fiddly bits and come up with wires connected to batteries that produced dead, flat nothing. Alan Brotherton had boasted he could do something with it and I grumbled 'it's all yours' and tossed the remnants of the kit, sliding around in its half-empty box, in his direction. He picked up a battery, one I was sure must be an utter dud, fingered some thin wire, threaded it lightly between the battery and the bulb— and:

'There!' he was happy, triumphant, bloody smug. He took his fingers away and the bulb went out again. It stayed out when I tried to do the same thing, though I was sure I had copied him move for move.

'There, like that,' he said in a patient voice as, back in his hands, it lit up again, silent and smooth. 'Simple.'

I was stupid enough to try again a couple more times, stupid enough to will the bulb to light, frowning hard at it, stupid enough to be wounded by its dumb refusal.

'It's *easy*,' said Alan, patient no longer, realising he was in the presence of a fool. He lit the thing up over and over, just to show me. All that light. Maybe I made mates with him so as I could borrow some. Though that didn't work.

Alan Brotherton loved to doss. Even as he gained bigger and better marks and praise in class he was forever planning the next 'good doss,' if he liked you he called you a good dosser, I was proud, swollen up, whenever he called me that. We'd clocked a place we called The Hole, everyone was fascinated with it, boys anyway; it was a room underneath the school and you weren't allowed in. There were steps down to it and these sloped metal doors and some kids said it was a dungeon, see, the school was dead old, like a castle, and it was a stinking pit where prisoners got chucked and forgotten about.

Only the caretaker was allowed in. He was this grey-haired bloke in a dirty blue one-piece suit and dirty, scuffy boots he never changed, he had a moustache too which looked grey, but if you got up close you could see was more like green, and he never opened his mouth, no one had ever heard him say so much as a word. Anyway, The Hole was his, he had the keys to it and he vanished down there every day and came out dirtier than ever. We were fascinated by The Hole and wondered what was down there; it looked exciting. Those who didn't think it was a dungeon thought monsters lived there, if you dared to get close enough to the metal doors you could hear these sort of breathing and clicking noises and this hum, a buzz that never stopped. Stupid little kids and girls believed it and were scared. Species Grogan, boring-smart and science-dull about everything, said it was just the boiler-room and nothing any good, but Species Grogan wasn't a good dosser, he never dossed, so we ignored him and ignored the dungeon and monster believers, we wanted a good doss and we wanted to doss in The Hole and didn't care what anyone said.

All we had to do was wait for the no-speak caretaker to forget to lock The Hole; so on loads of playtimes we lurked near those doors, ready to sneak in but never making it. The dirty man had this dog, though; he called it something daft like Lady or Laddie; anyway, one time he was coming up out of The Hole he turned and shut the doors but hadn't locked them when he heard this commotion; a crowd of kids was whooping and screaming and they had Lady-Laddie in the middle, jumping up and snapping, trying to get something from some kid's hand that he held up high and kept wobbling and waving. Caretaker moved his lips a tiny bit and there came out this amazing shrill whistle, a real ear-shocker, so this man had no voice maybe but he could whistle like he was miked-up, but for all that it didn't stop the kids from yelling and it didn't get the dog to go to him; in fact, the ring of kids got rowdier and the dog jumped higher and danced on its back legs as the treat or whatever it was got waved just over its nose out of reach. Another ultra-whistle didn't work and so the caretaker, for some reason trying to brush some dust off his front as he went, clomped in his dirty boots over to where the crowd was. I wanted to go too, to listen out for if he actually spoke to anyone, but Alan Brotherton grabbed my arm, pointing towards The Hole. This was our chance.

Alan pulled at one of the doors, got it just open enough to let him squeeze in, then pushed from the other side so I could climb in after. Then we kept flat hands on it, letting it come back slow and quiet, so there would be no clang. We could still hear the kids shrieking, there was one more superwhistle, but then the sound cut off and so did the light, as we eased the door shut. It was crazy-dark, we couldn't see anything, we were shut in with that ticking and that grumbling roar, much closer and louder now, and it was stifling hot too. It was just like you'd imagine an animal's den and I wondered quick and quiet whether the talk of monsters was the truth after all. The whole place smelt of dark and dust and heat and felt spidery too; I could touch powdery webs all around the doors. Alan Brotherton was somewhere further in, I could hear him breathing, somewhere slightly below me, and I found that out for sure because I tried to walk forward and realised too late that I was on a step, I fell and landed on Alan and he swore at me and lashed out. Because he was Alan Brotherton, he hit me as hard and as clean as if he'd swung his fist in good clear light.

And then there really was light; Alan had put out his lucky hand and found it, first thing he touched, a torch; he flicked the button and of course it came on, even if it had had no batteries it would've come on for him. Torch-light made the inside of The Hole look weird and flat, everything was either lit totally or jutting-back black. The place was smaller than I'd guessed, the walls all dirty brick and the floor was flat concrete patterned with dust. And yeah, there were dials and pipes and big metal boxes; the roaring and the heat came from the boilers. I hated Species Grogan for being right. Alan Brotherton wasn't disappointed, whatever it was he'd really expected. In fact, he looked as if he'd just won money or something.

'Great doss!' He grinned, put the torch under his chin, did a Halloween face and went 'Ooooo-ooo!' all ghosty, but he didn't scare me.

'How long we gonna stay in here?' I asked after a few mins; it was getting boring and stuffy.

'Frit already?'

'I'm not frit. But playtime will be over and Greeny will want us back in class.'

'What's Greeny gonna do? He's so nice he'll just tell us off a bit and that'll be it. No bother.'

'Hey, that caretaker, he'll put his dog away and come back and maybe he'll remember to lock the doors and maybe he won't look in here, then we'll be trapped...'

'Yitten.'

I told Alan Brotherton not to sneer yitten at me and he sneered yitten again and I got angry and my voice went up and so did his. Maybe if we hadn't have got to arguing like that we'd have heard the approaching clomp of dirty boots as they came down the steps to The Hole. We had bare moments to try to hide behind the big bodies of the boilers as the doors came open and the dirty-blue figure appeared in the gaping space, framed in brilliant light. I could only see his shape, nothing else.

'Out.'

Just one word, but he spoke. That was an adventure in itself.

Glyn Capstone

It was at this moment I found out that Alan Brotherton couldn't just create and weave light, he could also spin up a curtain of darkness and wrap it around himself: the caretaker had us right in front of him with daylight pouring all over, but he just didn't seem to see Alan. So I came creeping out in obedience to his terse command, light-stunned like a very sorry monster from the dark Hole, finding not just the caretaker waiting for me but an unsmiling Greeny standing by too and I got hauled off to the Head's office to be given A Telling Off about Dangerous Play. The man's eyes ranged about left, right, up, down, as if he were trying to locate something, they went in every direction except at-me and he seemed to be recalling a script, not addressing the boy before him in any real way. He finished with A Warning that A Word With Your Parents would be had and that made me feel even more as if I was made up of pure emptiness, as he didn't even seem to be aware that Your Parents were, for their different reasons, not available for A Word, and he would at best end having his Word with an Auntypoos who would be more bored and fidgety than a classroom full of sugared-up five-year-olds.

Alan Brotherton emerged from the Hole after me, unseen, uncaught and, by the time I got back from my Telling-Off, acting the innocent yet quietly taking the glory. I plonked down at my desk and waited to become a blankspace once again. This time I hoped for it.

'*Great* doss!' said Alan Brotherton as we went home later. He was on cloud nine. Me, I felt worse than when I'd been hit by that car.

Glyn The Pin

The big exam that scared everyone was coming, soon, and I'd decided that I needed to work like Species Grogan, not to mess around like hell; it was my decision, not forced on me. Perhaps if work and me called a truce and I gave to work what I'd given to dossing, I would find out I could be good at something, and that way maybe someone would pay me some bloody notice. I started quite well, but then my mates pressed round my desk, cluttering my head with sound, with movement and distraction. I carried on trying to gaze down at my book, then peered over the desk, as if I were driving, crawling along, trying to see through a fog. The lads were certainly blocking my view of the way ahead.

'Whassupwivyou?' Alan Brotherton flicked at the book, making the pages jump as if performing tricks for him, yet another thing that did as he willed it.

'Greeny's gone out a min,' he drawled easy, 'stop pretending, put that stupid thing up and let's doss.'

Brotherton was annoying me—again. Whenever we dossed, I fell behind and stayed trailing, whereas he messed about nonstop with or without me, but always came in among the chocolates, I mean truly, Greeny would hand out chocs for the top three in any tests. I often thought that Alan's knowledge was as natural as his cunning, that or he just cheated, I dunno.

'Got to do this,' I said, trying out a hard-voice and hard-stare on him.

'Haven't. S'stupid.' He flicked at the book again and it did backflips for him.

I prayed for the return of my invisibility, but that wasn't going to happen was it?

'Siddown and lemmedothis!' I told Alan Brotherton. I tried the tough voice some more, but it didn't work. He did look astonished for a moment, as if something had come out of his blind spot and fetched him one. I tried to read again but he riffled the pages again, kept doing it, then got bored with that and started riffling my hair instead, hard.

'Lemme do this!' I yelled, 'I wanna do this! You always doss and you always get me into trouble and I get bad marks and you get good marks and it inna fair!'

I pretty much emptied my breath at him, but he just smirked really annoying like he'd won already; he'd let me wear myself out good and proper and I'd got nothing left to throw at him.

'Big 'ead!' I used up some more puff.

'Little 'ead!' he came back: it wasn't up to his usual standards, but he wanted me to see that he wasn't even trying.

'Big 'ead!' I bawled; I felt bad, he was beating me again. I could feel it.

'Little 'ead!' everyone around was laughing—with him, at me. I was getting noticed, but as usual only when I was getting trod on. So I got madder.

'Big 'ead!'

'Little 'ead!'

I was getting out of control and Alan Brotherton was getting cocky.

Pretty soon he would say something really clever and totally crushing and everyone would laugh at me one last time and then I would return to being forgotten. I just had to do something. So I offered him on. Soon as it was playtime, Alan Brotherton and me: we'd fight.

I was angry enough to be blind in that scrap, blind to the fact that Alan Brotherton was a winner and I was a loser, and though he landed some lip-thickeners on me within the first few moments I realised that fighting didn't suit him, it was dirty and low, it was far more mine than his. I got in some real stingers and he fell back; I knew that this was my chance to get one over on him, to show that I was someone, someone who could punch out Alan Brotherton —no less. But there had, of course, to be something to come along and spoil it. I was blind to the ring of chanting kids too, blind also to the breaking of that ring and deaf to the dying of their voices.

Perhaps I thought I could turn on the invisibility when the teachers came for us, but I was visible and grabbable and I didn't resist as they hauled us off, tutting at Alan for 'letting yourself down. Clever lad like you' and just giving me glares that said *god, not you again* before their attention wandered back to Alan, but they didn't relax so much as they would let me go.

We got put straight in, in front of the Head: he must have been short of stuff to do, or in need of using his Sonorous Voice. The way that the Head spoke, he knew that Alan Brotherton was going to pass the big exam and go off to the Grammar and I was off down the secmod: to him, Alan was a boat on a river and I was poo in a sewer.

'Now look, you need to Think About Your Future. It's a Promising Future, but you'll face some pretty Hard Diamonds when you go up to the Grammar School,' he lectured Alan; this wasn't aimed at me, see, not at all. 'And they won't be so easily...' he paused, glanced at me, but with fading eyes, it put him off his stride and he quickly looked back at Alan, 'They won't be such... what I mean is that you'll no longer be a Big Fish In A Little Pond, if you get yourself noticed for the wrong reasons You'll Rue It, Boy. You'll not get away with it; they'll Make Sure Of That. Mark My Words' At that, Alan Brotherton got sent out of the room. He slunk away, obviously relieved, even more obviously not very sorry: he may have been caught this time, but he had bloody got away with it, bloody again.

I didn't move, waiting for my turn for a doing-over, a lecture on how better to manage my future. The Head looked up, the light in his eyes nearly gone; he went a bit cross-eyed as if trying to focus on the end of his nose; then his gaze slid past me altogether.

'*feh.*'

And that was it. I lingered a moment, but the butt-end of his pen gestured me away. That or he was just flourishing it before writing again. I could've pinched something off his desk, should've, he would never have noticed.

Glyn Capstone

After the big exam was done and over, Alan Brotherton went off to the clever-school, to the surprise of no one. That school had some Latin-type motto, which supposedly meant "Out of the Darkness" or something. He lit his own way there. The git. As for me, I got my due slice of destiny too, shunted off to the secmod, which was all of a piece with everything that had gone before. It was one last great-big '*feh.*'

How High Is The Sky?

Jilly Holdenbridge
'Questions, questions, so many questions!'

My prevailing childhood memory is of many, many adults saying this to me, or a close variation upon the phrase; all but one meant nothing particularly nice by it.

Questions were a burden to most people, a torture they could scarcely bear. They seemed instantly tired, their shoulders slumped as if I had loaded them with some back-breaking weight, their faces turned troubled, grey, their eyes fluttered and they looked frail, as if they were going to need to lie down at any moment. I inevitably felt sorry I had asked, but I told myself that I had done so only because *I must, I really, really must ask, must know*. Many people would flap the question away, as if it were a buzzing, annoying thing hovering uncomfortably under their noses—the more fearful would go so far as to flinch, as if dodging an enraged hornet. Some would attempt to supply me with an answer, but resentfully, almost angrily, as if the effort cost them something they were unable to quantify but knew they couldn't afford.

Lots of people are afraid of questions, I have found, then as now; as far as they are concerned a question is nothing less than a trap. They hate to show the slightest sign of ignorance, loathe the prospect of being wrong—many become spiky, defensive and touchy at the faintest sniff of a query aimed in their direction. They believe my sole purpose is to expose them to the world and dance and laugh and point and shout, bellowing to all within earshot, 'Look at him, he doesn't know!'

But I always asked questions because *I* was the one who didn't know, because there was a gap in my head I wanted to fill. Slowly, sadly, I became accustomed to people behaving like schoolchildren sulking at the back of the classroom, hoping to become one with the wall and not singled out and assailed with queries. Lots of folk are just busking their way through life—bluffing, pretending, putting up a front and keeping their fingers crossed, hoping for the best. I don't mind in the least if someone says, 'I don't know.' But nobody will do that for me.

When I was first at school, I had a teacher who was funny: she was in the habit of delivering lessons in a booming orator's voice that always made me feel she was telling a funny story to good friends in the next room but one. One afternoon she broke off, adopted a more intimate tone for her audience and said something that intrigued and moved me profoundly, 'The only way to learn,' she said in her bumptious yet likeable voice, 'is to ask questions.'

An electric excitement seized me on hearing this and I waved my upraised palm at her, keen to show that her words had inspired me and from that very moment my education had truly begun. 'Put your hand down,' she ordered, with a dismissive flick of her forefinger and then carried on dictating a monologue to an unseen audience that wasn't me, wasn't any of us.

She, like so many, had developed defences, ways of fending off unwelcome interrogation: such methods can be perfectly simple, really. You can treat the questioner as if she is stupid, imply or just state baldly that she is a fool and time-waster—only someone utterly *hopeless* would ask a question like that! You can issue a severe reminder of what curiosity did to the cat: questions can be dangerous, are you sure you want the answer? If you get hurt, it's your own lookout.

While I think on it, have you noticed how reticent people can be about asking? They feel obliged to apologise, 'Ah, silly question, but...' they say in a tight voice, their cheeks reddening. And that's the ones who actually dare to pipe up. So many seem content to sit and stew, hoping someone else will take the risk. I know that feeling, yes I do. The fear that the next sound following your '?' will be a building, rolling wave of mocking laughter, accompanied by knowing glances, rolling eyes, nudging elbows, 'Shit, what a *fool!*' Then you feel small, you are a low sort, a beggar, you wish for silence to swallow you. So perhaps it's no surprise there is a general assumption that it's best not to ask, for fear of causing embarrassment, attracting attention or falling victim to some inexplicable wrath brought by the simple act of interrogation. *You were asking for it—you asked for it*—and similar vengeful words. A friend at school once told me to do what she did; say nothing, look bright-eyed and when you're asked if you understand, 'nod wisely.' That works for lots of people.

There are people I can't blame, not at all, for their aversion to questions. I had a friend, Angelina, whose dad was the sort of man who likes to 'win' in life, everything a competition as far as he was concerned, and his daughter becoming educated and knowledgeable was a purest-red rag to him, more of a threat than a challenge; as far as he was concerned he *had* to know more than she did, it was essential for his pride, his very existence. And so he quizzed her constantly, demanding to know what marks her schoolwork had received and then deriding her if she ever fell short of perfection, asking her things beyond her age and ability, mocking her for how much she'd yet to learn, he tore her speech and writing apart, picking her up on simple errors and throwing her failure in her face. He spent hours setting traps, claiming that he was teaching her, but really so that he could tell himself that he remained top of the pile. She couldn't get away from her father, but over the years I witnessed Angelina equipping herself for the outside world and future life by developing stratagems to ensure that once she was free of this appalling man, she would never have to answer a question again.

'Questions questions, so many questions!'

My father was the exception: he prefaced any reply to my persistent why-what-whens with those words, but they were always accompanied by the warmest, most loving smile of approval and an unspoken, "Well done!" And he always gave me a straight reply, even if that involved admitting he simply didn't *know* the proper answer.

If I asked Dad what a word meant and he couldn't tell me right off, he'd throw his right arm in the air, pointing as if he was about to tell me to take wing and fly, and then he'd cry "To the dictionary!" as if he was saying "To the Batcave!" and that cry was never angry, he was always smiling. Also, he wasn't sending me away—it was my job to take him by the hand and pull him out of his chair so he could come with me; after all, we both needed to know what that word was, didn't we?

He nicknamed me The Inquisitive Elf and that made me laugh. The name came from a book I used to have when I was teeny-tiny: he loved reading it to me as much as I loved having him read it. I was happy being an inquisitive elf; it was an identity in which I could wrap myself to protect myself from my disappointment at others' disapproval. It made me feel good about asking my questions.

Dad could do something that I could not; he could read and listen to music at the same time. He loved to do this when the book was a comfortable old friend overdue for a reread and as for the tunes, they were always old, as ancient as his record-player; oh I remember its warm smell, powerfully evocative as the scent of a childhood dinner, and the tune I recall, over and above them all, was the summing of him, his theme tune, '*How much do I love you? I'll tell you no lie, How deep is the ocean, How high is the sky?*' Questions, questions. He had no singalong voice, no breath with which to do it, but he would smile and wave a finger in vague, faltering time and I knew that the song, in his mind, was for me—and for Mum.

When I picture Dad now, I indulge in what I know perfectly well to be sentimental exaggerations; I place his mind and personality into a setting that they should have had, that the man merited. The man I see in these loving dreams is tall, but his height seems trimmed by his generous girth, he is far more padded than he should be and yet this looks natural and correct, not remotely unhealthy. His surroundings play down his height also, for he is standing in a library, the packed shelves stand over him by his height and a half, and the books are everywhere else in the room too, stacked on the floor, over by the door, piled higgledy-piggledy on his broad, long desk, several propped open with whatever odds and ends came to hand when he paused in his studies, ready for him when the reading-mood takes him once again: and he hops from one to the other, chasing answers like an eager, harmless hunter.

His appearance is distinctive and eccentric; his hair and beard explode outwards in a leonine starburst and yet he is not remotely animalistic and he is certainly not threatening. He wears a waistcoat, which swells and only just succeeds in containing his bulk; one suspects that when he sits back at his desk to consult his books, the four small buttons will strain, give way and fire off like blunt bullets headed for the far wall. Naturally he sports a fob watch, its chain straining to maintain the unity of the two halves of that waistcoat, and equally naturally his shirt sleeves are rolled and held in place by expandable metal clips, baring arms made for the turning of pages, but which could adapt swiftly to any work, for this is a sturdy man for all his studiousness.

I see him in comfortable, rather baggy corduroy trousers and monstrously plaid carpet slippers; he is not planning to stray far from this warm, wood-walled room. Moreover, I cannot resist having him standing before a generous, yellow-red fire and, while he looks thoughtfully into the flames, adjusts his Victorian-era smoking cap, its tassel hanging over one ear like the fuse of a knowledge-bomb ready to fizz and pop with its benign pyrotechnics. He simply *has* to wear glasses, silvery half-moon glasses, which lend strength to his slightly sunken and yet sparkling eyes. This is a man whose pleasure is learning, whose joy is communicating and sharing knowledge.

There was never such a man: at least, I never met him. This man was a pure fantasy: the room he stood in would have swallowed the whole of my childhood home and still have left room for more. And my dad, my real dad, was as different from that robust, well-fed academic as it was possible to be. He was a little man, both small and thin; 'weasel-faced' he used to call himself, 'No need of a door, I can slip in and out through cracks in the wall.' He had no regal corona of hair, his stringy black strands deserting him as fast as they could go, retreating back inside his head so he said, and stubbornly reluctant to sprout upon his cheeks and chin. He sported no gorgeously idiosyncratic garb, he "wore what he had on" as he put it, in or out of doors, plain as plain, for he had no idea about clothing and no money with which to faff with finery. He had a sentimental preference for a moth-eaten cardigan my mother made for him just before she died, and her loss must have shrunk him because that cardie could go round him two or three times: like his opulent alter-ego he wore slippers, but they were worn and ancient, soles thin as paper. The only other things that the real man shared with my fantasy figure were that he had no wife, he had no work and he adored books.

Dad couldn't work, it was work that had done him in, a sickness that had sneaked inside and perished one of his lungs as if it were a neglected balloon. I could often hear him fighting for breath as he lay in bed at night and I never ceased to be scared by that sound, as it told me that his end could come at any moment. So there was to be no football, no cricket or long walks, no running and chasing games: he could barely lift me up after I turned five. The comfortable man in his library drew each breath with unthinking ease, but Dad had to pay dearly for every time he tried to take his fair share of the air.

Had mother lived, I sometimes wondered, would there have been room for her in our tiny home? There were two bedrooms, of which Dad gave me the larger soon after he became alone, and a tiny comfortless bathroom—and that was the upstairs mapped out, done. Downstairs was just the one room, plus the kitchen, with its small table and three chairs, one doomed always to be unoccupied, squashed between the ancient cooker and doll's-house sink. It was a cold house, always cold; it shrank from the sun but invited every passing chill breeze, and where my dream-scholar stood before a leaping, living fire, Dad and I had to make do with the hissy old gas fire that struggled feebly against the wall of cold air. Dad preferred the cold; he claimed it kept him awake and thinking. We weren't dirt-poor, this isn't lachrymose self-pity, we owned a TV and a radio and always had sufficient to eat; we were the same as everyone else for miles around, this wasn't the house of a pauper or miser. Dad was content; this little man hadn't much, but then he didn't demand much. What ambitions he nursed were centred on me.

He would sometimes say to me, 'if you want me I'll be in the study.'—always accompanied with a grin. 'The study' consisted of wherever he happened to be seated, either his favourite chair tucked into a corner of the living room, or at one of the cushionless upright wooden seats at the kitchen table if I was watching TV and he wanted his peace. He would also joke about "the library"—this jest being the origin of my vision of his alter ego, I suppose. My fantasy-figure stood in a room that held so many volumes even such a wise and patient man as he could surely never read them all; Dad's meagre collection occupied only three-quarters of a shelf of a little bookshelf on castors, three feet tall and two wide, which hugged the wall between his chair and the whistling, wheezing gas fire.

There was a Bible, a handsome if doomy old tome that he had been given at a very young age. He had kept it immaculate, only a slight yellowing of its pages betrayed its antiquity. A more time-ravaged survivor was a huge compendium of stories, fables, myths, moral tales and practical how-to advice entitled *The Children's Everything Within*. This hard-backed behemoth had been stripped of its spine and its covers clung to its vast body only by strings, thin strands, but Dad encouraged me to handle it, to read it—to love it. I lost myself in the tales of the Greek gods, the Norse gods, the inhuman children of ancient legend, the beginning of a life-long fascination. I was less attracted by the practical and moral advice for youngsters— aimed at people who were young long before my father was born, for I believe he inherited the book—stuffed-shirt advice about how best to clean one's shoes, how to address one's superiors, things one should always carry (a penknife, a notebook and pencil, plus small change), the insects you could find under stones in the garden, even how to tickle trout. I found it hard to believe that such an innocent—and yet stuffy—world ever existed, but the book commanded my fascination.

The rest of the part-shelf was filled with stout volumes called "The Home University", which presented the same type of homespun knowledge, but in far duller form, for adults. And then, finally, Dad's prized possession: the dictionary. For all that they were out of date and fading fast, Dad's books were not relics on proud and defiant display, they were old and still-living friends, especially the dictionary, and he sought its opinion frequently. He made deep acquaintance with many other books too, but they were always on temporary loan, from the local library, a one-time merchant's house half a mile away, boasting huge and magnificent rooms, but temperatures that made our home a hothouse. Dad was back and forth there more often than some of the staff, always taking away a stack of reading, never incurring a fine. So although our house harboured an elderly and mighty poor sort of library, Dad sought knowledge every bit as much as I did.

When the time came, the sad time, I found that people didn't like questions about Dad—what happened? where's he gone?—at first I thought they were hiding a nasty truth from me and I cried; I was tempted to shut up and ask no more because I didn't want to hear anything horrible, as if the memory of my sweet Dad was in danger of being fouled. But the questions kept coming as if they were rude I-can't-help-it burps and it was not long before I realised that nobody was protecting me from painful truths, they knew nothing and they just didn't want to admit it. I was presented with some prepared, glazed bromides that soothed me for a while, like the warm words that come with ointment over a grazed knee, murmured like a prayer, but I found that these were, quack remedies and inevitably the pain came back and the words and mumbo-jumbo didn't work a second time. I vexed some people when I asked more questions after that: 'Mind your own business, fry your own fish, keep your dirty nose out of my clean dish.'—that's what we *nya-nyahed* at one another as children. And it's more or less how grown men and women responded to my desperate, heartbroken enquiries.

It wasn't so much that Dad could possibly answer my questions (we all go through the phase when we think our old dad knows everything, but he never pretended anything of the sort with me), but that he made me feel good about admitting I didn't know and that I wanted to know. It wasn't a sign of stupidity or innate ignorance; it was the very beginning of finding out. He made me feel confident to admit gaps in my knowledge and track them down and close them. The measure of how much I missed him is what happened to me, what I allowed to happen to me, next.

It seems to me that everyone just busks their way through life, bluffing, hoping, pretending to know and praying that no one gets too smart with them. I've not known anyone since my dad who could manage a simple unashamed 'I don't know.' I don't mind being told 'I don't know,' but no one will do it for me, they all pretend. There's no one anymore to cry, 'To the dictionary!' That's how much I miss him; and I have to live with that one unanswerable question; why did he have to go? One day he would have told me how high is the sky.

Can't Do—Teach

Fizzmonger

Note to self: stop trying to be nice to Tobol; it is plainly pointless. I had seen him as a man whom I could help, lost as he is (and deeply mired as he is) on the wrong-road I had taken, I thought I could help him to extricate himself after my own example—but thinking about it, how would I have reacted when on that road, how *did* I react, to 'help?'

Charles Durant Tobol
'What is the name of the dauber who painted that miserable performance?'

I do wish people would not solicit my opinion of artworks; that statement, with variations to suit whichever medium, is my inevitable response. I wish that instead of marks or grades, I could simply issue it, rubber-stamp-style, to all hopefuls. Kinder and quicker than keeping them waiting and hoping.

Teachers are youngsters' first target for satire. Every generation brings some scabrous miniature Gillray who decides to burlesque the staff and then, ego-ridden, praise-hungry, passes his crude little sketches around his peers, awaiting popularity with all the puppy eagerness of the stupid young. These effusions usually find their way by one route or another to the Staff Room, where the thin-skinned get worked-up and swear revenge, the ones who want to be everyone's pal find something to praise and those with an ounce of sense essay to ignore the whole thing. My efforts to do just that have often been ruined by the insistence of some gauche, or is that malicious, members of staff in

134

shoving the wretched things under my nose as if asking for a critique—look it's art, what has the art master got to say? As little as possible, that's always best. Some, the revenge-seekers usually, want the art master to turn detective, to establish provenance, track back splotched colours to guilty, if studiedly stainless, fingers.

Reluctantly, I cast a wearied eye over one such gaudy splash-panel some little while ago. It was more thoroughly anonymous and untraceable than any of the usual product (even the simpletons of the staff room could recognise handwriting and, besides, there was no honour among kiddies, they would usually give one another away even before my expertise could expose the author) and so I was to have no peace until I had had pronounced on it: it was entitled *The Staff Portrait*. It was crowded, childishly over-busy indeed, derivative (the cartoon frames of Hogarth, Gillray, even Low, for a touch of spurious modernity, had been duly raided), basic and cruel: at once I estimated the maximum possible age of its executor as fifteen. Definitely fifteen. The artist (let us stretch a point) has plainly laid his hands on a new set of coloured pencils and wishes to test out every available shade and combination. He presents a chaotic, shambolic scene in which the staff assemble for a portrait—failing to arrange or even faintly organise themselves in fact—while a spattered-smock painter blobs pigments ham-fistedly, more on the floor than the easel.

The Head is there, as ever signally failing to provide anything remotely resembling leadership, with her 'coffee' sloshing to the floor to add a new tincture as she totters, roll-eyed inebriate, her silvery flask working its way out of her back pocket as she begins her decline and fall. The Head's instability knocks the arm of vain, preening Mrs

Cox, who is trying to prettify herself for the picture, but the wild smear of rouge across her gaping face is clearly considered by the cartoonist as an improvement on her day-by-day looks. Doghead, the bumptious chemistry teacher whom every child despised for his bellowing, bullying and utterly misplaced self-confidence (oh, but their feelings were not a patch on the way his colleagues spoke of him) is trying to position himself centrally and look important while also attempting to sneak a look at a private letter held furtively by a colleague standing in front of him and foiled only by the fact that his own unstable, waggling head wobbles and bounces too much, for his neck is not flesh but a vibrant, violent spring. It is true that Doghead (we all called him that, he belonged in the back window of a car, or preferably under one: and don't assume he was so-dubbed by any child) was almost as nosy as he was self-important. Bernard Lawton once sat reading a note with intense concentration and apparent absorption: the trap was sprung in short order and over the old man's shoulder the stinks-master spied the message 'FUCK OFF DOGHEAD.'

Wayman is there too, an absurd parp-parp toad figure jammed grotesquely into a kiddy-car with his legs, arms and tripes of spare flesh spilling out of the windows. He is skidding out of control, panic on his ugly face and a payload of poorly strapped books tumbling off the car's roof and threatening to crush his colleagues' feet, those whom he does not seem doomed to run over bodily. His immediate victim is Mr Mumbles, the man with the inappropriate name and the foghorn voice, who is oblivious to his danger as he has his head thrown back and arms spread orator-style, still pacing about and dictating notes (from memory, he liked to show that he did not need books and nor, by extension, should any able pupil of his) even though there is not a single bored schoolboy there present to ignore him. Another distracted figure is Old Wash-Hands, up to his elbows in a foaming bowl. His mind is clearly on other things, higher things of course, and from his fevered philosopher's head come steam-puffs of thought: 'on the one hand... on the other hand...' Those who knew the man didn't need more, they were aware that he was musing his way to capitulation, total and inevitable; it only remained to work out who and what to, this time.

In the midst of this moil, tuxedoed as a concert conductor and sweeping the air with a broken baton, jagged in the middle, its tapered tip also broken and hanging on by a thread, is little Weisel; Weasel, the boys called him, his name was not his fault, nor were his unfortunate, starveling rodent face and frame, but it was his fault that he could not control a classroom. His lessons were a riot of noise, but there was never any music therein, the boys ran wild and either baited him cruelly or flatly ignored him, doing as they pleased in feral joy as he gesticulated and fumed, enraged but impotent, at the front of the class. The same happens here, his face is twisted in horror, rage and disbelief as once again disharmony reigns. A dozen other minor figures add to the ruck; a square-headed sports master whose name escapes me now but whom I remember not even possessing the semblance of a brain; the dry mathematician rendered as an abacus (broken, a few beads bouncing away); the Geography teacher rendered as a fat world-globe made of corduroy; the Physics master with the dead-eye touch and a board rubber taking pot-shots at hated colleagues; and all around chalk in choking puffs and pathetic, splintered sticks, leather-patched elbows aplenty.

The painter-within-the-picture is a little man, a ridiculous near-homunculus with a huge head, untidy hair and beard (both dripping paint) who has a vacant, helpless expression; and, look closely now, there are no eyes behind his TV-screen glasses, just blank whiteness, as if he cannot see to paint, cannot see at all, has no connection with light whatsoever. It is clear that even if his subjects, by some miracle, become still and paintable, the picture will be a masterwork-mess of grand incompetence. On the painter's smock (too big for his tiny body, he is tripping over it, blind clown: look closer, it is no smock but a babygro, with the backside hanging out of it), along with paint-splatters, are the letters CDT. They stand for 'Can't Do—Teach.'

Fizzmonger

Tobol's problem is that he spread himself too thin; he did a bit of this, a bit of that, he dabbled and he daubed, he never mastered a medium, he simply became multi-mediocre. Perhaps I should say that that is just one of his problems. Another is that he subscribes, did so and presumably still does somewhere in recesses of his head, to the myth of the tortured artist, or rather his own vain variant thereon; he believes that all he needs to do is to keep on going, keep working at his little projects and, in time, for some (unknown) reason, some (unidentified) patron will see the great artist's work (quite how—unknown) and tell him what he has been waiting throughout his whole existence to hear, that he is a genius whose brilliance will make history bend like light through a prism, transform the face of modern art, and who, having found him will then fund him, puff him, protect him from his enemies, place him aloft, among the wheeling stellar heights where he belongs. The flaws in his thinking scarcely need picking over.

Charles Durant Tobol
Whoever told Alfred Wayman he could draw did not know what he was talking about. Assuming anyone did, of course; and whatever their opinions, he was unlikely, overall, to listen to them. That wretched performance, that artless, amateur cartoon, reflects no merit on him—none whatsoever.

The glaring herald of Wayman's authorship was not the portrayal of himself—it protested too much, it was too savage, he was railing too loudly by far against himself, but that was not it—it was the lack of any portrayal of his beloved professor. Of Bernard Lawton there was no sign and only one person upheld that man as being above criticism. Wayman could throw mud at himself to obfuscate his ownership of the piece; he might confess his own ugliness and inadequacy and parade it in plain sight, but he could not bear the pain of doing the same to his hero. Humph; an artist, if we may presume to call him that, tyrannised—this time by his own conscience. He has a conscience? Then, QED, he is no artist.

I've said before that Wayman doesn't *know* people and so when he plies his pen people-wards, the only possible outcome is caricatures. I believe it's not a failure of interpretation but vision, that all his eyes can see is stickmen, grotesques and semi-animals, all grossly absurd and rendered with a laugh that carries with it nothing but scorn. Wayman never did belong at people-level, he considered himself above that, his cartoons declare it; there is no other way in which they may be read.

His other work, let's call it his serious work, shows something a tad and a scrape better, a modicum of hand-eye coordination and that is creditable, I suppose, and although he also demonstrates the virtues of persistence, patience and application, technically his talents are nugatory. If that sounds like an end-of-term report so be it, such an approach has become a matter of habit. Be that as it may, Mr Wayman's output does not impress me; his little cosmic drawings are competent perhaps, but then again he is using his—pardon me—skills to record facts, scientific data, not to record impressions or explore any feeling except gosh-wow-look-at-that. Like a kid. His subject matter has no appeal either, not emotional, not artistic. Clear, cold night skies, no, no, no. 'Clouds—blight his sky!'—that's my motto. The problem with Mister Wayman's beloved sky, from the point of view of colour and variety, is that it has practically none. I have turned my eyes aloft at his behest and I have seen a series of insipid sploshes, various shades of white-ish, conveying to me precisely nothing. Wayman, the connoisseur, has argued fiercely that there are infinite, boundless alien rainbows out there, but for all that he can point out a faint blue tinge here, a sickly yellow there, a dying-ember orange elsewhere, there's hardly any more than that. He has shown me his drawings, the ones he sketches at the eyepiece, convinced that only the hand and eye can do the job properly, and he has demonstrated a few episodes of green, just dots and flashes, in an infinite universe it represents nothing whatsoever. The little sky that we can see is unexciting to the eye.

'It's not a particoloured palette for your personal edification!' huffed Wayman. I told him that he was missing the point. Wayman's sky is no fit subject for art.

Fizzmonger

Tobol regards me as a sell-out and by his lights I suppose I am, in that I managed to sell at all. I worked out what I was best at and stuck to it, honed and tuned it; I kept an eye on rivals and I didn't sell out, it's just that in relation to them I sold differently. That's how I survived. I once tried to talk to him about how to promote himself, about the right people to talk to, about basic marketing, but his eyes turned to blank ovals and his jaw dropped, not from astonishment but from instant, consuming boredom.

If I wanted to infuriate him, I could tell Tobol that this bubble-existence, the puritanism, the otherworldly detachment from crude realities (and who knows, perhaps the secret, self-consuming ambition too) reminds me very much of someone else.

Another thing, I don't think Tobol thinks so much in terms of tortured artists these days. Of torturing artists, more like.

Charles Durant Tobol

Although his paintings often addressed the tops of heads down to the gentle slope of shoulders, our painter was always thinking of his models… shall we say from the neck down? It was mainly the women, no particular discrimination about age, as I understand, and I don't think he was averse to dipping his brush into a quite different sort of pot from time to time. That was his reputation when I knew him and it was also what filtered to me later on; the grapevine never really withers, does it? His reputation also embraced the capacity to abandon his avowed ideals and find the quickest way to market-market-market, sell-sell-sell.

But what I noticed most clearly about his work, it called out and signalled wildly to me and yet it seemed invisible to others, was the rottenness, the bitterness within his every brush-stroke, especially in his portraits of the women: the more beautiful, the more rotten, the more bitter. There are portrayals within his portraits, unseen and yet obvious, rank and hateful. Perfect for my requirements.

Fizzmonger

I can scarcely describe the pleasure of drawing faces: the infinity of expressions and angles, the imperfections (which I always at least hinted at, even when under considerable pressure to conceal them), the light and shadow, the glows, the intimations of the secrets hidden beneath the skin. Skin: the skin I saw—some of it like leather, some like paper, some resembling a repellent breed of sponge. The study of faces reveals more than does nudity, which is a distraction because the viewer is always looking at the wrong thing—come on admit it all of you, even the connoisseurs.

Charles Durant Tobol

I resent, *resent and hate* the tyranny of the artist. It's self-hate, true, but not foremost. I can paint, plying knife or brush or whatever you would have me do, I can score and injure stone, throw pots, mash and bash metal, mould any medium; just name it, it's mine. The skill is in my hands, strong threads connect through my arms and up to my head, my eyes and the dark places behind where there are visions, so many, that could set my hands so easily to work: and the work I could do, well that would be a sorrow to the sight of other artists, who would know they were beaten hollow, outstripped. But it shall not happen. I refuse it; I *refuse*. To strive for a world without art, that is my aim. I am a subversive, a subverter; it's my wish not to re-educate the young about art, no, but to *de*-educate them, drain them of any capacity for it, for its appreciation, its creation, its working and worth. I want to numb them to its absence and make them glory in that emptiness. I desire everyone, one and all, to want nothing but bare walls, colourlessness (oh domestic magnolia, take every room and douse it, douse it, drown it!). I am the doom of the rainbow, the spectrum's assassin. The statue-hammerer, the acid-hurler, the metal-melter, the gallery-burner, the Anti-Artist, the Anti-Art.

Fizzmonger

'I wanna be a drawer.' I made that statement of intent at the age of, oooooh, six. All we children were being asked what we would like to become when we grew up, the answers generally predictable enough and plenty who didn't have an answer to give, children who hadn't even come to the realisation that they *would* grow up—to them, children and adults were separate species, immutable, unmixable, not part of a pupa-imago-adult lifecycle. For myself, cynical at six, I suspected that we were only being asked this premature question so that the adults could laugh at us later, 'Wasn't he *cute* when he said that?' But I gave my answer nevertheless and stuck to it. I hope that nobody else stuck to theirs.

I have the perfect story to illustrate the inextricable interrelation of art and bullshit: it was a lesson learned, literally, for me at an early age. I'd say I was no older than six, I remember being at school: there you are a little, *little* one, just learning to use brain and voice and hands. You'll probably recollect being asked to draw and paint a picture —usually of mummy and daddy in my day; I wonder if they still do that in these days of easily fractured and dysfunctional families—and you will probably recall the colours, the brushes and the pots full of water, the mess, the smell, the thrill. Many things began the day they put all that within my reach; but anyway, I digress. The teacher told us what to draw and how to draw it, what to do with the paints, what the water was for, I forget the details and I wasn't listening in the first place. We were being given our start in art in the way we were intended to go on, we were to be directed and micro-managed, producing a result exactly as demanded; after all, anything else wouldn't be art at all, would it?

Each child was presented with an oblong of paper and set to work. My memory goes hazy as to what happened in between, all I can remember is the fascination of working with the paint, of the shapes I could create, the way I could push and pull it and spread it and pool it and scatter it and slick it, colour on colour, colour on colour, lost in 2D, eight inches by twelve and only surfacing from my chromatic bath when forced to do so by the eruption of a piercing, querulous voice, the teacher standing over my shoulder. I hate being stood over: I really, really hate it. I cannot work if someone tries to stand over me, whatever I am doing comes to a halt, whether painting or pissing. Perhaps this is what started all of that.

I crashed those sheets of colour across one another, into one another, with the same primal, breathless joy I crashed the cars from my toybox, for they were not there to be treasured, certainly not to be raced in search of a winner, they were there to be cracked, buckled, bent with the greatest possible violence and excitement. My mother used to refer proudly to me being 'let loose with colours,' but I was really let loose against them, as their tormentor and destroyer. I just couldn't leave pretty colours alone; they had to go.

'And *what* do you call all of this?' demanded this woman, in the glass-shattering voice she employed to intimidate errant infants. I looked up at her, I had this queer angle on her face and neck, her protruding teeth, her geologic rumples of chins, her venous, hawser-tendon neck bedecked with pearls—or some other substance, tacky as seaside plastic—and then I looked down at the soaking-wet piece of paper. It was no portrait, it was daubs and blots, a seething wall of blue paint partially admixed with a shapeless swell of yellow, with the rest of the rainbow swimming and drowning here and there too. It was nothing but a paint-doodle, merely the results of me playing, but, remember, I was supposed to have made a *picture*. What *did* I think I was doing?

Question—do you remember your first big, big lie? The one you proffered in desperation with pain in your guts, with the feeling of your heart being there only to drumbeat the awful passage of time, when with each thump the cold sweat had made it just a little further down your brow? That was my moment for all of that and as time pumped blood I fumbled wildly; it was a picture, it had to have a purpose, an explanation; I had to justify myself.

Perhaps it was the sense of peril that I had created in the midst of my excitement that gave me the idea: 'It's a sailor, lost in a storm at sea.'

'Where is the sailor?' she asked, skimming the flat surface of the picture, searching for a figure. She was *that* stupid.

Fizzmonger

I used to be a portrait painter but somewhere along the way I lost my taste for faces. For a time I was completely blocked, left without a style, it was a form of bereavement. People gave me gentle hints and well-meaning bits of advice, but it was all useless and just plain irritating. You can't raise the dead, can you? I suppose I could have 'had a go' at all sorts of styles, as they suggested, but it would only have been in an uninterested, soulless sort of way that would reek of cynicism and cash-hunger; it would have turned me into a sort of Tobol. Pity those who made *certain* suggestions to me, for I couldn't resist giving them both barrels about their choices: if you have a day or two to spare, for instance, I will give you my opinion of Still Life. 'Death And Decay' is my expression for it: let that suffice for the moment and I'll get back to the subject if there's time. Landscapes? Do me a favour; lumpy and banal, predictable browns blues and greens; still-lives with just a little more breath in them.

In frustration I took to drawing, at whim, the scene before me wherever I happened to be. At the moment, remembering all this, I'm in the upstairs bar of a riverside pub, one of only four customers; business is slow and the barman and the barmaid, teenagers and obviously lovers, canoodling, sitting together on the tall stools in front of the pumps, moving only when rare drinkers arrive or someone wants a refill. I should sketch them as I see them now, reflected in a three-by-four-foot mirror on the wall opposite. I can't see them directly unless I move from my perch and I'm not much minded to do that until my glass is dry. If I did it, they'd be drawn in reverse, framed on a wood-panelled wall, a portrait within a portrait. Or I could sketch what's directly before my eyes, a view of the river as a slack tide starts to flow more strongly and all the boats moored on the buoys start to turn in obedience to the water... if I could capture the slow inevitability of that movement. A fine, misty rain casts a haze over the scene, droplets dappled over the three enormous windows overlooking a courtyard which in summer must be thronged with thirsty tourists, but which is now greyly wet and deserted, its tables washed with rain and its cobblestones damp and darkened, the parasols closed on themselves like fly-trap plants that have gone out of business for the duration, tied up tightly to prevent the long-fingered wind tearing them open. I could try to think in less concrete terms, try to paint the sweet, gentle, unusual music that the lovers at the bar play—more for themselves than the punters, I think, 'their' tune, without a doubt, and doubtless played in breach of the brewery's diktats about what bland rubbish they should inflict on the drinkers. Or I could turn my thoughts to the emotional force of the elements, the wind and waves outside, imagine myself amongst them, pulled and dragged, tugged and drowned. If I were free again to draw.

Spontaneous sketching was the way I tried to rehabilitate myself in the use of pencils and paints once the faces had deserted me. The process of relearning finally came on with the return of my ability to forgive. Ah, that too had left me for far too long. But let's not rush the storytelling, let everything come in its own time: that's another lesson I learned during what can only be described as my recuperation. Every now and then as I talk to you, to pace myself and keep a firm anchor in reality, I will pause and flick a pencil over a blank page, sketch for you the scene around me, showing you where I am. To show you—and remind myself, of course.

I have had to relearn another art: that of being alone. It's odd in an artist, the inability to bear thoughts of solitude; it doesn't fit in with the traditional image, does it? I dreamed as a youngster of having my own studio, of abandoning myself to my muse, working all day and night too if need be, letting ideas flow over me like sustaining waters, losing all sense of time and forgetting to eat, drink or wash as I brought my craft to perfection. Stupid dreamer: I became an artist because I fancied dabbling with dyes at a board by a big window, in glacial isolation form the rest of the world. Idiot. That idealistic phase didn't last long, I soon realised that I could only really function in a crowd, in an environment where my image-artist would have been drowned out, unable to survive. Stupid, stupid dreamer, you're not me anymore, stay away from me. It got to the point, of course, where I needed not just to be not alone but also to be out of my head, and I wasn't too fussy about what substance did the business. Christ, how close did I come to death? But there I go again, jumping the gun, leaping ahead in the story when there's so much more yet to tell.

Charles Durant Tobol

There is nowhere more arid, more depressing than an art gallery, especially one that contains your own work. It's like looking at hunks of meat on butchers' hooks, I get that raw-meat smell in my nostrils whenever I set foot in a gallery, the charnel-house in which my pictures are slowly decaying. I hate art, I hate artists, I hate their haunts and hangouts, I hate their work and its hanging. I applaud every vandal, every art-thief: more power to them. And let me be clear I don't include photographers, not that I care for them at all; they are no threat to me—they are cheats, frauds, image-stealers, non-artists pursuing a non-art. My sympathy is with the Stuckists—I mean, what the hell is happening to art? You can call anything art these days, what's the point of that? I love being a fogey, you can't wound me with that allegation, far from it; I'll just grow more proud and still more stubborn. Art needs a complete rethink; and I mean that whole godforsaken lot, not just my work. These days, if it makes you puke, it's art. What fucking good is that?

I used to aspire to something so pathetically simple; a vision of the artist that was as clichéd as it can get, with smock—and beret too maybe—holding a palette like a flat shield, smeared with colours of human and inhuman blood shades, knives, brushes, pots, the easel and a slanting light illuminating my chosen subject.

Fizzmonger

Art lessons, I scorned them—at first: what use were they? None. All the teachers contradicted one another; did anyone else notice that? Art isn't something you can *learn*, that was always my argument; you're either capable or not, what's *wrong* with you?

I just did what came to me, I've never taken to being told what to do; I've never needed recipes or manuals either, what happens, happens; if I want art then I flick my wrist and make a picture. I can fill my mouth with paint and just spit and there it is, the result I wanted. It comes. Came. Others spit and claim that the resulting mess is art. They just can't do it.

Charles Durant Tobol

'Art, artist, artistic! Can't we ever hear the last of that stuff!' Another great writer said that and he was right, more so than ever he knew. I would not delete or burn his writing or any other, I am no savage; it's what you can see in the frame, on the plinth, in any smug setting you like, that is my target here.

I had a friend who wanted to go and live in Ardendale. Idiot. It's not that Ardendale isn't the most beautiful village in creation, not that it hasn't landscapes that would exhaust the paint supply of every age of history before it could be done true justice, but he didn't want to go there just to paint. That I would understand fully, but he wanted to go to be among artists, to be part of a self-appointed 'colony,' a huddle and hive of paintbrush-twirlers all head-patting and back-stabbing, forming cliques, breaking them up, gossiping, plotting, scheming, I cannot think of anything more appalling than being in a fucking artists' colony. I avoid artists for much the same reasons as I avoid rats—nests especially. Never let them gather, never let them settle and breed, or there will be easels and daubs everywhere, galleries on every corner, art that is not about art but about artists. I cannot conceive anything more worthless.

I hero-worship the art-destroyers. Step forward the Italian, Piero Cannata, the man who took a hammer to the foot of Michelangelo's David and assailed a Jackson Pollock, a man who attacks paintings, frescoes and sculptures in a mission to attack what he calls 'ugly' art. Even the most Philistine amongst us would gasp with horror at least at his first target, most would say that he is mad, but not I. Take your place Piero Pinoncelli, he who attacked Marcel Duchamp's 'Fountain' at the Pompidou Centre in 1993, returning it to its proper function by piddling into it. Duchamp said he had made an everyday article something novel and aesthetic: 'Fountain' was voted the most influential work of modern art—by whom, pray, and what were they on? I read in the paper that public art in Italy is under attack and attrition, the authorities and connoisseurs bewail the loss, but bah—let the movement prosper and spread worldwide, whether it be careless and unthinking abuse of some artwork that has been dumped down in people's way or calculated assaults on even the greatest of the world's treasures, let the destruction commence!

There was one Stephen Murmer, an art teacher who got the sack when it was discovered that he painted with his bare backside—at last an honest artist, a man who truly earned the $900 he got for every piece!

I respect smashers everywhere: destruction itself is art, good and pure, not stale posturing. The only point of "art" now is to wait until it is wiped out. If I had my way, art would be an endangered species; every gallery would be under siege.

What's it got that nature hasn't? Artists are amateurs, slapdash dilettantes. They're too quick: nature builds slowly, slowly but perfectly, just *wait* for it and it is all you will ever need. Compared to that reality, all that even the greatest brush-plier will ever serve up is a series of comedy breadboards.

Fizzmonger
I owe so much to the stars. I lost my anger in the stars.

Maps Of The Stars

The Astronomy Club

Sabina Faslane

I had believed that once I could secure Alfred's approval and involvement, then everything and everyone else would follow. I had tested and gauged the interest among the kids and it seemed genuine and sufficient, so all I needed was for Alfred to break his solitude and share the stars (he had never joined a club or society in his life, as far as I could tell) and I would be in business. I thought, 'You know what thought did'—that would be my mother's response. On the afternoon of the inaugural meeting of the school society, I was seized with cramps; what if it should descend into the anarchy, the maelstrom that had been my first effort, The Astronomy Club?

Jilly Holdenbridge

Teachers become famous, if you can say that, for their little sayings, their catchphrases. Mr Wayman had so many you could make a book out of them. He had a 'Yoooooooooo-uuuu!' that could wake dozing back rows several rooms away, possibly in other schools. It wasn't wise to do a take-off of these tics: offenders got a good bellowing-at and a short, sharp gulag sentence.

Faslane, Miss, she was famous for just the one—'Do you understand?' The emphasis was transferrable from word to word depending on the situation; it could be a friendly summons, a demand, a near-command, a plea bordering on despair, an outburst of impatience (more a Wayman trait than a Miss trait). But to me, it showed her sincerity: she was not there to stuff little pre-exam munchkins with pre-digested facts; she really, really did want us to *understand.*

Sabina Faslane

You could see it as my first, faltering step to braving a classroom, or as the dawning of my career as a bossy bloody cow. Either way, it was not a great success. The experience haunted my teacher training; when we discussed how to control a class I knew by my encounter with the Astronomy Club that I could not, the task was beyond me.

In forming the club, I leapt to and for all too long held to a host of shaky conclusions, as an overconfident ten-year-old might; as I was so passionately interested in the stars, it followed that others were, ought to be, *had* to be, but that not one of them could be as keen as I, not one know as much as I, and it was therefore my job to make up their want of knowledge, to make them *understand.* So, on this dubious premise, I corralled a random, scraggy collection of street-friends and school-friends, set a date and time, (and a place, the garage at home, when I knew the car would be gone, my parents safely off out shopping) and I commenced my crusade, to teach my class and lead them. Yes, I had a very definite direction of travel, as the buzz-phrase goes, even at an early age.

There was Biff, who was not so much into stars as what may come from them, a convinced junior UFO buff, he was awaiting an imminent, inevitable alien arrival and wanted help to watch the sky for anything that glowed and hovered and looked like it was about to extend landing-gear. Shooting-stars, planets, satellites, aeroplanes and car-lights all excited him wildly and then disappointed him utterly—but his faith was unbreakable. Angela Crane was, we all said, tall enough to touch the stars, but, for her, all my star charts were fortune hunter's maps, pointers to the riches of her future: she seemed to believe that I would impart some arcane secrets to her that would help with her ascent to happiness through love and money. We fell out, regularly and shrilly, about the truth of the stars. Years later, her daughter was one of the key schemers who shut down our whole school for the sake of a string of world-shaking wanderers.

Then there was Europa Lee—yes, that was her name and yes we made her suffer for it, cruel little swine that we were—who only ever wanted to talk about the Moon; she was calm and attentive if I talked about her pet, but her mind drifted back Moonwards if I ever attempted to direct her elsewhere. Had I known Mr Alfred Wayman then, I would have handed her over to him; what would he have made of her?

There was also Melanie Hooton, Hootin' Mel, who, when she deigned to listen to anything that she was told, found it knee-slappingly funny, no matter what it was and who said it, and Perry Ward from down the road, single-minded, easily-fixated Perry who at this time had discovered the word 'sex,' and used it as often as he could, seeing sex everywhere, in everything. Last, and most disruptive, of all, was Tilly Pease, pretty but hard-faced, frown at the ready as she braced herself to argue any toss that happened to be given. She would challenge anyone who pretended knowledge, simply by taking the polar opposite view to theirs and flying her flag of defiance with her catchphrase, 'How der *you* know?' It was as if I had gathered together a disorderly ragbag of the uninterested, unlistening and unteachable, to make mock of my ambitions and portend my own future doom.

At the beginning of meetings, I would, (as a little girl playing teacher, for all the fierceness with which I would have denied it) take a register—correction there, I would *attempt* to do it.

'Biff, Angela, Mel, Per...'

'Pugh, Pugh, Barney McGrew, Cuthbert, Dibble, Grub!' Perry would call out every time and that would start Mel off loud-laughing, and the others would then chatter through, play during, or simply disrupt my chosen lecture for the evening.

'Tonight we're going to learn about the sun. The sun is a star and the Earth goes around it...'

'Isn't!' burst in Tilly Pease, 'The sun's a planet!'

I scolded her gravely and repeated my truth.

'How der *you* know?' Tilly brought up her rhetorical big guns. I responded with what should have been a killing-blow, a book, ready to hand, open at the correct page and proving my point entirely. But I was dealing with Tilly Pease.

'What der *they* know? They said planet on TV; I heard it, plain. Planet!'

'*The Sun*'s a paper with titties in it!' enthused Perry, setting Mel off hooting, deep, loud, breath-stealing whooping that even the sternest disciplinarian could never have stemmed; no, not even the legendary Mr Wayman at his fiercest.

I made matters worse: after my earnest talks had been disrupted by previous semi-riots, I had appropriated my dad's old football ref's whistle, sure it would call all attention back to me. I emptied my breath into it, but its

158

terrifying shrill simply set Perry off Pugh-Pughing again, redoubling Mel's helpless hyena sounds: so as Tilly continued to berate me, Mel to do her klaxon impression, Perry to slaver and await a sexy future, and the others to dream variously and serenely among the chaotic, all-consuming racket, of Moonbeams, love, wealth and green-skins, it left me and the stars without an audience, and I had improved the minds and increased the understanding of precisely nobody.

The only time that I got their attention for more than a moment was when I was, for once, a child alongside them, girlish, excited and joyful. I had overheard my parents arranging to buy me my first telescope and I was being eaten alive by the anticipation, I simply had to share my news and so I told the club members, hoping, boasting, projecting. I scrabbled at my books yet again, this time showing off pictures, the finest, the prettiest, the glossiest I could find.

'When I get my telescope I'll be able to see the Lagoon Nebula, The Horsehead, the Veil, the Crab the Andromeda Galaxy too, all, as good as they are here in this book.' I boasted and boosted my hopes, working on myself far more than on any of the others, to bend my credulity so that I might believe it true.

Perry gasped, struck breathless with wonder; it was as if I had finally communicated my passion. 'You could use it t'see nudie people in their bedrooms,' he slobbered.

'Not if the kertins are shut,' Tilly countered sourly.

'It will be,' I said, recovering my schoolmarmliness, 'an *astronomical* telescope. For looking at the *stars*. Plus,' I added in what I hoped would be a final, crushing demolition of

Perry, 'the image will be upside-down. You'd have to stand on your head to see your stupid nudies.'

'I'd stand on my head for Mrs Collis.' Perry was all talk; still is, from what I hear. It was lucky I was never foolish enough to talk in front of him about getting an image-erector.

'If your telescope can see as far as the stars...' mused Tilly, now back at her usual occupation, looking for a way for me to be wrong.

'Yeah?' I sighed.

'P'raps it could see through kertins. Like an x-ray.'

'Sexray.' Perry truly was unstoppable.

Europa demanded that the Moon be the first point of call for the new telescope.

'*I'm* more interested in deep-space,' I pontificated, 'The Moon's too near a neighbour.'

'I wanna look at the near neighbours—there's no nudies on the Moon!' cried Perry.

'How der *you* know?' came the Tilly Pease challenge, followed by voluble discussion of and disagreement upon which nudie neighbours would be 'worth a look.' In desperation, I tried the whistle, but Perry was so far gone he didn't even lapse in to his chant. Pandemonium, I mean greater and worse pandemonium than usual, ensued, and after the others left in boisterous spirits, still arguing about nudies, I slunk to my bedroom, to dream, alone, of my promised telescope and how it would finally connect me to the stars.

That was the last meeting of the Astronomy Club. I never taught anyone a thing. I never communicated my love, never passed it on. I was just a bossy, fussy little girl, frustrated, impatient, impotent and unable to comprehend that others weren't interested; they didn't *understand* and didn't want to. Disheartened and deflated, for a while I put my precious books in a box. I very nearly took down my star-map.

Glyn The Pin

I couldn't resist it, the opportunity. It was there, in bits and pieces and waiting to be put together. Though I usually managed to spot such things and assemble them into a half-baked scheme, I was often also far, far behind someone sharper and faster, such as Alan Brotherton of course, someone who had clipped the wires to the batteries, made the circuit and set the bulb bright alight while my reward was darkness. But this time, I don't know why, I hadn't been beaten to it and it was mine; I made the circuit and did it quicker and better than anyone else: for the first time I'd taken a lead. Leader. Me.

The news was full of it, it was on the radio and the telly and all the papers except the boring ones; people talked about it, especially when the celebrity stargazers got hold of it and were on the speakers and screens, fate-telling for phone-ins, making people tearful and grateful and also more than a bit frightened. If you watched or listened long enough there was the odd boring bloke who'd spit his outrage about how it was all bally nonsense, but nobody wanted to listen to boring blokes, this was too good to miss. Anyway, science couldn't save anyone from this thing, what had science ever done but help them make special effects good enough to fake the moon landings?

The celebrity fortune-tellers didn't really agree with what was coming up in the papers, they soft-soaped it, spun it happy and said it wasn't the end of the world at all but a turning-point, that a 'new era' would start after the line-up, everyone would feel the good forces of the planets, a lost harmony was going to be restored and humanity would feel great, they were going to stop being gits and hating one another, they would get rich and fall in love, better still someone was going to save us effort and heartbreak and they were going to fall in love with us, someone we'd been watching from a distance and who so far, in the age of bad vibes, had been completely stubborn about even giving us a look. Far as I was concerned this was candyfloss, it was almost as duff as the no-no-no boring blokes who said it meant nothing. I was with the newspapers—what they said was far more exciting.

The papers called it a 'once in a lifetime line-up' (the boring blokes said it wasn't at all, but as I said, they weren't needed), but there was to be no lovey-dovey new era. They printed stuff from people who said that the line-up would create a 'standing gravity wave' that would draw the planets closer and closer till they filled the sky, maybe they'd clash and click like the sliver beads on the stupid desk-toys that all the bosses had in all the TV programmes, and more, this coming-together would affect the sun, draw out of it this big finger of flame, a 'cigar-shaped deadly solar flare' that would flicker up and down the pinned-together planets and finish the business, brunching up all the bits that weren't already rubbled ruins. Basically, end of the world. End of all the worlds. See how that was better?

The nuns had it better still. There must have been something good in their holy water. The clubbed together and went off to see the Pope, stopping off with some notebook-wavers on the way and giving some big talk, saying that once everything had crashed and burned then a swoop of angels would hurtle down from heaven with dustpans and bushes and would put everything back in place, but only the good and the righteous would get glued back together—the rest would be shovelled off to the burner. No hope for the white-coats to save us, no goody-goody new era, we were all gonna roast.

So this sort of talk got round the school; the talk at home had been of nothing else, kids carried it in with them in armfuls, grudges and pending fights got suspended, teachers found it hard to get any focus from anyone, even the mean ones struggled, old Wayman gave up an entire double period, set aside his toy-soldiers of history and tried to explain that it was all total crap, that we were wasting our time, but only the usual creeps and keenoes were swung by that. The Physics teachers stopped putting their heads out of the Staff Room, they were nursing sore throats, and unlike Wayman they had the sense and self-preservation to recognise defeat. No one asked Old Wishy-Washy the RE man, he'd have ummed and ahhed, not said one way or the other; he missed the chance to take the lead on this, they all did. So I took it.

I'd intended to go to the meeting of the star-club; the one Fastlane and Wayman were starting. I didn't like spending any extra time at school, I'd got too many deets to want to hang around anymore, but a load of us had figured out that if it was going to be an after-school thing then maybe Sweaters would go home first and change into something a bit more—y'know—even better than the sweaters. We all built up a fair bit of enthusiasm on that until someone pointed out that Sweaters lived miles off and the meeting was only half an hour after school so she'd never have time to go and do the thing, there'd be no short skirt or sexy dress and well, that was it for the enthusiasm.

We might still have gone just for the ordinary sweater, but then I got the idea to steal their crowd, call my own meeting, I set the word running and my club grew and the star-club died. That was when Wayman raped Fastlane, of course, alone with her in a musty room. People still believe that.

I reckoned my strike would fall apart once Wayman started lecturing people—I thought they'd listen to him about anything to do with the sky. After all, he lived there.

Sabina Faslane

Fifteen years old, confidence as fragile as a shell, I'd gone off on my own; oh, I'd told my parents where I was, this was no rebellion. I'd half-expected they wouldn't believe me, that they'd think I was off boy hunting, but there was more trust there than I'd ever suspected. I took the bus; quite a first step, to walk on to that shuddering platform alone and announce where I wanted to go, to offer money, get my sums right, (I'd shifted the money from palm to palm about twenty times as I watched the bus come up the hill—after all it did demand *correct change only*). Everywhere there was the shadow, the hovering potential, of someone with an ugly face and a loud voice materialising out of the ether and shouting, *shouting—whatyoudoinginheregohome—* I thought it was going to be the bus driver, but it wasn't him, not tonight anyway. I opened my hand and let the palm-warmed coins trickle in the amusement-hall slot at the driver's elbow and as my ticket skirled out moments later I snatched at it and shot off to a seat, keeping ducked low as if I were eloping and afraid of interception, and then searching my pockets repeatedly, *where had I put that ticket?* After all, the moment it was well and truly lost, an Inspector would get on and I'd be for the high jump.

When I filled in the form, I'd been full of myself. I had neat handwriting, my application looked impressive. I had lingered, havered, over the question, 'Would you consider giving a talk to the group on a subject on which you are an expert?' I felt momentarily fearless of standing up in front of a group of strangers (the teacher, making another premature appearance), but that burst of self-assurance didn't survive the border-crossing of my bedroom doorway, and it was a demure and minimal application that I then sealed and posted, with the inner expectation that it would be treated by the Membership Secretary as if it were a begging-letter.

But a Member was what I became and so to that first meeting: Waveway Astronomical Society, Cartwright House, Enderley Street, Waveway Town. In my head it was a palatial building with marble portico, a grand hall leading to a grander staircase, guarded by twin armillary spheres some ten feet in diameter past which the Members would file in silent awe up the sweeping curve of the stairs, breaking off left and right, to the imposing doors of the wood-panelled lecture theatre that was the meeting-room, adorned in its turn with star maps and marble busts of Galileo, Copernicus, Kepler, Giordano Bruno, William Herschel (I added his sister Caroline too) and then portraits, tall, broad, gold-framed, of the more-moderns; Hale, Hubble, Harlow Shapley, Bernard Lovell, and on to Sagan and Moore, a pantheon of honoured heroes. Thin pickings for heroines, admittedly, but then I knew that one day I would supply my name to bridge the deficit.

I almost missed the distinctly unimposing red-brick building that was the real Cartwright House; a sign outside said 'WEA', not 'Astronomical Society', and the room I eventually found was a square, wipe-clean space with no indication of its purpose other than a hand-written notice on the door. It was not full, but there were sufficient numbers there for my nerves to grind and for me to become, without cause, shaky, intimidated and braced to flee. I crept towards the door, expecting interception, interrogation—*hooryoogerrout!*—or perhaps a querulous quiz to check my competence at basic Astronomy before I was allowed in. The Moon was an average of 250,000 miles away, Saturn took 29 years to orbit the sun, the Aurora, I tried to recall, was caused by ionised particles hitting the atmosphere, but what was an ionised particle, what sort of particles, what was ionisation, what did *I* know? I only went through the door because someone had spotted me and it was too late to take to my heels.

I was welcomed with smiles and gladness, any club welcomes new members, especially young ones, but try telling my fears that. With a school-bound mind, expecting roll-calls, demands for close attention and castigation of wandering wits, I did what I did on the bus, made at a don't-look-at-me crouch for a seat in a spot both inconspicuous and that also afforded a clear escape-route should it be needed. I had stick-out teeth and legs like match-tails and my hair was messy and disgusting and everyone was looking at me but no one would talk to me and-and-and; good god, the memory of that adolescent terror, it remains so strong, I'm blushing and cringing even now. What a long way I've come.

It was just my luck to choose an AGM to make my debut; I settled from panic into creeping, anaesthetised boredom tinged with disappointment as reports were made, officers elected, business discussed, any matter not astronomical in fact.

Glyn Capstone

I admit it; I was worried the whole time that I would lose them. I had got them away from Wayman's little meeting easy enough, who wanted to go if Sweaters wasn't going to be all dolled up?—but after that I was afraid that the plan wouldn't work, that people would get bored or scared, or that they'd start to look past me again, that I'd fade into the light yet again. I needed stratagems for continued visibility. Luckily, someone very visible came along to help out. Luckily in the short-term, that is.

Sabina Faslane

They say that young people gravitate together, but that wasn't true, not that night. Perhaps it was my fault. There were youngsters there, a small group of boys who, in the exact reverse, I suspected, of their chosen placings in the schoolroom, sat at the very front, lolling luxuriously in the only three or four cushioned chairs (armchairs, but not of the grand sort that would have cradled us in the noble meeting-house of my imagination) and although there were plenty of older people there that night who looked like they could do with a nice comfy seat, they didn't demand them and the boys didn't offer. I didn't even try to go near these youths; they weren't interested that a girl had come into the room, they all looked at me, sure, but only to glare the message *don't try to steal our chairs*. I took their message of unwelcome and steered clear. I wondered if everyone here was equally scowly and unfriendly, and re-laid my plans for a quick and early exit.

When the AGM finally proved itself not to be interminable, people relaxed, there was a break and they began to move about the room, chatting. Head down, back straight, hands on my lap, I stayed as still as possible and hoped not to be noticed. Someone ignored my refusal to engage and pressed near; all my danger signals flared and tingled, but when I raised my head and took a cautious peep (dammit, that look could have been mistaken for being demure) I saw it was a woman, friendly, motherly, large, harmless. She was carrying booklets full of yellow tickets, it was raffle time, she said, don't be left out, there's some lovely prizes to be won. My watery smiles were outdone with ease by her generous sunbursts, and quickly she persuaded me not just to buy a strip of tickets but to stand up with her and have a cup of tea, eat cake, chatter a little. I assume she was trying to "take me out of myself"— oh hell, she was, wasn't she? My attempts to reclaim anonymity were further frustrated as my raffle tickets were coloured with luck and I was propelled to the front of the room not once but twice, to collect first an Astronomical Society pen, then a huge tin of chocolates. I tried to retreat again, made it back to my seat and then sat there frozen in a pose, my prizes clutched nervously in my lap, my legs juddering as if ready to run, the instant someone came to take my things from me. Again I was invaded, a figure loomed, leant, dispossessed me without being troubled by my feeble resistance, took my prizes from my stiff hands and then set them down on the floor underneath my chair.

'There. Perfectly safe,' said the mumsy-woman, all-smiles still.

It was a relief when the break ended; at last the meeting began, the real, true meeting: and we talked about the stars.

Glyn Capstone

You could say that she was the leader, almost as much as I was. She ran the messages, did the legwork; well, she'd got the legs for it. She helped me keep their attention, their faith, but it was still mine, my thing, my strike, my name as leader.

Sabina Faslane

The badge made a lovely contrast with the shade of my school blazer; it was about half-an-inch in diameter, a circle of midnight-blue, bearing the image of a brassy telescope pointing at an array of brassy stars, one of which blazed far brighter than the rest, a four-spiked splash rather than a mere dot, outdoing them all in its metallic sheen. The name of the society was picked out around the curve of the badge. I loved that badge; even though in reality no star outshone all the others quite like that (Venus does, I suppose, at times, but then it's not a star).

'What is that object, please?' snapped Stuffed Shirt.

'It's a badge.' I replied flatly, adding 'Sir' after a suitably perceptible delay. Predictable as ever, a fish in a barrel as well as a Stuffed Shirt, he bridled.

'A badge of what sort, please?'

I told him, leaving the 'Sir' longer this time.

'And this society, are you one of its elected officers?'

Stuffed Shirt didn't recall, why should he remember one trivial interdiction among a lifetime of trivial interdictions, but we were performing a word-for-word encore of an exchange that had taken place two years previously, when I had first become a Member and had bought and proudly worn the badge for the first time. On the first occasion, he had threatened to confiscate the offending item as I was, apparently, too humble a Member to be allowed to wear it.

'Yes, Sir, I am one of its elected officers,' replied the newly-elected Membership Secretary, fresh from the latest AGM, at which she had blushed but accepted both the applause and the post, with the mumsy-woman next to me, applauding and smiling the most of them all.

'Well, remove it anyway, it is not part of school uniform. And if I see it again I shall take it away from you.'

'You bloody well won't, "Sir".' I muttered at him as I unclipped and pocketed my precious badge; those churn-ears were all for show, they often let him down and they were not at all attuned to the *sotto-voce*.

The other thing to mention, going back to the AGM, was that it was also the night I gave my first talk to the group, all still gathered in that anonymous and yet somehow cosy little room. It wasn't really all that much different from a schoolroom. The talk was about the history of women in Astronomy, The Forgotten Stargazers. Some of the men, the scowly young lads in the comfy seats especially, looked shifty and sceptical as I spoke, but I never allowed anyone's attention to wander, I made my points, got some laughs and yes, I think I got them to understand, if only just a little. My own course was set; I was ready to begin.

Glyn The Pin

I never saw much of any of them again, not after the strike broke up, and they saw very, very little of me, even though I was there before them. Especially her. We'd made our point, it was all done, the world had never ended, the midday sky had never gone dark, there hadn't been even a single threatening shadow, not even a raincloud to make it look for a minute like it was going to come and happen. And everyone was already starting to forget. Especially her.

All In A Row

Sabina Faslane

And lo, the Moon, though full and clear bright, shall by gradations lose its lustre, without a sound its light shall die, it shall tarnish to the dullness of an old, worn copper coin and then a tide of blood shall overwhelm it and thereafter it shall be consumed by encroaching darkness, until it may seem that it will never return, as if it were never there. Lament aloud, strike at bells and gongs, any sounding thing you can, to drive away the unseen demons and call our Moon back into being, for we fear to lose its soothing light.

There: in suitably doomy, larded language I have over-described a lunar eclipse. It isn't a frightening event at all; it's inspiringly beautiful, but it's possible to make something natural and beautiful sound horrendous if you try hard enough. Note how I don't explain in any way that the whole process has an ending and the Moon shines "full and clear bright" yet again every time no matter what bells and gongs are or aren't struck and, notice how I throw in "without a sound" to make it seem sinister, whereas if you think about it, everything about the Moon and all that up there happens "without a sound". Note how people are called to fear, urged to *do* something to drive off the unseen threat. This is how easy it is to be a prophet of doom. I just couldn't resist "and lo". Apologies.

Charles Durant Tobol

'Would you believe that a ragbag of people, grown men and women, vanished up Bayliss Hill last night, to wait for the Moon and Mars to start spinning around one another like a pair of bloody ice-skaters! A group of grown adults with the vestiges of common sense, plus information available to them if they could be bothered to check it, trooped up that hill and there they waited, like Millerites in their annual The End camp; and for what?

'What the hell did these people think they were doing? How did they think these things were possible? A planet hopping off its orbit and trundling fifty million miles to pay a day-visit to us? How could they have fallen for it? There is only one way; it was a lie and yet it was a beautiful and fascinating lie, whereas the truth was mundane-dull and, to them, no-good. Brain off, intelligence opt-out, love the lie and revel in it—even when the lie is made plain and the Moon rises alone, no big red companion, and everyone is made a fool by a lazy rumour—or rather by their own laziness in the face of a rumour. Mars, meanwhile, was guttering like a dying coal on the other side of the night. Why, why, why do people cleave to the lie every damned time?'

It wasn't enough for him to rail at the discomfiture of the gullible—Wayman never did understand that human foolishness is as unbounded and eternal as his beloved skies—he had the arrogance to believe that it was his job to correct it.

Sabina Faslane

For the second year in a row, the story had had plenty of exposure in the tabloids and even some raised eyebrows in more respectable quarters; Alfred was enraged by it, but people in general liked it a great deal, they took it to their hearts, even when it turned out to be specious piffle, they gave it a second chance. Which enraged Alfred yet more. 'Public disbelief—permanently suspended!' he growled.

The planet Mars was going to be visible, alongside and as large as the full Moon in the late August sky, that was the tale, but it was a case of hurry-hurry, one night only and it's all gone. That the whole sideshow would have required the temporary cancellation of several laws of nature didn't occur to anyone and the intervention of earnest scientists and angry history teachers didn't deflect the story from its course. Experts and know-it-alls were unwelcome party-poopers; people wanted drinks and finger-food, and to watch the Moon rise with a thrill of anticipation and not a care for what may or may not be true.

Alfred was to be enraged again a little later, far more enraged; even more planets were recruited for this, a true spectacular. People's story-hunger had increased.

Old Wash-Hands

As revelation (intended, intended) is my trade, it was understandable that some of them would come to me for advice, for an unscrambling of their remarkably ecumenical misunderstandings. Some had imported stories of cosmic disaster from cultures of which they had never heard, of which they would never hear. It was the first sign, for me, of the pick-and-mix spirituality that would dilute and adulterate faith thereafter.

The other thing that struck me was how few of them went away assured; they were as immune to my ministrations as to the careful explanations of any science teacher, or the bull-roars of a certain history master.

Glyn The Pin

I don't know how it ended up being mine, I mean my thing, people were talking about it, some were joking but some were worrying, even one or two got to crying about it, I mean in the school. It was all over the TV and the papers too and there was talk and talk and talk, but very little listening, especially nobody listening to the killjoy scientists or Wayman or Fastlane when they said it was all just stupid. People got round to the view, joking or not, that something was going to happen, 'You can't say for sure that it won't,' that's what a lot of them said; it all sort of ballooned from there. I don't think I was even the one who suggested the day-out, the strike. But it ended up being mine, people said it was mine, and suddenly I was the leader, calling them all out for a cause I didn't really believe, didn't really understand, but which meant that for once, the first time, maybe the last too, I was visible, my name known.

Charles Durant Tobol

'Ye gods and little fishes!'

Wayman stuck a spoon into a large, unlabelled tin, measured out two heaps of brown dust, added hot water, milk and sugar, agitated the mixture, then set both mug and spoon aside, watching the pale tan vortex swirl.

'Ye gods and little fishes!' he reached for the mug, thought better and sat in a way that could easily have been mistaken for abject collapse.

The pickets on the gates did not interfere with the teachers, but they scuffled and bawled if any child attempted to enter. Those who attempted to resist soon surrendered and joined the mass. There was to be no school this day, for what is the point of learning when you are at the end of days? It was rather an easy day for me, for anyone prepared to relax and accept the situation; turn up to work, make coffee, sit and watch the fun. I enjoyed it thoroughly. May I make so bold as to describe it as the one piece of "performance art", however inadvertent, which has ever brought joy to my soul?

Attentive little Fastlane hovered, tending, nursey-like, to the apoplectic Wayman, attempting to calm him, restraining him from storming to the gates and dragging children back by the scruff, to be re-educated by force. "Empurpled" is how I would describe him. It was wonderful, so rewarding.

'I cannot abide *twaddle*!' Oh how he bellowed and how impotently. It was a good day, a very, very good day.

Glyn Capstone

Don't imagine me standing on a platform or a soapbox, megaphone in hand, caw-cawing to the crowd, telling them what to do and think, pronouncing my will disguised as the callings of fate. That was the way some people operated in those days, but it wasn't my style. My message went out, but not my face. I suppose that's the way things go for me, has been and always will be; that's one fate I can call. Even my name didn't keep its shape as the word went about; Glyn, Glen, Glym, Glem, Glom, Glum, goodness knows what, even in an effort to make myself at long-last visible I ended up blankspaced, but it was the message that mattered, wasn't it? And it aided my security I suppose, made it easier to dodge the blame if the scheme went to hell. And then I could return to outer darkness, gone and finished with.

I didn't even know if anything at all was going to happen, I'd sold them on a cosmic spectacular, but it was completely unlikely to show up, I knew that as well as

Wayman did. It wasn't what the whole thing was about, not for me.

No soapbox then: it was done through whispers, mouth to mouth (shouldn't that be mouth to ear?). I had just the hard-core, the faithful few who attended to me, then they spoke to others who spoke to others, you know the spreading, branching way of it. Friends spoke to friends who spoke to friends and the word spread far further than poor, see-through Glyn the Pin could achieve, and somehow the walk-out, the call to strike, caught on like a blazing playground craze, like platform shoes, clackers, tartan-trim trousers, passing fads that take a grip for no very good reason, then grow claws, dig in tight, grab a hold till nearly everyone is crazed or complicit and those who aren't don't count anyway, and there is nothing anyone can do to stop it, not even Wayman and his tirades against "twaddle". Everyone against me got turned invisible. There was no HQ, no meeting-room for the teachers and disbelievers to raid, no notes or papers for them to intercept, no list of names to line up for punishment.

So I brought the school to a stop. For a day, half a day, an hour would have done, it was me, my doing. I never wielded such power, before or since.

Old Wash-Hands

Four—or was it five, why ask me?—planets were said to be "in alignment", which was what the fuss was about. It sounds portentous, that phrase, although like all such sonorous jaw-exercises it was fine to say, and practically meaningless.

Now, in my humble submission, there is a considerable difference between a mystic and a mystifier. A mystic is a still-point of true wisdom, one who attempts to discover hidden meanings and make them plain, for the benefit of all. A mystifier has no interest in either meaning or plainness, he is there to wallow in the mire of confusion, to stir that confusion into a vortex and turn the resulting chaos to his own very tidy profit. He will be long-gone before anyone starts to think straight or ask searching questions.

It was the mystifiers who ran amok when the planets lined up. I could almost bring myself to sympathise with poor, frustrated Wayman and his ilk as people who never once looked up at the sky began to see horror and doom come their way, via a hell-brew of jumbled, scrambled predictions tossed around like hand-grenades by the mystifiers as they emerged from the woodwork and flooded the media, proclaiming themselves *experts*, announcing the coming of storms, floods, hails of fiery meteors, war and famine on Earth; the planets would be flung from their orbits as if they had been smashed by some great cosmic tennis-racquet, the music of the spheres was to become a terrifying cacophony and the poor little earth, should it survive the horrendous poundings that were its due, was to be consumed in solar fire, even unto the last, littlest blade of its sweet grass.

The children took in so much of this it quite astonished me. To my mind they absorbed twenty-dozen lessons' of information in just a few short days and this toxic unlearning lodged firm where even the most diligently-taught curriculum could not, in a way that should have gladdened my teaching-heart for at least there was hope that other learning, better for their hearts, minds and souls, would find its way there eventually. But that would have been excessively, foolishly optimistic, like looking forward to a child's ability to drink pure water after it had just gulped a bottleful of paraquat.

The tuppenny-ha'penny doomsayers could not even agree what this 'phenomenon' would look like. Did this 'line-up' include our little world, or were we just onlookers? Some claimed that the planets would be strung across the sky from East to West, horizon to zenith and down again, as if hemming us in; some that they would hang up there clumped like a gang of conspirators; some that they would appear huge and imposing; others that they would be as nothing more than bright stars, but with a sinister power that belied their innocuous looks. Others still claimed that there would be little to see, as the planets would line up one behind another, so that only the foremost would be visible, but by way of curious compensation that this would be the deadliest of all combinations, for, all in a row, the planets would 'exert an unprecedented attractive force' on our hapless island home, our Earth would leap out of its little round rut of an orbit and go careening through space, shedding its atmosphere in its slipstream and suffocating all who drew breath, until it collided with the first of the queue of other worlds, which would spin away and strike the next, which could do the same, and so on, so that it would not be simply the end of the world, but of all worlds.

It was not just our little school that caught the bug; it was the whole town, the entire county, the very country, all the world was awash with alignment-fever. Millionaires offered bricks, whole hod-loads, of cash to NASA, to the Russians, to anyone who may have a spare rocket or two to help them escape the impact-zone (where they thought they were going afterwards does not bear scrutiny), that famous group of nuns bought themselves one-way tickets to Rome and presented themselves appointmentless at the Vatican, beseeching His Holiness to abjure all sin and wickedness and abandon strong drink and pornography, for the wrath of the Lord was upon us all. I try not to be a cynic, and their words may have been misreported, but this group did rather imply that judgement was come because the Pope had secreted his very own cache of whisky and girly-magazines.

It was not only the mystifiers who made a mint from this hysteria. Little gas-masks went on sale (to spare the wearer from the coming 'cosmic gases'—how they could help him cope with an absolute absence of air was not explored, even in the small-print), there were silvery-sleek 'space survival suits' with rather fetching fishbowl helmets, for those who wished to outlive the sundering of the Earth and float in the void post-apocalypse, working out what to do next. Absurd insurance policies boomed, the betting-shops must have resented having to close their doors and, most horribly, there were reports of a roaring trade in DIY suicide kits.

In the midst of all this, our leaders faltered; the scientists, the spiritual leaders, could make no headway, they could not halt the mental anarchy, the panic and profiteering, and it seemed that the world would end, but though hysterical self-rending and not any exterior force natural or otherwise. There was a fever of so-what hopelessness, where a dangerous number of people came close to surrendering all to a curious, infective despair, and while it raged this foolishness was quite something to behold.

I know my reputation, and I shan't waste time defending myself, but I was not awaiting a majority-verdict in this matter; I knew the right of it at once. I needed no science to do so and I do not necessarily align myself (intended, intended) with Wayman and his ilk on this matter. What troubled me was the matter of faith: plainly, we had failed to teach our children the difference between faith as it truly is and slug-witted, open-mouthed credulity. Faith is a search for truth, the work of the mystic, not a capacity to believe any and all absurdity, which is what the mystifiers want from us.

I don't quite know what inspired our own pupils to do what they did, I hope it was not despair—they were all too young for such a harrowing, hollowing emotion. I ascribe it rather to a form of cunning, the ability of the young to exploit the weakness of their elders and not-necessarily-betters. Opportunism, nothing more. I believe that I am right.

Jilly Holdenbridge

Who would have expected such pluck, especially from the timid little girl with the tight-folded arms and the chin tucked down on to her breast? Jilly the Shuffler, the girl who broke the strike.

The class was due in double-history at ten and Faslane, Miss, was there in that big empty room, sitting at her desk on the dais, marking the work of an absent class; plotting her revenge too, for when they came creeping back? She seemed surprised when I struggled my way into that room —those old boys'-school doors are so heavy, why are they so heavy?—she didn't quite say 'I wasn't expecting *you* of all people,' but came close. There was an awkward silence and a little nervous laughter from both of us; I wondered what would happen next, would there be a lesson, a just-me lesson, or perhaps just a conversation, my first chance to have her sole attention, be treated as a temporary grown-up, perhaps. And it happened, a little bit of lesson, a little bit of conversation, perhaps with too many unfillable gaps where neither of us could smooth over the strangeness. But she smiled at me, that gap-tooth smile that made her look almost as young as me, so pretty, and the *fwoar-fwoar* boys weren't there to see it.

'Well done, Jilly, I bet that took courage.'

Yes, I suppose it did; but then again it makes it easier when nobody likes you or cares what you think.

'It takes a lot to go against the will of the majority, even when they're dead wrong,' that smile flickered again, it was even more girlish, almost naughty, 'you could talk to your RE teacher about that if you'd like.'

Old Wash-Hands; I wondered if he had come in, if he could ever make his way past the pickets on the gates.

'It may just be that I'd be in more trouble if I didn't come in—with my family. School is where you go during the day—you have to go where you're meant to go, that's what they say.'

'But what about the end of the world?'

'I sort of don't believe in that.'

'Sort of?'

'Don't believe in it. Never did.' I managed a firm voice. Well, it quivered a little.

'Good for you. Any problems at the gate?'

I shrugged; my chin sank back on to my chest, that's how I got through; head down and shuffling.

'No one even shout?'

'Not at me.'

'You've really achieved something today, Jilly, you have truly stood out from the crowd. That's not been your strong point before now, has it?'

'No, Miss.'

'You should be proud. You stood up for something, not like them. Barely a one of them believes in their little death-watch, at first it was a laugh and then it was popular and then it became something everyone had to do because everyone else was doing it, it's not easy to resist that sort of pressure, well done.'

I shrugged an it-was-nothing. Because it was, it was a nothing-achievement from a nothing-person, but it was good of Faslane, Miss, to try to make me believe I was brave.

'Like I said Miss, I'm more bothered about my family.'

'So it's just that school is where you should be?'

'Yes Miss. But I suppose I mean it in a different way.'

'Oh? What way?'

There was no other way of getting her, Miss, to understand. So I told her about my Dad.

Old Wash-Hands

School windows—the sort provided in our noble edifice if not in the appalling little educational rabbit-warrens of later times—afford a goodly splash of God's light and, of course, a jolly good view of the surroundings. I stood in the window of the Staff Room, sipping my third coffee of that day to make up for having arrived rather earlier than usual so that I might observe. A thin trickle of youngsters was beginning down the long avenue that led to the school and its smaller side-street tributaries; cars and school buses ambled along in time, vomited forth their little charges, and made off again.

A few youngsters began, without much resolve, to make their way towards the main school building, but (I could hear no sounds) they hesitated, as if they had been called back, and they wandered, unhurried, to the gates where a growing knot of scruffs and spotties was accumulating, agglomerating, slowly. I watched with interest, how I do enjoy being the onlooker, to learn if the mob would stiffen and sustain, or give way, split apart and spill back into the waiting classrooms. Would there be signs of dissent, disagreement, push-and-shove, or, as the lads were content to call it at that time, "aggro"? Something was bound, surely, to happen. To begin with, there could have been barely a one who truly believed in their avowed purpose for gathering there clotting up the gates (intended, intended). Indeed, had they truly believed that it was the end of everything, they would hardly, as their final act in this life, have abandoned their beds and dressed for school. No, they were, whether they knew or not, testing, nay, proving, the sheep-effect. If there was any single one among them who was strong enough to breach the barricade, start a counter-movement, then that would be the end of this little 'strike.'

I wondered if the contrarians, the ones with argumentativeness in their blood (or their DNA, if we really must), or those raised and trained in their school careers by such bad influences as Mr Wayman, would make their way forward, if only for the joy of arguing the toss and feeling the "buzz" of opposing the hive mind (intended, intended), the dumb mass-will: but all was disappointingly quiet. The gates and pavement were choked with milling children, I was surprised by how few spilt out on to the road, and a few even leaked towards the school, but only to the field, engaging in ragged, desultory games. But still there were none who seemed intent in running the gauntlet or even wagging a finger at the self-appointed pickets. Thanks to the sheep-effect there was not to be any school today, it seemed. I was not really sorry.

'Good morning!' chortled a familiar voice, 'Amazed to see you're here. I wouldn't have thought you could bring yourself to cross the line.'

I gave Wayman a thin smile and an even thinner good morning and I was careful not to let on about my time of arrival at work. I am not in the business of inviting mockery.

They had hardly been set a good example, these our children, by the adult world. The newspapers had stooped to levels of ill-informed sensationalism that scarcely seemed possible in our, ah, enlightened age, and there were plenty of reports (both tongue-wagging and probable truth), of supposedly responsible adults using the fuss as an excuse to cheat their bosses (and us all) of a day's productivity by taking a sneaky day in bed. Tobol told me about this; I told him that the bosses should not take matters lying down (intended, intended, but he missed or ignored it entirely, the humourless little troll).

It was well past nine o'clock and the only movement to and from the school building was of frustrated teachers attempting to supervise, control and cajole their refractory pupils. The Head stood, with her coffee in her gently tremoring fist, a characteristically irresolute and ineffective equidistance between the school and its missing pupils. I bet that concoction of hers was even less coffee by-volume than ever by lunchtime. I took myself to my timetabled classroom, partly as that was where I was supposed to be, partly out of curiosity, to see if any strays made it to lessons, but also to quit myself of the company of the increasingly agitated Wayman, inveighing against "twaddle". It was an interesting morning. Very interesting. Indeed.

Glyn Capstone

It passed off without so much as a shadow on the sun. Shame really. If only there had been something, a comet maybe, just a sliver of an eclipse would have done, but there was not a short-lived flickering of the light, not even a funny-shaped cloud. It was just words and feelings, just a story. The only other suggestion I'd made was that we should all get together to look at it, the phenomenon that had brought us together, all those pearlstring planets, so that we could see as one the thing that had given us Armageddon and a day off. But you had to get up early to see it—Wayman would tell you that little Mercury, at the very least, never strays too far from the sun, you had to ride the dawn to see them, all in a row, the cause of all the fuss. But nobody wanted to do it; some said they'd 'have a look,' but in the vague way they'd promise to look in on a duff TV programme. They were no more interested in the planets than I. We had found a use for the planets and now we weren't interested anymore. I was going to say "they", but it was we.

I woke up early that morning—come on, I was excited and nervous, it was a new sort of day for me, a frightening one too, so sleep was a forget-it. I abandoned my warm bed and broke my old rule; I went to look up at the stars, the planets that spelt my fate—for that day anyway. I got outside without disturbing the Aunt, but there was a setback. I knew the planets were strung along, rising in the East, but… I didn't know which way was East. I worked it out; it wasn't that hard I suppose. So there they were, all in a row, a diagonal line chasing away from the still-hidden sun. From the horizon going up, they went: pinkish flickering one, yellow brilliant-lamp one, red ember one, bright but milder yellow one, a faintish other one that looked like it was a million-billion miles away, just a dot.

And just for a few moments I got this queer feeling, this mix of feelings, was it really going to happen, I mean really, was the sky going to rip apart, or the ground buck and go-wild, was a tower-wave coming to swallow us or a hail of meteors like bullets from a gangster god? I realised that those planets were just there, hanging in a cold, dark sky, and they were tied up in their own business. What happened with us wasn't their lookout, they were simply far-off and indifferent. But that feeling stayed, this time as a sort of frosty wonder, so that for a moment I realised I was feeling a little of what old Wayman felt as he looked on high. Hell, he'd be there right now, looking at that same string of lights, self-satisfied and not afraid of any sky-break or ground-shake or other imagined cataclysm.

Well, I re-thought, maybe this little whirl of dizziness isn't fear or wonder; maybe it's just lack of breakfast and seeping cold. The cold reminded me I was no Wayman, I had seen what I'd set out to see, so with cold air clinging to me, finding its way through gaps and holes in my hastily-donned clothes, I darted back into the warm house, dived into bed still bathed in that persistent night-chill and shut the stars out once again. Those planets had been a wonderful sight; nothing like the blazing, whirling discs in the TV pictures or papers, those artist's impressions that always oversell; no, it was actually *better*. But in the end, those planets had made me feel sort of small, sort of lost, and I'd had enough of that, all told.

Jilly Holdenbridge

I made sure I was wrapped snug and warm, and that made me feel as if I had done at least something right, as to do what I was doing, to creep out of the house long before the safety brought by the light was a very, very wrong thing indeed. I had never been specifically told that was so, but I simply and truly *knew* that it was. The Love Cloud's rules were never written down in any book, but existed in blood and bones, so if you were of that blood, those bones, the rules were written within and no book was needed. I was doing nothing that could harm anyone, nothing they would ever need know about, and yet my guilt was unbearable. Guilt and fear; I might be kidnapped or murdered in the dark, locked out of the house and forgotten, and whose fault would it be, eh?

Faslane, Miss, she would be looking at this very sight too, probably at this very moment. So would Mr Wayman, come to that. Something in my imagination placed them together, gazing up, but aware of one another, touching, holding hands perhaps. I knew it was nonsense, but there it was anyway.

My best friend was upset by the whole thing; the planets formed a chain that linked her star-sign and the next, and from somewhere she had got the notion this meant that all the good luck, love and money would drain out of her sliver of horoscope and into the other, and of course vice-versa with bad luck of any sort you could name. She talked about it all the time, and yet never took one look at those

188

lights as they shimmered in the sky. Her bedroom even faced them, dead-on, but she never even opened her curtains a crack, that was what she said. And soon the great line-up would be over, that was what Miss said; she said Mercury would be swallowed by the sun (or something, that can't be right, it sounds more like the newspapers than it does Miss, I've got mixed up) and the other planets would move off too, slower but breaking the chain: and my friend's luck would stay the same, planet-line or no. Miss Faslane had tried to explain it, to show us that it was a pretty sight, a trick of perspective; she turned herself into a science teacher for a short time—and a lot less boring she was than the usual white-coats—but however short, it was time wasted. I don't think anyone truly believed it was the end of the world, but they all fell in with the strike; well, why take the risk? Why study if we were all going to die? Another day's knowledge would be neither here nor there. Better to hold out for one last carefree day.

A little breeze ruffled my hair, gentle and indulgent as a kindly uncle. I knew no harm could come to me in this dark, not ever. I thought about Faslane again, Miss, and perhaps a little more about Mr Wayman too. I let my eyes rest on the twinkling diagonal above and began to plot my silent re-entry to the house, undetected and then to be as-normal, up and dressed and ready for school, not that there was to be any school that day, but appearances mattered, *really* mattered. They needed not to know that I had been out; they needed not to know that I had looked up.

Glyn Capstone
I supposed at the time that they thought it was appropriate, clever maybe, to send their message via one of the group,

one of the faithful who had already pretty much forgotten me even through the thing I most wanted was… from her… you know… There was female cunning lurking in that decision, which was my guess anyway; it was a clever, poignant, rather cruel touch. But at least it meant I was noticed by her one last time, so maybe there was kindness in it too.

I had expected to be summoned, arraigned, punished, but I'd thought it would be a march to the Head's office with a couple of big, sweaty prefects for an escort, not being told in a gruff voice by a girl who either didn't want to look in my direction or genuinely couldn't locate me, that 'They want to see you. Room 33.' I set off, trying to saunter, unconcerned. No Head then, the message came from Wayman and Fastlane. When I got there they were marking books; I thought for a moment they were going to pretend I wasn't there, let me suffer. I'd seen it done on the TV.

'Ah,' said Wayman, looking up. 'The cult leader.'

They smiled, but not bad smiles; I mean, not the smiles of those about to enjoy someone's suffering.

'It's a rarity,' said Wayman, looking dead-at me. I was no blankspace here.

'Sir? What is?'

'For a cult leader, when his predictions of Armageddon have fallen flat, to fade back into obscurity. Most of them find a new angle, a delayed date for the end of the world, a new scam, a fresh way to fleece the flock.'

'But…' I was interrupted by Fastlane, who spoke gently.

'But that wasn't what you were doing, was it? That wasn't your game. All you wanted was…'

'What I got. I don't want any more.'

190

'Fair enough. One more thing, though. Did you believe at any time—in any of it, any at all?'

'No, Miss. No, sir.'

'Hmph. Off y'go.' Wayman looked down at his stack of books and Fastlane smiled at me once more before going back to hers. And that was it, my punishment. There was nothing more.

Evelyn—A Summer Evening

Evelyn Lawton

'Sabina, Sabina dear, a word.' The poor girl looked perfectly terrified; I suppose it was my tone, hushed, urgent and sleeve-catching. She hardly knew me, so she hardly knew what to expect from me. As, of course, I also barely knew her, I didn't know quite how to speak to her; I regret the "dear", it made me sound like a patronising old relic. Perhaps, to her, I was.

What had terrified her so? I supposed she feared it was interrogation-time, the third degree, 'Are you and Alfred…? I mean really, isn't he a little old for you, I can't even say that he's well-preserved… oh my dear, are you sure what you're letting yourself in for, shouldn't you be out and about with people of your own age, I mean after all…' etc. etc. Truly, I believe that she was braced for this sort of thing. Her relaxation was visible, sinuous, top-to-toe, when no such assault was launched on her. Of course, I never suggested that she and Alfred were having any sort of liaison; far too many things militated against that, and I do not mean the age-gap. After all, who am I to lecture on the subject of age-gaps?

The only thing the two had in common—teaching set apart, that is—was the star-watching, the sheer enthusiasm, which was a mutual love indeed, a passion shared. I hissed my urgent question to Sabina because of that love, because she would know the answer. The garden chairs were set out and the sun three hours gone; the sky had adopted a rich depth of velvet darkness that had not been seen since the abdication of the spring-time, the stars shimmering and the

Moon hidden discreetly so as not to interfere with the proceedings and annoy Alfred. We had snacks and treats in bowls on little tables, plus drinks aplenty. We four were going to sit out and enjoy Alfred's annual summer treat, his sky-festival.

'Sabina dear, what are we supposed to *expect?* What are we actually going to *see?*'

'Has he not told you?'

'Not ever. This is normally his private show, but for some reason this year he's asked us to share. He's been doing this for so long he's forgotten that others are usually long-since in bed by the time it starts and we don't know what to do, how to do it or what we are going to see, beyond what we've seen in the papers and educated guesses. And we are far too embarrassed to ask him.'

Sabina laughed; it was a kind, fond, silvery sound. I had been right to like that girl.

A disclaimer, please. Bernard and I were most definitely not attempting to be match-makers or magic-weavers; we would not do that, it is unfriendly, manipulative and ultimately self-centred: *once upon a time a grumpy older teacher met a beautiful younger teacher and they fell in love and all was happiness forever, be like them or be inferior.* We were more interested in a meeting of minds, four people who could get along nicely, with sufficient in common to make interesting talk, but not a monotonous chorus of unthinking agreement. I do however confess that our invitation to Sabina, which was perfectly legitimate on its own merits, also contained a little selfish motivation on our part, as Bernard and I could at least plan the evening in the certainty that one of our two guests would show and that she would also take time to talk, play guest-host a little, rather than staring endlessly, wordlessly into space.

I have to say that I can defend myself from accusations of match-making because I knew already about Keith, who was not so much her unspoken secret but her quiet, happy pride: they lived together, much to the disapproval of his parents and the indifference of hers, well away from our town and the school with their abundant prying eyes and tattling tongues. Sabina was already appalled by the staff-room chatter, name-calling and mock-moralising; I had come to know her extreme distaste, intolerance even, for gossip, for adulterated stories and histories. I had my reasons for sharing her sentiments. But her *cordon sanitaire* could not protect her from the sour outpourings of the grapevine; people knew people who knew people who knew things (even though they may have made them up). *Miss has got a boyfriend, she lives with him and they int married!*— that was one runnel for whispers, the purse-lipped disapprobation of those-without-sin in the staff room another. These thin but acrid streams mingled and fed off one another and may have shared a single source.

My link with Sabina was forged some time before she was even born. I was once the look-at-'er of the story, the one to whose name dirty rumours and hot-knickernames were tagged. To some of Bern's colleagues I was known as "Lawton's Attachment". For the sake of clarity, they did not mean an emotional one—to catch their drift, think rib or excrescence. They head-patted me, called me sweet names, damned my intelligence and demeaned my teaching; to them I was not much more than a nanny, a bossy little starch-bosom whose only true function was to free the hands of busy parents for a few hours and let their offspring play out a few last pointless games before the real, joyless schooling began where they would learn to clamour, bite, scratch and trample one another in the relentless rush to *succeed.* But education for little people is not little education, it is not cheap at the beginning and then worthy in later years, you can't ignore or throw away a child at one stage and then recover them at leisure. They may not still be there to be recovered. I was not some nursemaid to distract brats while they were quietly trained up for a life of failure. Bern used to joke I prepared his victims for sacrifice; I never took this amiss because I knew precisely what I was really doing and so did he, and what's more, he approved; it wasn't just at senior school that the Lawton Plan was at work.

I did not know, never did know, if Alfred was even aware of Sabina's young man. But that doesn't matter, does it? No, it does not.

Sabina explained what the meteor shower was, what we may see and when, and in a way that made it plain why she was a teacher to the marrow: I felt informed, buoyed and not for one moment a fool who could have and should have asked before. I was able to step out into the darkness, Alfred's territory, equipped in mind as well as body, and my next drink, to celebrate my relief, was taken without any remaining shudder of nerves and for that tasted doubly delicious. I knew what I was about and Alfred would be neither offended nor embarrassed by my gaucherie. I noted that Sabina even managed gently to correct Alfred himself —Bern always called him a slip-tongue—that he had spoken of the Per*seads*, Sabina of the Per*seids*. To my shame I was tempted briefly to put my trust in his version, thinking he was the senior, the one who must know best, but Sabina was right, that was that. Perhaps if things had been just a little different that lovely Sabina would after all have made him a good—*now stop that!*

The three of us had been chatting happily for some time when our wayward guest appeared, barrelling out of the gathering semi-darkness with his habitual awkward movements that always looked painful (a rolling gait, ache in his hip I'd guess, caused by his bulk), but he was affable and smiling.

'Ready?' he asked me, as if he were about to light the fuse.

'Ready.' I was firm. Bern shook hands with Alfred; Sabina simply smiled welcome at him and betrayed no surprise when he took his seat, reclined in it as far as it would go and looked aloft, without a further word to any of us.

'There's one! There's one!'

'Woowoowoooo, look at them go!'

'Powpowpow! Pcccccchhhhh!'

'Do any of them ever make a noise—a proper explosion?'

'Not really—very rarely.'

'Awwww!'

'There's another—wheeeeeee!'

'Oh no, I missed it!'

'Oh, there'll be another along soon…'

Sabina started it; Bern and I joined joyously, we were children at the fireworks. Alfred remained as silent as his sky, but he was smiling to himself, indulgent and benign, the uncle-in-charge. After all, this wasn't a *serious* stargazing session; had it been, he would never have been with us in the first place. But of course. The Earth was doing some cosmic cleaning, sweeping up motes of dust from a dead-and-gone comet and the upper air was a furnace in which they burned, briefly, brightly, some like tiny, flashing scratches appearing on and then vanishing from the face of the night, others more spectacular and enduring, jagged magic-lantern scars, bursts of fluorescent flame that left glowing trails flickering, dancing like illusions in our eyes, long moments after their immolation. No wonder Alfred always scorned the expression 'meteoric rise'—meteors don't rise, they fall; and they burn.

Perhaps I had caught a little whiff of Alfred's stardust, even then. Before he arrived, even before Sabina, I left Bern to finish the preparations for our little party and sat in one of the garden chairs, watching the summer sunset, the gradual change as the bright blue of the August sky began to fade, acquiring other, deeper shades, red and gold flecks, the few scattered clouds as white as scraps of angel-wing, accompanied by short-lived flickers of changing light, creams and greens and violets in a kaleidoscope show. I watched the first intimations of darkness gather their forces in the Eastern sky, creeping across, encroaching to extinguish the slipped-away sun. Soon I could make out the beginnings of the stars, faint twinkling points attempting to assert themselves against the slow-fading brightness, I began silently to urge them on, to will them to win the struggle, for them to brighten and the sky to darken.

A glass full of dark, promising liquid was thrust across my eyeline and my sky-written poetastry was at an end.

'Jobs all done, everything ready—drinkies time,' chirped Bern. He looked at me, waggled his eyebrows, grinned like a fool, as was always his way when breaking in on my thoughts.

'What's this? Playing at being Mr Wayman are we? So: how does it feel to command the heavens?'

Alfred's face was a composition in the shades of a summer night's semi-darkness. Relieved of the harshness of intruding, abrasive light, it was softened, rapturous as it turned up to the place where more than most he truly existed. Semi-dark and shadow; they forgave his imperfections and brought out his long-buried boyishness, wide-eyed and profoundly contented with something simple, natural, supplied without human effort, art, intrusion or human cost. Light was never tender or gentle with Alfred, it made him look creased, pitted, blotchy, permanently tired. That's not to say it didn't reveal the truth: outside of power-maddened politicians, I never knew of anyone who slept so little or whose face was so weathered by time and unrevealed experience. The softer tones of a summer night were a sweeter companion for him than cruel daylight, part of the environment in which he thrived. Alfred never thought of his face as one for being seen, it was for seeing, for looking, for looking *upward*. He never cast a glance at any of us; he was absorbed in his task of second-guessing the sky. When he spotted the brief-lived burning, eerie-silent flashes and scratches in the sky, his smile was of the purest, most joyful satisfaction. He would be such a cheap date, you know— *stop that, I told you!*

Sabina was almost as rapt—although a little less the unsullied child of the sky, to the extent that her gaze, her hands too, would wander to the food and drinks from time to time, I'm glad to say. We had over-catered as usual and Alfred was touching nothing. I also noticed that from time to time she would take a peep at Bernard and me too, with the sensitivity of a polite guest, checking for signs of fatigue, of that's-enoughness, in her hosts. Alfred didn't do that. We could have removed the food, drinks, even ourselves, gone to bed and left him there alone and he would never have taken it amiss. As it was, Bernard fell quietly asleep in his chair as the very last of the summer day's heat leaked upward to greet the meteors. I coaxed him gently to bed and left him there, re-joining my guests under the midnighting sky. I am fairly sure that neither noticed our going, or my return.

Alfred Wayman first crossed our threshold some months after he joined the school. Bernard had talked of this 'queer fish' of a new arrival, this mis-shapen, mis-fitting lone man (lone—lonely? I was ready to test for that) who had come along to teach history under Bernard and had already acquired a name (several actually, mainly derogatory) with the boys as well as a mystique that came along with his characterful face and his failure-refusal to apply the past tense to himself. I was not at all sure if I liked him: he was too self-defensive, a man who pretended to sport a cast-iron outer skin but whose armour was plainly pitted with weak-points. He was touchy, suspicious of our every line of friendly chatter, as if each were a reconnaissance mission, or a feint prior to all-out attack. I confess I was not far from losing interest in him, leaving him to Bernard's (on this occasion) greater patience and tolerance.

Something about him impressed me, however, and allowed me to persist even though I absolutely hate it when one has to make all the running and is compelled to conduct oneself entirely by rules tacitly set by the other person. His disadvantages were many; I could have taken against him and pounced on any and all of them. He had all the hallmarks of bachelor self-neglect, he had the smell of the man who never lets his clothing dry properly, I could almost have borne the niff of tobacco better than that breath-stealing mustiness. When he thought himself unobserved, even for a moment, his fingers drifted to his mouth or nose; I never liked biters and pickers, it quite turned my stomach. He was only faintly ashamed if he were caught mid-meal, so to speak. Not to mention the inconsistent application of his razor, his excessive devotion to elderly, ragged favourite items of apparel, his inability to boil an egg.

He rarely relaxed; he sat as if impatient to get away and conversed like a moody fourteen year old unless his pet subjects, history and the skies, came to his rescue, in which case he would become animated and embarrassingly over-energetic. I suppose at least he did not attempt to wrench and wrestle the conversation to his pet subjects with the sweat-stained effort that I have seen from far too many others, but he was constantly checking the tide and when it flowed his way his turnabout from semi-sulk to fluent talkativeness was leadenly lacking in charm. So many disadvantages and yet... Bernard saw the good in him far more quickly, but Bern would be the first to admit that he had more time with Alfred, worked with him, observed him and talked to him day by day. At first, all I had to judge from were tea-table anecdotes and character sketches, unpromising portraits to say the least, before we decided to invite him over for one or two more-or-less successful short visits.

For a while the chatterers of both staff-room and schoolroom tried out 'confirmed bachelor' (hint-hint) on their new grotesque, behind his back of course, and the phrase spread around the school, accompanied by every possible offshoot of inference. When Sabina came along, that rumour shrivelled completely, but what took its place was uglier by far. The boys nicknamed Alfred 'The Daylight Dodger,' which had a species of logic attached, absurd as it was, as he spent his daylight hours right there before them, and it showed a sort of respect (rare, from them), a recognition for the night-creature he was. The same nasty little sprigs dubbed my beautiful husband "The Coffin Dodger" with a great deal less respect. Bernard knew and didn't care, dismissed it as trivial.

Sabina, although of course, was a far easier guest. Oh Alfred was easy enough as soon as you knew how to make him comfortable, positively agreeable if he got what he wanted, but Sabina at least observed a little more than just stars; she knew some social skills and codes, I mean the necessary ones—not any fussy, silly conventionalities but the guide-posts that allow a conversation to go forward, without leaving anyone out or causing crass, avoidable embarrassments. At first I wondered if she was too careful, too studied, a card-player who would try to match you as an opponent, only revealing when you revealed, dropping her guard when you dropped yours, but I'm sure now that was just nerves and she was very soon flowing, natural, elegant and open. I noticed that although Sabina had brought along some wine, she didn't touch any. She said nothing about the matter until rather later, but I guessed the reason. It was not feminine intuition, I'm not sure I even believe in that, it was good old fashioned deduction. I was secretly proud of myself for knowing that on that night there were five heartbeats and not four, though one secret and very new beneath that late-night summer sky.

Another thing I liked about her was that although she quite plainly lived with and loved somebody, she did not invoke him every other sentence as both protection and boast. I always tread carefully about over-broadcasting our domestic bliss when Alfred is about, after all he could be secretly sensitive on the matter, he could find it an insulting attempt to grind his face into his own singularity and I was pleased when Sabina, too, chose discreetly not to attempt to mock or punish his loneliness. I shouldn't, but I feel sorry that he has that absence in his life. I really shouldn't; he seems to get along quite well.

We broke the party up at about 3am; Sabina had slipped away into sleep, breathing lightly; against her will, her eyes had closed and she lay there like a sunbather in negative, overwashed by the night. When she woke, she laughed at herself and decided for home. She had been almost side-by-side with Alfred, (wide awake, but of course, and still watchful, but with no eye on anything occurring on Earth). He would tidy up and close up for us before setting off home. As I got in bed I couldn't help but stifle-giggle the thought that I could set quite a rumour running should I wish—Miss Faslane had slept with Mr Wayman! Well, isn't it true(ish)? Isn't that what certain others would say?

It is August once again, meteor night once more, and I am here, seated in the same chair, watching. But I am many Augusts on and so much has changed. I am here alone; unlike Alfred's isolation I did not choose this. I was often drawn to wonder about Alfred's self-selected solitude and, yes, in spite of my better instincts I sometimes conspired ways to bring it to a happy end, to relieve an unhappy state as I saw it, deluding myself he would be grateful because he *had* to be grateful, *ought* to be. I suppose Sabina would call that a false story, tinged with romanticism and sentiment. But I always took possession of myself, I never tried anything, because I knew in my heart Alfred was alone because he chose that state. He was not making the best out of necessity. I don't believe he ever craved company and most of the time he neither sought nor enjoyed it; I have always enjoyed company, equally I have never hated being alone and I have been fortunate in my life, privileged, I have never really been forced into the one condition while my happiness depended on the other.

Sabina is more like me; she is now enjoying the happiness of family, the joy that Bern and I once shared, although perhaps it has become a little sporadic of late, our sons inherited a mass of their father's best qualities, but neither possesses his easy mastery of staying in-touch. They live with their phones connected to their bones and yet never seem to call home... but that is perhaps an old woman's quibble, a variation on a traditional tune; our sons and daughters have their lives and have to declare independence at some point.

Alfred is still very simple to find—locate him by the stars. He will be there you can be sure, gazing aloft on any clear night. He is usually alone, apart from his visits from that oddity of a portrait painter, still calling on him with the regularity of a devoted son. What a strange pairing; as far as I am aware, they have little to say to one another these days, what needs to be understood between them is understood and in amicable silence they paint the portraits of the stars.

I need to see Alfred. There is something I need to tell him.

Jilly the Shuffler

Jilly Holdenbridge

Remember her? The girl who never raised her eyes to heaven. Head bowed, in fervent prayer perhaps? When she moved, she did as one who was already good and old, arms wrapped about herself just below the breast-bone, gazing always down, feet never quite breaking contact with the ground as she walked, slow-shuffle-scrape, through a childhood that seemed to have begun in physical dotage, as if she had been schooled in her movements by her arthritic Nanna. Spring, bounce, high-step, dance, all absent, never-there, she was half-lifeless in her carriage at a tender age. She was the timid pet victim of the crowd, the one that gathers in every schoolyard, everywhere and forever, it howled at her, harsh and vicious. 'No one likes you, no one likes you!' but Jilly the Shuffler did not look up, her bowed head nodded, slowly. She already knew; she was equable about it. She accepted. But then she knew that nobody *had* to like her; she did not need them, she was better off without them.

Sabina Faslane

Children, the tales that you hear are true; your teachers talk about you all the time, we speak of nothing else! We gather together out of school and out of time and we recall you, analyse you, tell each other cruel and hilarious stories, zoom in on your most embarrassing moments, your failures, howlers and imbecilities and oh, how we laugh! Well, that's what I used to believe and there remains an echo of it in my mind even now: there's that flaw in my confidence, yet again.

Just occasionally it's the truth. Not the cruelty, but the discussions—sometimes they oil the wheels, the social ones I mean. When I was first introduced to Bernard and Evelyn Lawton I was terrified (confidence, you traitor!) because of Bernard's formidable reputation as a great man, emeritus, of the profession, and because Evelyn was a wholly unknown quantity. Their natural likeability—let's be more plain, lovability—overcame most qualms, Bernard was not the least grand or full of himself (I had allowed that sagging morale of mine to let in poison-leaks from persons whose opinions I should have discounted without hesitation) and Evelyn was friendly, relaxed, relaxing and, as it turned out, a former teacher herself, the retired head-teacher of a local Infants' School. Bernard had been retired for eight years, Evelyn for rather less. Teacher-talk was inevitable; the how-are-yous followed with speed by memories, anecdotes, comparisons of Bernard's school— then with my school-now, occasional terse interjections from Alfred, seated, contentedly uncommunicative, in a corner: and then there came a remark, unintentionally stunning, from Evelyn.

'You must have your hands full with Jilly.'

'Jilly?'

'Jilly Holdenbridge, she's at your school now, isn't she? I remember her even though it was so long ago; I suppose we all have our favourites over the years. Jilly Why-Why, we used to call her. The little raised hand, the serious, furrowed brow and the unceasing questions.'

Jilly, the silent, shoe-gazing child who would scarcely even meet my eyes.

She was a curious, forthcoming and forthright child before her father's death, a bookworm, a grub of the species anyway and not sorry or shy about it. Jilly Holdenbridge wanted to *know* and she didn't care what anyone else said: she would ask, ask, ask. What forces could have borne on her to make her fall in on herself the way that she did? It was surely not just the impact of her mourning, her loss. Children of that age, surely they recover, even from such grieving? There had to be something else, another, powerful influence: somebody took great pains to train her in timidity, in that ground-held gaze and the crick-neck, breast-hugging slow shuffle that was her protection and her all: *do not try to put knowledge into my head,* her carriage said, *for it will be useless, just as I am useless, purposeless and without any future that does not consist of acquiescent silence, deference to the convenience of others and listening with respect to their loud opinions; with this I am surrounded, by this I am caged. Do not attempt to release me, I am where I belong and I can go no further, raise me no higher, the sky is for others, not me.*

From that time on, that night of discovery, I knew, *knew* that Jilly Holdenbridge was a prisoner, held against her will: thus was rekindled the determined, headstrong evangelism of the founder of the Astronomy Club—it was not just my job but my duty to reach her, to help her to recover her ability to look upward.

Evelyn Lawton

Jilly Why-Why vanished from sight—she was removed from it, rather. Not that she disappeared physically; she changed out of recognition, the bright child who had showered me with eager questions arrived at primary

206

school dragging her feet with her head hung low, silent, listless, questionless.

Teachers do wonder what became of former pupils, of course they do, and I thought that I would perhaps one day bump in to her, or at least spot her somewhere around town, but Jilly vanished with a decisiveness that meant I, everyone, lost track; my sources of information were scant, lines of communication stretched, and there followed a gap in her history that was, simply, a blank, one not even hastily back-filled with rumours or half-baked stories. Those why-why questions had come to an end, that essential spark gone. Her family were there too, clustered in formation as if to fend something off, and it was only in school she was alone, and there truly alone, stripped of that protective phalanx, friendless, silent, incurious, unquestioning and minimally responsive.

One teacher had tried to encourage her, draw her out, and had encountered such sullen dullness she had gone quickly to talk to the family. Was the child on some medicine? She had seen it before, a young and lively child who transformed within weeks into a somnambulist, drained and foot-dragging, from whom the questions and answers were gone, with his former bubbling curiosity not sated but removed as if scalpel-cut. The previously bright and happy child was also apt to burst into tears at the tiniest provocations, indeed in provocation's absence. Urgent but gentle questioning at a parents' evening revealed the story —the boy's doctor was trying to treat persistent bedwetting and for some reason had hit on the idea of prescribing tranquillisers with a net result of conjuring water from both ends so to speak, and the teacher's concern was already felt a hundredfold by the parents, who were emboldened by her intervention. The tablets were withdrawn, plans redrawn and a small star shone again in the classroom. But there was no such neat and happy solution to the vanishing of Jilly Why-Why: the teacher's enquiries to the family in this case met with polite, cool, unshifting nothingness.

Charles Durant Tobol

Were I a character in a book, I should like to be the villain: that is, someone regarded as such by the dullard other-characters and any softheaded reader. A schemer, a plotter, but a successful one, that's the key, subverting the usual run of melodrama. Wayman should accept that sort of thing; it fits his empty, godless universe, his moral desert. And what would I scheme? The downfall, of course, of him and his kind. And there would be no last-minute reformation, no conversion to 'goodness' and no turncoat confidant to betray me, no cheap coincidences to deliver mundane justice, no squeaky-clean *deus ex machina* miracle to thwart me at the last. Not even Old Wash-Hands could stop me, with his queer sense of justice and dithering deity.

Wayman and Fastlane, Bernard Lawton too, they break the iron rule laid down by Capital-Haitch. That was our name for the headmaster—Headmaster, he would have insisted—of the primary school where I first developed my arts. The only resemblances he bore to Wayman was a peculiar, oversized appearance and an apparently eternal tenure as a teacher. Capital-Haitch was enormously tall, statue-like but with brutal, unfinished edges; a rough-cut sculpture come alive that would have turned Pygmalion white-haired on the instant. There was, I decided, in an obscure place somewhere within the cellar walls of that little school, a niche, jagged-edged and full of shadows, over six feet high and half-that wide, looking a little like an unfinished cupboard, and yet step back a little and the overall effect showed that it was almost man-shaped: it was not that it had been hewn out of the wall, but more as if something had formed within the wall, dragged itself clear of it and was now walking around. That was why Capital-Haitch never left the school; he was part of it, literally, and could only be destroyed with dynamite or a wrecking-ball.

He was fond of dispensing wisdom from his craggy height; he loved above all else to deliver A Good Homily. This one stuck in my mind and its applicability is obvious.

'Some Of You have been trying to do something—out of genuine Goodness Of Heart—but I am here today to tell you that you have been making A Mistake. When you find a baby bird in the school grounds, one that has Fallen From Its Nest, your first, kind, instinct is to pick it up, nurse it, try to keep it alive. Some Of You have even borrowed cotton wool and little boxes and gone out Looking For Them, trying to Save Lives. One child was even found Warming A Bird In Her Hands at her desk! But in every case, The Bird Has Died. In each and every case, it would have been Better To Have Left It. I can understand your intentions, but you only prolong their suffering and it is better To Be Cruel To Be Kind. And for that reason, you're Forbidden to attempt to rescue any more birds— From Now On.'

There were shrieks of protest, sobs and tears, Capital-Haitch was whispered of as a villain and a beast by the children (who had been mentally poisoned throughout their short lives with sugared stories and saccharine idiot-box happy endings), but he was right, the monolith-man. Those little things were barely-formed, broken creatures, tiny-headed, slit-eyed as if light pained them, feathers only existing as traces like unfulfilled ambitions in the shrivelled pink-brown skin of their bodies, with useless wings like thin strips of broken bristles. They were hopeless, their sole comfort in being left to their fate; anyone with common sense could see that.

Now, for the avoidance of misunderstanding, I would not be of the breed of villain who would tread on the poor, defenceless creatures, nor would I find their nests and tip them out, laughing as they fell. But I would be of the sort who refused to countenance 'good-hearted' rescue attempts, who would accept the death-spiral of the flightless for what it was. The sort of villain, in short, who accepts the inevitability of destructive nature and was Cruel To Be Kind. The sort of villain who was *right*. Who was, in point of fact, no sort of a villain.

Jilly Holdenbridge

I call it the Love Cloud. That isn't what I called it then; I didn't call it anything then, it was simply how things were, it was normal—it was what had *become* normal. It was like a dream-state, with fuzzy edges and a breath of drowsy happiness, a safe haven with no prospect of nightmare. Imagine the feeling, unending, of being carried upstairs to a warm and welcoming bed. There can be no desire to escape the Love Cloud; within it you are safe and warm, there is no stress, danger, threat, and never will be. All you need to do is remain where you are and allow yourself to be loved, there is no need for anything more.

Talk is fine, chatter too, and laughter is always welcome. You can express opinions, criticise, even fall out with others, just so long as it's about someone's face or hair or dress sense, or something from the telly, or whether tomorrow will be nice or what your stars say today. But knowledge, discontent, dissent, argument (for they are its children) are most unwelcome in the Cloud; after all, little birdies in their nest must always agree. There are limits within the Cloud, you know them as if by instinct, and you know that to breach them would be cruelly wrong, ungrateful. And you know that light is your enemy, it is folly and presumption to bathe too long in light. Outside the cloud are monsters: stay here, cling close, they cannot get in. One of the worst things you can do is to find something out, find by seeking, for that something will be unwanted, from outside of the Cloud, possibly unhelpful, even inimical. Cosy-wrapped in that Cloud, why would you want to quit it, to disappoint and hurt so many who only want the best for you? Why would you do it? Who would wilfully forsake a feeling of warmth and belonging for cold, empty aloneness?

It took the arrival of a powerful force to disconnect me from that existence, and make no mistake, I'm glad that it came to be: and yet sometimes I yearn for the lost Love Cloud, I (almost) wish for it to swoop back down and carry me away, protected, provided for and happily helpless.

Sabina Faslane

I tried to protect her as she changed, developed, as she learned to raise her eyes and even, skies be praised, her hand. I tried to protect her from mockery, undermining, bullying, the day-by-day cruelties the world directs against those who are coming-up. I suppose it was a little too obvious and in some ways I didn't do her any favours; from being picked on for being defenceless to being picked on

211

for being defended. There are those who told me to leave well alone and I heard and ignored them. I believed, believe, that I was right, that I was vindicated by the results. I released a prisoner who would not otherwise have had a single sight of daylight.

Jilly Holdenbridge

I was not so much adopted as assumed—they *pre*sumed. And I was too young to have any choice or understand what was going to become of me. They were family and so I went to them. I took nothing with me bar a few clothes, not that there was anything really to take, though given the choice I would have liked to keep Dad's puny treasury of books. I just went along, did my own little bit of assuming —that the books would follow me somehow. I was never told what happened to them. You could see me as a traveller between worlds: the world I now lived in possessed, if you like, the advantage of simplicity. There were boy-things and girl things, coded blue and pink. Book-learning, questioning, hows and whys, were very definitely blue.

I could cast this lazily as a wicked-guardian story but that is precisely what it would be—just lazy. But looking back at this remove, lessons learned and hindsight at full strength, I see perfectly well what happened to me. At the time it was not clear in the least, it was a step-by-step plod, with an enormous weight of grieving and loss pressing down on me. When you have that, your head goes down and shoulders slump, moment by moment you can see your feet as they make shallow prints, but you have little idea of forward motion and even less notion of what is around you.

I idolised my dad, still do, and nothing can poison his memory or undermine my faith in him; he was and is my guiding light. But dark ages can happen and happened to me. I didn't fall among villains or cruel people; in many ways what befell me was worse. I was surrounded by the inert and what they expected from me was inertia. A power was exercised on me: the power of stopping.

No, they were not wicked, nor stupid; indeed, they were kind and helpful in so many ways, but in their hearts nestled the belief, inasmuch as they believed anything, that you are born to a certain station and your life is fixed, determined at that point. To wish to change, to move on in any way, was not regarded as any sort of evil, it was not punished or persecuted, it was simply utterly futile. You were met with a rictus smile and a slow-shaking head that didn't say 'no-no-no,' but 'not-possible, not-possible, not-possible.' It was an ethos, an atmosphere, they inhaled it and suspired it—we all existed in it, subsumed. They were harmless in all but one way. They immersed me in their air-bubble and its weight pushed, dragged, all the harder on me.

The family considered that Dad had attempted to rise above his allotted station in life and that his illness and death, though cruel, sad and regrettable, were inevitable and just. If he had stayed quiet, minded his place, he would have lived longer. My dad believed in self-improvement, his family did not. To rise above one's station was as hubristic and impossible as to seek a crown. I had started school with a mighty force behind me, plus much cheering and clapping, and sometimes someone who learned alongside (I think Dad played down his understanding to encourage me), but when dad died, my forward momentum was lost,

213

the weight bore down and my guardians instilled the philosophy of stay-still. They accepted schooling was required, normal and everyday, a fact, one law and authority demanded be done. But had compulsory schooling been done away with, they would have regarded it as true nature reasserting itself after an era of artificiality, of un-nature. School was a ritual, an observance, to be done within the limits of what was required and then finished with. I was to attend and do what I was told, but as soon as was decorously possible to make my exit, shed my burden of knowledge. I was not born to it.

They believed in destiny, though not of the sort fixed by the positions of the stars and planets at the moment you pop, but rooted in the deep past, family-born and heritable. This destiny was not to be resisted, but noted, submitted to; the only way out was to depart the family, which was unthinkable. They didn't so much preach failure or denigrate success, they engaged in a form of passive resistance of taciturn, remarkable tenacity.

I was never afraid of them, never angry with them; better that I should have been, you might argue. I might have agitated, pushed, fought to be free, but the truth is that I was steeped in their atmosphere. I was far too young to realise what was happening, too contented to resist, and not clever—*developed*—enough to stand a chance working out what to do. Dad had shaped my world at first, for too short a time, and now it was the work of these people, these kind and safe people. I was no longer living with tiny rooms and inadequate heating; I was no longer living with illness shadowed by death. It was a better life, better, don't you see? It was not to be refused; it was, after all, all I had.

I learned lessons though, that spirit could not be killed entirely; my dad lived on, the struggle to understand continued. For instance, take the business of Graham the Mongol. That was his name, as uttered by all; my family, the whole street, his family and I, knew him as nothing other. Graham had an allotted fate, too, and he had to adhere to it. To do better in life, he would have needed people all the time, to do things for him, to help, to act for him. For me, Graham the Mongol was a monster of childhood, a creature let loose from the framed cage of the cinema or TV or the prison-margins of a book and given flesh and breath. He was a street-corner beast of intense real-nightmare fear, the creature that really-really was going to *get you.*

He was small, yet seemed huge, rather fat, a man bursting out of a child's body, his face was… not… not *right-shaped*, not his eyes, not his brow, not his mouth, and his mouth, wet, slack, didn't make talk or chatter or prattle, it made grunts, but most of all incoherent, scary yells. His physical station in life was on the low brick wall outside his mum and dad's house—a low wall to a passing adult, but king-of-the-castle high to we the small; his elevation made it harder to tell if he was small like us or big like a grownup. He sat there in a closed off part of the neighbourhood; we were blocked from going round the corner to the sweetshop, we had to take an exhausting round trip just so that we did not pass Graham the Mongol on his wall, not even on the far side of the road; there he would sit, grunting, yelling and bawling in his terrifying non-language and if we came too close, growing bold or playing dares, he would leap down, land clumsily and come after us, still bellowing as we fled, squealing in highest trebles of true

215

terror. Not a game, no; how I feared Graham the Mongol, a deep, uncomprehending, mortal fear. How I wanted him to *go away*.

When he did *go away*, when the wall was empty and the street free of his misshapen form and his angry, inarticulate cries, I was relieved; we were all relieved, although puzzled that change could come to our unchangeable world. I wanted to ask what had become of Graham the Mongol, but by then I had long learned that questions closed mouths and it was better to feign incomprehension and boredom, to hang around the ragged edges of adult conversations, hoping to snatch a share of a whispered confidence, snaffle up some forbidden knowledge.

By such stealth I gleaned that Graham the Mongol had died, suddenly and at an age much younger than I had thought possible; but his sort, they did that you see, they lived short and unhappy lives, sat on street-walls and scared children and adults alike and then were gone. That was their lot and it was not to be altered; destiny was not to be bucked. All his mum and dad had to do, when they knew Graham was a mongol, was to allow him to play out his mayfly fate and pass away to the regret of nobody. It was their place to wait, ours to run and scream, and his to sit and shout out his time before death.

That family had its dogma of incuriosity. Downward-looking, you watch your feet, concentrate on making sure you don't trip and look a fool, don't attract attention, clutch your secrets such as they are, to your pigeon breast, meet no eyes, no gaze, be humble. Without knowledge of hubris or yet of nemesis, my family feared a force couched so deep in life that to name it was unnecessary, which, like Graham and the nightmares, would come to *get you* if you tried too hard, reached too far, craned your neck and looked up too high.

Yes, I know they called me The Shuffler; when people think you're stupid, their voices are stripped of subtlety and shame, since what do they care if you hear? Were such a thing possible, you could go and ask Graham the Mongol; he knew about that. Anybody's shoulders would wilt under the accumulated antiwisdom of generations of meek acceptance. At school, they taught meekness, for to be meek was to win the long run; waiting was required, otherworldly patience. So why look ahead, why yet look upward? Shoulders down, head follows. Proceed, but not forwards. Jilly the Shuffler, going about life slowly, not rushing because there's no point, taking her time because nothing matters. She can do nothing; she can make no difference, none whatsoever. She's alive just because she's alive and then one day she'll be dead; she simply bows her head and accepts. She will achieve nothing, change nothing, with no work in progress. What an existence—an inert, inactive stopover from the land of the dead. You have to be so accepting, already so nearly dead, to shuffle along like that, never slowing to a complete stop, never speeding up to a proper step. Going nowhere. Slowly. So you are pointless and meaningless, yet you are comfortable and you are loved too. It is easy to settle for that; after all, what do "achievers" actually achieve?

The Book That Waited

Glyn Capstone

When I spotted it, solid and undeniable, my first instinct was to tell myself that I was too busy, that I had things to do and other places to go, and anyway it would be expensive and I didn't want or need it. But even I couldn't make myself repeat an old mistake.

You wouldn't, even now, dot me as the kind of bloke who's seen to haunt old bookshops, browsing dusty shelves and chin-stroking while all the interesting stuff goes on in the good daylight outside. I wasn't there by choice, I was (as usual) tail-coating someone, just tagging along, and I hadn't really been paying attention; it was her absorption and not mine, but she decided to move on and didn't even look backwards, understandably confident that I would continue to trail in her wake. Either that or she had forgotten I was there at all.

It, the book, I had to reach out, to touch it. I was fated to do more, fated to take it, read it. Well, what else do you do with books? It was old—a little dog-eared, but not ruined, the damage just to the paper sleeve over the hard covers. I slid it from the wedge of old, forgotten books, picked it up, hefted it; it was as heavy, as imposing as I remembered; it dragged at my hands as if trying to escape me. I got control of it, began to handle it with confidence and following a strong instinct, turned to the fly-leaf, the page where people put dedications: dates, names.

Jilly Holdenbridge

I was there when Mr Wayman took poor Glyn Capstone by surprise and set his teeth rattling with his demonstration of "Romanisation". I was there another time when Wayman was far gentler, but the result much more shocking to Glyn. Of course, I had a shock or two of my own to come too, in due course.

Glyn The Pin

Is there such a thing as bookophobia? If there is I think I've got it, had it for quite a while. I reckon that that there's not much good comes out of opening a book. Much the opposite, in fact. I always go and find things that would have been better to stay between the covers.

Some people look at the first page of a book and give up right off if they can't get on with it. Some go straight to the end and give up if they don't like the look of that. My reckoning is that both of these ploys are too risky. I tend to go at books only when I have to and with a presumption of defeat. It's the opposite of how I eat; with a meal I go fast and hard as if I have to get it all in quick, that the plate has to be conquered and cleared; I need to get the stuff in me before someone else comes along and takes it. I reckon I'm just a caveman, in many ways.

I look at a book, I can see how many pages there are and I feel weighed down without even touching the thing. I can feel the sheer tonnage of every bloody page, I know how much each line will make me struggle and suffer, not because I can't read (I can, so no saying that again), but because it never gets me anywhere, I'm no better off. Not like a meal, at least at the end of a meal I'm full and feel good. Who needs to read? There's nothing in books for me.

Sometimes I dream of having money and a big house. I sometimes wonder what my library would look like, if I had one; a bit thin and sick looking I'd say, every weedy volume with a bookmark stuck fast on the title page, all stranded even before reaching Chapter One. Scrap the library; make it a games room. That's better.

Sabina Faslane

'Mr Capstone said something interesting today,' Alfred spiced his words with little muscle-pain groans as he eased himself into a chair after handing me a coffee.

'Mr... Glyn? I thought he might stay quiet after last year's farrago...'

'So did I, but to my surprise, there he was, speaking up. He wanted to know if it was really true history is always written by the winning side. He wanted to know if the losers ever got their say.'

'Not original I suppose, but from him...'

'There is more joy in the Staff Room over one late developer...'

'Amen. But how did you respond?'

'Offered him this.'

'Ah.'

Glyn Capstone

I wasn't accustomed to teachers like Wayman. He was a madman, a whirlwind, a storm of noise and gesture. He was unpredictable, mercurial, sometimes terrifying, even to a hardened sixteen-year-old from the secmod. He seemed on the verge of frenzy half the time; he was rarely the least bit calm, rarely at rest. He would burst into a room, teach in a flurry of hands and arms, chalkings and verbal tirades of information and comment. There were probably jokes in there too if you could but keep up. He only checked that there was anyone to listen to him when the storm was spent, but he expected you to have learned. He loved to set snap tests, which you would only know was going to happen when he hurtled through the classroom doorway—whether or not the door was closed to bar his way seemed of absolutely no consequence whatsoever—and bawl 'Nuuuuuuuuuuuuuuuuuuuuuuuuuuuuuuuuumber one!' and began to rattle off questions. Complete madman. But he was far better than most of them. Teachers, not madmen.

Glyn The Pin

There was a big exam that had everyone worried and afraid. That was the start of my big-school career, such as it was. It ended with even bigger exams that everyone was even more afraid of. What linked them was the stark sense of failure at either end. Apart from the bother brought by Alan Bloody Brotherton, I had been more-or-less-happy at primary school, especially when I could make my light-bending obscurity work for me, but getting sluiced off to the secmod like a shit to the sewer made me unhappy, unhappier, because I'd failed the big exam and I felt it so, I was *meant* to feel it. There were no Waymans around then, to tell me that it wasn't all over and it was okay to be a "late developer". Perhaps I'll develop like a picture—nothing but a blank that then comes, slowly, into sharp focus. Like emerging from a chrysalis. Yep, that's what I told myself. Still do.

The only comfort (cold as school porridge, lumpy too) was that lots of others got swooshed off to the secmod too, not bona-fide failures like me, I mean brainy ones, talented ones, kids who took the big exam with all good and due confidence (everyone around them confident for them too) only to find they'd ended up with "secmod" stamped on them just as unremovably (that a word? See why I failed?) as I had, feeling the same shame as I, but for them also shock. Fact is, the big exam was less like a test and more a plague, in that it took people you didn't expect and didn't take those you would. It left Rosin, who was brainy and talented and wimpy and girly and just right for clever-school, and left Species Grogan swooshed and stranded, even though he was well on the way to knowing everything. Other way round, it took Stitch Witcherson (the stitch was in his head, from where they fish-hooked his brain out years back) and Feet Murphy too. Feet was in size twelves by the time he was ten and he could only think by putting one of those big plates against his head. We knew that the clever-school had twiddled the results to get Feet in, as he was an ace kicker and they wanted to stock up on rugger players so a bit of cheating didn't matter. Stitch, however, was just a big mistake, so everyone reckoned.

Glyn Capstone
'I have always tried to cling to the idea that there is no such thing as a silly question, Mr Capstone, but in your short school career so far you have rendered that notion quite, quite obsolete.' By my 'school career,' the RE teacher, the old godbothering gremlin of the chalkface, meant *that* school, *his* school. Anything before didn't count. I didn't try to answer back, I was still a little awed and surprised to be there, but then again I couldn't really be at the secmod anymore as there was no more secmod, just a flattened

space with brick-dust hovering over it. Progress had paid a visit.

There were other survivors from the secmod with me too; Species Grogan, who was growing a white coat instead of skin and Rosin, still with his fiddle. They landed in the place as if they'd always belonged and had a letter explaining that failing the big exam five years ago had all been a clerical error, like the reverse of Stitch. I just slipped in only half-seen, still feeling as much out of place as I did... well, anywhere. Oh, but Alan Brotherton, he who'd passed the big exam easy and sly, he wasn't there any more, nobody remembered him much, they didn't know why he'd gone or where. Perhaps, I hoped, his light had gone out.

I didn't like the old man and he didn't like me. He told me that I wallowed in 'a morass of ignorance' and did his laugh, like dry sticks rubbing together, when he realised I didn't even know what a morass was. Actually he didn't seem to like anything or anyone date-stamped after about 1895. He didn't seem to enjoy teaching, but he still seemed to be fighting off retirement as if death lay immediately on the other side of it. I just wished he'd get on with it. I'd been told the only way to get him friendly in any way was to ask him about Pontius bloody Pilate, but there were only so many times you could do that while still having fun. He taught us Comparative Religion; 'This week: Christianity!' as the wags always said. The comparative bit was him telling us how his religion was best and everyone else was just a bunch of idol-grovelers.

But anyway, what was I doing studying religion? What was I doing studying history? What was I doing studying at all? When they sewered me off to the secmod I thought I'd at least have the pleasure of being a failure amongst failures, but like I say, there were Rosin and Species and plenty of others like them still trying to work out how the hell they failed and got sewered too, and once again, overtopped and obscured, I felt like a piece of empty air, a blankspace and a rank underachiever even at that. I got used to this new obscurity and planned to slip away as soon as I reached sixteen, but by that time the queues out of the dole office were a sight to see and most of my mates were little dots in that straggly line; what chance did I stand in that overcrowded world, who can be overlooked in an empty room? I gulped hard and took my chances. There was no other way of doing it, nowhere else, and that also went for sticking around at Auntypoos's house as opposed to putting my claim on a sleeping bag in a shop doorway and a share of the winter wind. At least she was accustomed to me and she reckoned I'd be less nuisance to the world still contained behind a school desk. Less nuisance to her, she meant: she could continue to farm out the job of blankspacing me to others.

And why did I go for history and RE? I suppose you could say I got interested in truth, or rather lies—why people believed things, especially why they chose, no, loved, to believe lies. After all, I had good cause to wonder about that. But I need to tell about the books. That'll make it easier and will better explain how I got to... where I was.

Jilly Holdenbridge
I still say that I learned best from Faslane, from Miss. But it was Mr Wayman who made the remark I'm thinking of.

This next lesson should appeal to you and to Mr Capstone, I think. The two of you being the future historians in this class...'

I'm afraid I can't remember the lesson, just the remark. I spent the whole period trying to work it out, while trying to look attentive and intelligent. It was the first time anyone had bracketed my name with that of Glyn Capstone, but more remarkably it was the first time anyone had projected a future for me. My heart hammered and I thought I would faint. I didn't even look at Glyn; I was too busy dealing with my shock.

Glyn Capstone

There *is* a word for fear of books—bibliophobia. I gather from a quick skim on the computer that it's usually fear of the contents of books. Repressive leaders are prone to it, so it says. I had nothing to fear from books and yet I did fear them. Why?

I know that Auntypoos had a distinct thing about books. For her, they were things that were not to be shelved and displayed, still less read, but avoided and, where that wasn't possible, contained, caged. My old Unc, dead and gone before I uttered my first baby-yell, had been the opposite: a book-fiend right enough, he had piled and scattered the things everywhere, so that they spilled from him as he read and shed them. The house was a chaos of random tomes, waiting to be perused or kept for another little look later; it was like a library that had been hit by a hurricane (Auntypoos' words, remember, I never saw this), there were bookshelves of course but they seethed with life, the volumes pushed and shoved against one another, bookends and shelf-ends proving no barrier. Just like that stupid kiddies' song where there are too many in the bed, they shoved one another out and the pushed-out ones found a billet wherever they could.

Aunt had the tendency to get squiffed on sherry from time to time and under the influence she'd tell me the tale. I got the vague impression that the Unc was dead *because* of the books and that Aunt had remained alive owing to her abstemiousness. She never claimed this, didn't have to, but just let the idea percolate through to me.

As soon as the old Unc was cold enough (it was a car accident, not a ton of loose hardbacks falling on his head that did him in; life is cruel in random rather than poetic ways), Aunt donned her clean-house clothes, dug out every suitcase, trunk and sturdy box she could assemble and packed up in every book in the place. Her only system was what fitted best where, removing every one of them to the dungeon darkness of the disused coal cellar underneath the house. That she kept hold of them rather than selling them off maybe seen as an act of sentiment, but I think that to her it was better to keep the books locked up and harmless than to let them out into the world. At least they couldn't come back to haunt her. Even my schoolbooks had to be 'tidied away,' Auntypoos was happier if they were out of sight. She preferred me to bring none home and at the time her sentiment chimed with me.

Glyn The Pin

On the whole, I got very little out of books. Perhaps the bookophobia was the right thing after all. Books don't tell you what you need to know, they end up telling you that the thing you are trying to avoid, the thing you've run from and denied forever and want to go on denying, is the plain, burning undeniable truth, and that it has caught up with you—*boo*!

But then again, deliberately not knowing doesn't change the facts, does it? They're still out there.

Old Wash-Hands

Nobody is a barbarian born and bred, but all of us carry the barbarian spirit within. It depends, then, if we care to chain and shackle it, or feed and blood it. If the latter, the chains will never go back on. Wayman was a believer in that will-o'-th'-wisp, the late developer; in encouraging him. It was his way of restraining the barbarian and he would press his campaign even when all others declared it too late. Is it permissible to say that he resisted the darkness? That was the secret of the loud and impatient Stentor at the forefront of the classroom, bawling at the skivers and those whose brains had lapsed into desuetude, 'There are too many indolent expressions in this room!' he would bellow. It didn't help when someone inevitably asked him what 'indolent' meant; truly, it did not. But he worked on, fool's errand as it may have been, to deliver them from the inevitability of their history (intended, intended).

Glyn The Pin

'You will be civilised! You-will-be-ci-vi-lised!'

The damn madman had me by the neck, practically lifting me off my feet and shaking me like he wanted my eyes to bleed.

Later, Species Grogan, who was trying for a white wig as well as a white coat, told me I should sue Wayman 'for assault.'

'Better not,' said someone else, 'he'll murder you next time. Didn't you know he was once in the Marines, he can kill with one touch?'

'That "we" are both civilised and civilising is just one more tall story, another of the repeated lies of history. But of course it resonates, sounds far better than the truth, and so that's what people mistake it for.'

Nobody was listening as the teacher carried on; they were all looking pop-eyed at Glyn Capstone, not just because Wayman had wobbled him around rubber chicken style, but because most of us hadn't, until he dangled before us like a thief on a gibbet, even realised that Glyn was there.

Glyn The Pin

'I've been thinking about what you said, Mr Capstone,' said Wayman, and hell, he was almost friendly about it. 'It reminded me of this thing—been on my bookshelves for a while. Borrow it if you like.'

And so there it was—*They Are No More—The Casualties of Progress.* You just wouldn't be able to believe how frightened I got at the idea of carrying that thing about with me. What if I lost it; what if someone took it for the sake of a stupid laff; what if it got damaged; what if it got ruined like Aunt's friend's books when her cherry brandy leaked from the cocktail cabinet above the bookcase? But mainly the terror came from the book itself. It was tall and broad, fatly many-paged and (I could tell without looking) more than a bit short on the blessed relief of a picture or two. It was a five hundred page battlefield.

I got about twenty pages in before I took it back to Wayman. 'I just can't, er... get into it, sir. Sorry.'

He looked at me, an odd, penetrating look; I thought maybe he was going to have one of his anti-ignorance, anti-indolence, towering rages, pinion me for being so stupid and cowardly in the face of a bundle of bound papers.

'You come from a house where there's not many books, don't you son?' the question was put as kind and gentle as I could ever have wished. Christ, someone was trying to understand me; nice of him, but I'll always be the human equivalent of invisible ink. I'm a fade-away, a goner.

Glyn Capstone

One thing I learned from that book, Wayman's book, the one that waited and then became mine: don't be an aborigine, not anywhere, not anytime. Don't get in the way, not of progress or commerce or religion. Even if you can duck the bullets, don't breathe in. It's the historical equivalent of going down to the cellar in a horror film— just don't do it, there's always hell to pay. Ask the Arawaks, the Guanches, the Gundungurra and Dharawal, the Hottentots, the Bundjalung, the Aboriginal Tasmanians, the victims of Gippsland, the Apache, Cheyenne, Arapaho, the Daur, the Yakuts, the Ainu, the Namaqua, the list goes on, if you want to go further get the book; I've a copy for sale. Used.

Those loser-histories are interesting, sad, I mean melancholy-sad. The echo of a loss. The writer can't check the facts—because anyone who could have told 'em is dead. The histories of these people are either found, all unfinished and shattered as if by the conqueror's boots, or they are the work of the survivors, or rather their thin-seed posterity, full of empty self-justification, irremediable anger and history so rewritten that you can see the crossings-out and the enraged, marginal scrawlings as they thought out their approach: we didn't fail, we were betrayed—usually that's the way. '*It wasn't like that, it wasn't like that, listen!*' Or the winners wrote the loser-histories. Maybe with a little tear in their eye and a pang of conscience, but hey. We are where we are and where would we be without all that effort, eh?

I learned a lot about human beings, reading that book. Empire-builders, empire-wreckers, big talk and lots of killing, treaties, plague-blankets, promises given with big saucer eyes and then welched on with a sneer, more killing. That's life on this planet, forever. No wonder Wayman turned his face away—to the unconquerable stars. Nobody's going to plant a flag on them any time soon. Barring the Moon, which I know doesn't count anyway.

The slaughtered, the massacred, the destroyed, the deleted. The people who left no mark, got blankspaced good and proper, and no wonder I felt an affinity with them. But usually somebody at least wanted something from them, even if it was just their stuff, their precious stones, their gold, their land, their lives. Me, I'm out in the void without anyone wanting anything out of me. They just make me into nothing and that's how I stay. I'll be one of those old losers whose body gets found three years after he died. 'Oh dear!' the world will say. And then a faint '*feh*,' as it forgets again.

Some of the conquerors used to have their pictures taken standing over, sometimes on, a pile of moribund natives and it looked like sport not war. Those pictures make me uncomfortable, not so much for the horror and cruelty of a dead and gone past; no, they make me think that if I turn just one more page there will be yet another proud plate and it'll be me, down and helpless, dead-as, with Alan Brotherton, chest puffed, eyes on the camera,

230

steady and full of himself, grinning bright (no flash needed), with his foot pressed firm on my neck.

'The Capstones don't exist any longer. This was the last.'

Bernard's Star

Evelyn Lawton

There was a time when I held power over Alfred Wayman; and then there was a time when he held power over me. It was what we each did with that power that is telling.

Sabina Faslane

A disclaimer: anything I now reveal about Alfred Wayman's past was certainly not learned from him. But I have every reason to trust what I have been told and those who told it to me, albeit piecemeal, implied, spread over many conversations over many nights. I may also be guilty of a little unhistorical speculation; addition, fiction? I'm not perfect, after all; perhaps I'm as bad as everyone else. Perhaps I have made the story what I would like it to be.

'Blunt. Not a subtle person. Not a *nice* person.'

Alfred Wayman's self-assessment may have seemed more of a self-excoriation, but there were some words to which he applied somewhat irregular meanings. True, he admitted that "blunt" was 'a word used by rude sods in an attempt to make a virtue of their bloody rudeness,' but "nice" was, with him, a term of scorn; "Nice people they are over there, very *nice* people". With Wayman, it was always a question of possessing a keen ear for emphasis. He was awkward, spiky, difficult to get to know and frequently hard work even when you did know him well. "He tells it like it is", said some shell-shocked people, looking charitably for the best in their fellow man, or perhaps agreeing with Wayman's definition of "blunt". "Pig. Pig. Pig.". Another view and one far more commonly expressed. He was not completely antisocial, but he had, "The, ahem, *unfortunate* manner that makes people keep their distance". The critique is again his own. He knew what he did; he just didn't see any good reason for stopping. He was perhaps too accustomed to employing the heavy hand required to keep his schoolroom under control.

Many who met him once left it at that; most of his acquaintances and colleagues assumed that he had no real friends, but it was not so. In his way he was friendly and friend seeking, just "selective"—as he defined it. What friends he had, he kept in silos: philosophical ones, of course. Wayman saw his friends one-by-one; perhaps two-by-two but rarely more; rarely mentioned or introduced one friend to another; and satisfied that they didn't know of one another's existence, although many in truth knew each other well. He had, at a guess, the benefit of his bright friends' considerable discretion; they refrained from discussing him. Among the brightest and most discreet were Evelyn and Bernard, for whom Wayman harboured a respect that deepened, more than he would ever care to admit, into a peculiar devotion. The brave—or reckless—would call it love.

Bernard, thirty years his senior, once taught at Wayman's school, at first as a sniggered-at master (Wayman's caricatures of his teachers were legendary, especially in the staff room) then as a respected mentor and then a colleague and an unshakeable friend. Look no further than Bernard for Wayman's passion for history and desire to teach. 'You don't have to *like* 'em to want 'em to do well, to want to be part of their shaping,' Wayman would philosophise grumpily, acknowledging his inspiration. Evelyn had been Bernard's 'bit of stuff' in the lost language of the schoolrooms of Wayman's adolescence, but although younger than Bernard by some fifteen years she was even then his wife, his equal and eternal love.

There are some who knew Wayman who promulgated, some still do, the tale that he was honeypot-attracted to the couple's happiness, envious at a remove and yet fascinated, and that he spiralled into their ambit as he found them easy, unaffected, genuinely affectionate and, most importantly and fortunately of all, broad-minded and tolerant. Spiteful commentators whisper that Wayman wanted somehow to draw, to leech rather, on the couple's love, to divert some of its uplifting, rejuvenating power to himself, possibly even waiting for "the old man" to die so that he may appropriate his wife, as he might inherit his academic mantle. Wayman the love-vampire; now *there* was a scenario to excite the fabulists.

Evelyn Lawton

It was not true, what I know was said of him. Like all the stories about him; most, anyway. Alfred was shy in his idiosyncratic way, averse to displays of overt emotion (apart from his usually confected schoolroom rages) and allergic to sentimentality: some speculated that he was, possibly, immune to real love. He was not poised to take anyone's heart; he truly would not have known what to do with such a thing. I may nor may not have been the first woman he was accused of plotting to claim; but it was his awkwardness that led him to be overly-attached and his only, mild sin was quietly to steal a vicarious charge of lasting, companionate joy: he placed a high value on friendship, sported an excessive and sometimes bloated honour, and, ever secretly, an even bigger, but attenuated and fragile faith in faithfulness, something he was confident he himself would never have to see tested.

Sabina Faslane

Bernard and Evelyn were his ideal, the wellspring of what happiness in people he possessed: this man without family, few friends and wholly without a knowable past. And so the jokes began, among the less discreet, about their "adoptee", although in truth everyone appreciated it was fortunate that there are always those who are formidable and flexible enough to take on and take care of the misfits and the unplaceables. It may be safely assumed that Wayman was grateful too.

If Bernard recognised Wayman's devotion—it may just as comfortably be assumed he did—then he saw it for what it was and perceived no wife-stealer, not even one in-theory or daydream. After all, trust was one of the many virtues Wayman admired in the couple, a trust that never came into question and did not expire before its time. Bernard extended that trust to Wayman and he was sure in his heart it was right and proper to do so.

But it was Wayman's tough shell that showed to most and so they probed in idle malice for weaknesses and found them where they did not exist; they lacked the perceptiveness of the wise. Wayman prided himself in having few qualms about confronting fools with their foolishness and yet the truth was that he would let even an astrologer off the hook if that breed of fool shied from confrontation; he would not attack a retreating enemy. His enemy, he said self-importantly, was foolishness itself and not those who practiced or committed it. Some quality of mercy, rather than piggishness? But there was to be no such mercy for the foolishness that makes hay from the foolish. He despised sharks and cardsharps, money-wheedling tricksters and charlatans of all stripes.

Wayman was not what you would call a regular guest; oftentimes but irregular, perhaps? But he was also unreliable, especially as a dinner guest, for after sunset his priorities did not include human beings, even ones as precious as Bernard and Evelyn. He would abandon even them—appreciated, respected and yes, loved as they were—for the night's stars. Bernard and Evelyn bore and forgave Wayman's vanishings and non-arrivals and persisted in inviting him. Fortunately for Wayman, they understood passion, and although neither shared *his* passion, nevertheless applied their intelligence and understanding. Evelyn would scold Wayman, occasionally and gently, but more for what he had missed, such as Bernard's superb red-wine-and-herb potatoes, than for the annoyance and disappointment they had been caused.

Evelyn and Bernard even became dilettante weather-forecasters in their way; when working out whether or not it was a safe bet to invite Wayman, they would sniff the air, eye the clouds, attempt to work out if they would have a clear sky, or company. There were some relaxed summer evenings in their garden and even when the clouds stayed away darkness fell slowly and so Wayman did not flee the scene immediately. The early stars pricked the evening blue and Wayman would sit with his friends and in lecture-tone yet with gentleness school them in the contents of that night's sky. Evelyn and Bernard would share with him the cooling of the sunset air, the slow-dying glow lying to the North of West, the hardening of the sky's blue, the poetry of the fall of nighttime.

If a person idealises another (and note how close that word is to *idolise*; only mis-tongue it slightly and there it is) that person runs grave, deep and dangerous risks, the least of which is disillusionment and the greatest of which is betrayal. But even betrayal can be inadvert, and it was in this way Bernard—honest, loving, undeceiving, dependable —betrayed Evelyn and Wayman, and by the simple act of ceasing to live, 'The last thing I ever want to do,' as he always said, producing the line from a shiny-worn but treasured stock of hoary old wheezers. Bernard, affable and loved and ever-there, became an absence, a memory, unrecoverable: and those who loved him felt, simply, helpless.

Evelyn Lawton
I led the way into the living room, the room filled with Bernard's absence and still telling his story, and Alfred, my first invitee since my heart's loss, followed, looking both at home and at relative ease; those feelings froze however when he saw the low-level table set out with two glasses and a tall, elegant, unopened bottle of amber liquid.

'Glen Alford,' I said, with a lack of expression that almost drained my voice to silence. Alfred noticed, and yet did not quite note, the folded papers also there on the table (he may have wondered faintly—a brochure? a map? was I planning holidays already?) but they did not seem important, they did not achieve significance, not, set as they were against the compelling presence of the bottle. Alfred Wayman quailed, physically shivered.

Glen Alford.

'Glen Alford,' Bernard would say, ever careful to pronounce it "Affud". Evelyn said it that way too. She said nothing else as she gestured to her guest to sit. Wayman hesitated; he would trust Evelyn to the ends of the earth—but of course —and yet he knew that betrayal and humiliation are known to be dealt out by closest friends, under the cover of intimacy and friendly confidence. The bottle before him bore a meaning, in fact several possible meanings, and one made him deeply queasy.

It wasn't the whisky itself Wayman feared; he was not at his best in his cups and generally steered clear of alcohol. He knew it to be a powerful enemy: one he never came away from feeling his life had improved. Bernard had harboured no such cowardice in the face of a bottle: he had made something of a totem of his collection of whiskies and enjoyed sharing them even with the lily-livered astronomer: the night they tried the first Glen Alford was a memory Wayman had permitted to gather dust; indeed, he had attempted to shovel a little extra obscurity on top of it, in an act of wilful, hopeful entombment. Now, he sat in fear of the exhumation of a memory of the purest shame.

He had that night, in theory, been sharing his glass with Evelyn, a drinker good and true, but who shied at the choking burn of whisky and declared she would 'try a sip or two from Alfred's glass,' knowing that any incursion on her husband's, one who would normally deny her nothing, would not be in the least welcome. The conversation had been cheery and companionable, the whisky warming and peat-tanged and somehow, dram by dram, Wayman lost count of the sips and how these turned into gulps. He also failed to notice that Evelyn had barely taken a sip from his glass, that she had ceased very early on to sip from it at all, and yet its level kept falling low and the Glen Alford, miraculous, had renewed its golden self, and in Bernard's too. They had begun to chuckle and talk a little more loosely and foolishly than they might usually, laughing away Evelyn's concerns and then warnings and in due course she had to limp Bernard to his bed as he laughed and cried at once, and to make the sofa up as a spare bed as Wayman was 'unfit to travel' in her curt understatement.

At some blurred, unfocused point during the course of that incautious evening Alfred Wayman knew that he had said something to his friends he would never have uttered to them, or of them, in any other circumstances, and the moment he had said this thing, this urgent thing he had ached to say, he could no longer call it back to mind and had gone to sleep in fuddled forgetfulness and was cotton-wool thick in the head when he awoke in stark darkness and didn't know where he was or what he was doing or where to go. He was violently, stinkingly sick on the sofa and, worse still he tumbled back to woozy sleep in this reeking puddle of spew for some time after. His efforts to clean, when sober enough to make them, were ineffective and he remained for half the day after, still "unfit to travel" and asleep in the spare room with a duvet over him and the company of a bad conscience, a hammering head and a fluttering stomach and with the threat of humiliating recall poised over him the whole time.

He knew too well the one thing that he had done with his mouth—and this proud and arrogant man, begged forgiveness, abased himself in abject misery. But however terrible he felt about that, far worse did he feel about the words, the other escapees from his mouth: when he found the courage he asked Evelyn what those words had been, but either kindly or cruelly she declined to reply, at that time or on further application, and Wayman gave up asking as her voice came in a thin, strained tone that betokened to his frightened ears the last draining of her patience. For a while he feared the end of the friendship; that he had caused some offence that lodged deeper and more noxious than the unkillable smell of his vomit on cushions and cloth.

Wayman had never been sure either of them had ever forgiven him for the incident. 'After all, they even moved home right afterwards!' he joked, but somewhere in his guilty head he feared that they were fleeing the lingering stink. He had steered clear of Glen Alford since and shuddered at the faintest, even imagined, allusion to it. Evelyn's avoidance of the subject made Wayman feel as if it were perhaps too distasteful, too harmful to her regard for Wayman: Bernard, steady, unjealous Bernard, had never referred to the incident; Wayman could almost hear a schoolmasterly and magisterial 'the matter is closed' hidden somewhere within his tones. Wayman perceived and imagined all sorts of distaste and disapproval in his friends; he picked at the scab of his own mortification even though precious few fragments of recall would ever assemble. He hated being the butt of jokes, the object of pity, the subject of tut-tut talk and was haunted by fearful speculation about their pillow-talk, anecdotes to chuckling friends, their concerned head-shaking at his failings.

Glen Alford.

Here is the voice that Alfred expected to hear: '*Now Bernard is no longer here to stop me, I want to tell you just how appalled we both were by your behaviour, here are all the foolish things that you said that night, I shall now revel in your twisting and burning humiliation, I have waited all these years to pay you back...'*

Wayman's imagination was an effective and diligent torturer and Evelyn's continued near-silence gave him no relief as he took the bottle from her—her hands arthritic and painful now and she could not get the awkward wrapper from the top of the bottle—stripped away the metallic cone from the bottle-top, eased out the stubby cork out then set the bottle down for both it and himself to wait their fate.

Evelyn Lawton

'It's not what you may think,' I hastened to assure him; it was simple to tune in to the clattering alarms emitted by Alfred's racing thoughts. 'But we are going to drink this stuff, you and I, a dram or two anyway, for Bernard. See: I have my own glass this time.' *So; she remembers*, I could see into his head with a clarity usually denied to me, to all. But he could take hope that my voice remained even-pitched and not rising shrill, I hoped he could see that there was to be no seeking of belated revenge, no impaling a man upon his old misdeeds. I was, after all, nervous myself: fearing punishment and hoping for kindness.

The first glasses caught the light as they we raised them to a lost friend and love. Glen Alford. To Bernard. For some time we spoke of him, our memories and the joy of him, and the whisky fell and rose again just as it had on another night long before. Neither of us minded to cease, or even to slow down.

A new short silence fell between us, but now I knew that Alfred could detect no awkwardness within it, no coming accusations or long-dreaded scolding. But at last, my gaze on the bottle rather than on my old friend, and somewhat whisky-loosened myself, I came to it at last; I spoke of it.

Sabina Faslane

'Alfred. If you're wondering—you *have* been wondering—what you said that night.'—she did not need to explain what *that night* had been—'It was love, Alfred. You spoke of love.' Her tone was not hard, not accusing and yet Wayman's fears rose again—love, he had spoken of *love*? What had he said, had he demanded borrowed, unearned love, had he abused his host for being so unfairly privileged in being so adored, blamed the married, happy man for the loneliness of the unapproachable, self-isolating bachelor and perhaps demanded he surrender, or even share, his wife in the name of some corrupt conceit of friendship? *What did I say, just how twisted is my mind, how jealous and sick am I when I cannot control myself?*

Evelyn found her voice and it was balm and relief to Wayman. It was love, indeed, of which he had spoken that night: but of love, amicable and not envious, of love for both of them, how he had never felt so close to anybody in his whole life, that having friends like them had helped him to hold back a tide of despair that sometimes threatened to swamp even the stars.

'Bernard wept—remember?—and I packed him off. You'd both ceased to make sense by then anyway, but he was moved. Moved, Alfred. Rather embarrassed too, both of us were, it was all mixed up together, but we were happy that you opened up. It was only that once. Wayman cringed at *opened up*, but it was not a barb. The matter of *that night* was now closed. Evelyn's mind was elsewhere.

'Glen Alford.' She refilled his glass and her own. 'Bernard.'

Alfred was, however, correct in thinking that this was a test, not of his ability to withstand vengeful mockery from close-range as first expected, but a test nonetheless. Soon enough he was battling to contain his words; but this time not clumsy dilations on the healing power of friendship over sadness and isolation—nothing sentimental, mawkish, tear-clogged or so very unlike Wayman. He was to be, mouth oiled and slack on Glen Alford, battling to keep a righteous rage in check, holding back words and tones of anger and condemnation.

Evelyn Lawton

I needed a little more of the golden glow before I could broach the matter; I could see Alfred's surprise, bordering shock, that I was now trembling in fear of judgement—his judgement—every scintilla as much as he had dreaded mine. A confession was on its way, one that admitted of no outcome but the most outspoken damnation.

'Alfred, I need to talk to you—I think I may have done something a little foolish and I want your opinion, please.' My voice may have trembled from any number of causes, but I sounded, at best, on the terrified side of intimidated. Remember that I knew Mr Wayman's ways very well.

'I wanted to do something for Bernard, something that would stand out, which would survive my death too, something that would be... eternal. Oh yes, I know my own death is coming and I don't care, I didn't care even when Bern was still alive, not when I realised we couldn't enjoy the time together. So I thought, I planned. A little brass memorial plate on a park bench? Too easily ignored, never mind vandalised. And too soon gone. I'd worry about it every day, is it kept clean, is it used, is the plate still legible, does anyone ever sit there and read it, would passers-by ever catch its glint in the sun and stop and wonder who this man was and how he lived? So no bench. A library would have been nice, appropriately scholarly, but I'm no moneybags; I couldn't build some pile of bricks that would carry his name into the future. Some people pay for prayers; you know what he'd say to such an idea. I'd endow a poetry prize, but... no moneybags. He loved poetry, you knew that of course.

'It came to me that what I wanted was something untouchable, ever-present, lasting and which was beyond human power to destroy. Alfred, there was only one thing; I named a star after him. There are companies, they advertise; it was ever so easy and it cost me something that my pension could stand and now there's a star that bears Bernard's name. But now I feel a little badly about it; I don't know who has the right to name stars and doesn't, and I know that the stars are your province and I wonder whether I should have sought your opinion first. But it was a spontaneous sort of thing you understand, the final decision I mean, all done so quickly and when my mind was full of him after we laid him to rest. I decided that his name should live on and that was the way I decided it should be done. I always loved the way I could point to a star and you would be able to tell me its name; I just wanted you to be able to point at the sky and tell me, 'That's Bernard's star.' Alfred: have I done wrong?' And like a child proffering work for approval but fearing the worst, I picked up and handed over the folded paper from the table. It was a map: a star map.

Sabina Faslane

Blunt. Not a subtle person. Not a *nice* person. Alfred Wayman had to approach gentleness as if he were reading from a manual, or slowly joining dots. He knew of the art, he had even applied it in the past, but so rarely and so long ago that he was definitely rusty. When a dear friend did a foolish thing—how was a man like Wayman to respond? For him, fools deserved scorn, and scorn scoured and cleansed the soul. He had not been known to make exceptions. But he had now to battle to gain control of his tongue, set aside the coming torrent of words and find others, the true words, to offer Evelyn what she needed; comfort, help, reassurance. She was the supplicant now, ashamed and humiliated and expecting angry condemnation. '*I wonder whether I should have sought your opinion first.*' He had heard her voice catch and falter; she had so nearly said not *opinion* but *permission*.

Evelyn Lawton

Who has not feared the towering rage of a schoolmaster, not cowered at a desk as the voice rolls and rises to castigate stupidity and stubbornness, whether of oneself or a neighbour; perhaps the voice is even a room or two away, yet everyone and everything stops to hear it bellow out like a hellfire preacher. I was assailed with unhappy memories of classroom terror, after all teachers in my time were far less gentle than the modern breed and I had always fancied Alfred perhaps belonged to the ranks of fierce old timers rather than to the fluffy modernists. The frustration at lessons not learned, facts unassimilated, wisdom ignored and neglected; I may as well have sworn open allegiance to the overcomplicated clockwork of the Ptolemaic heresy, with its tricky, cheating epicycles and other sense-insulting, gravity-defying geocentric asininity. I had placed myself so far away from Alfred's favour.

For him to withhold a killing blow would have been to show true love indeed (though still the love of a friend, let us not stretch matters too far) and a tenderness with the foolish with which he had never yet been credited. And I was very, very cognisant of the fact that Alfred Wayman could not abide *twaddle*.

Sabina Faslane

As Evelyn could, all too well, I can hear the voice, picture the angry face turning ever uglier with puce rage and supply the words, the spluttering, enraged tirade as Wayman strides the room, occasionally reading from the pamphlet, but more usually waving it as if it is a contaminant to his skin as well as his mind.

'I had truly thought the stars beyond the corrupting touch of Humanity, but now they have *monetised* the sky; the one act I would have thought beyond even the voracity of human greed! They have laid their grubby mitts upon the stars, *my* stars! The stars should be beyond reach and yet, *poisonously* yet, here are these little creeps purporting to offer the stars for sale. Is there nothing they will not try to *spiv*? Well: now I know there are greater and more shameless rogues and frauds out there than the damnable astrologers and their tricksy horror-scopes! Star-sellers! *Star sellers*! To sell something, do you not have to hold title to it first? What do you call someone who sells what he does not own? And just *what* do you call someone who buys from him?

'Even as I age, I learn. Humanity reaches out for the stars; pah! *Per ardua, ad astra*; pah! But nobody, *nobody* owns the sky. Nobody! The sky is truly above us, stateless, free and independent It cannot be nationalised nor privatised, no greedy little swine can take title to it or patent it or stick a flag in it or slice it up and parcel it out to his cronies and bum-suckers, flogging it at high-high prices to the unwary and foolish! So I had thought, anyway. The criminal arrogance of these star sellers! Star sellers? Star stealers, they are, the basest frauds; no doubt they flog the same twinkle-twinkle a hundred times over or more, sending out bogus star-maps amended in cheap biro with a lost, loved name about which they care not at all! Human dishonesty, preying on delusion, on grief, on the desire to memorialise someone who was deeply loved. These people, they are simply evil, parasitic; on both people and the sky. Selling stars! Do they do a bulk deal on a whole damn constellation? Hawk the whole zodiac as a loss-leader?'

'*Your star is a memorial candle; no wind can blow it out. It is eternal.*

'Hades, what a thought! A sky of memorial candles, twinkling lit-up tombstones. Filling the night with death? Idiots. And, by the way chaps, no star is 'eternal,' do you know nothing? Any star you look at now could be no more than a memory in ancient light; stars die, but they die far away and the news is slow in coming. For short-term profit you would sell a sky-full of emptiness to the vulnerable and gullible? It's bad enough that you'd do the latter and think it justified, but the former? How low can you stoop? Far lower than this, I'll warrant, this is probably just amateur-hour. Now I know there are greater and more shameless rogues than the astrologers. Nice work. There's a short word for all of this: F-R-A-U-D. Emotional fraud, financial fraud; and piracy of the stars. Contemptible.'

And Evelyn would never be able to be sure that the last word was not meant for her.

Evelyn Lawton

I waited for the brutal tsunami of angry words, the judgement from above, with head hung as one who knows that any, all punishment is deserved. Alfred sighed, picked up the map and looked at it, glasses perched academically on the precipice if his nose. He sighed again—and once more.

'I can find that star for you; the Right Ascension and Declination are given on your certificate. It's quite easy; binocular object, mind, it doesn't blaze at you. Bernard's Star, a modest star but named after a great man. It is, after all, consistent with the tradition of placing heroes and demigods in the sky.'

I knew then that I had found a new side to Alfred. I had found his capacity to lie—for love.

The Triumph of The Light

The Loser Histories

Sabina Faslane

And Lo it came to pass that the day of reckoning came: and I stood before a class alone and unprotected at my new school for the first time. My sense of mission joined sickening battle with my crumbling confidence, my head whirled and I checked to ensure the exits were clear. There they sat, silent for the moment as we eyed one another with tense, mutual suspicion. I swept my gaze across those promising young faces (I wish I could say eager, but of that I was unsure) and a terrible thought crossed my mind—out there in that cluster of young minds, not with the same faces or voices of course and thus hard to identify, was this new generation's Biff, fixated on irrelevance and impervious to fact, a Perry who would hear not "impervious" but "perv", and have little difficulty in homing on the sleazy side of history, a Hootin' Mel who would be set off aloud and along by their antics, a vapid moonshine-worshipping Europa and, worst of all, a dug-in, defiant anti-knower, a stubborn new-generation Tilly Pease. My fears came close to claiming me; I was sure to be caught out, shown up: still a little girl, still playing at teacher. When would the riot start?

I introduced myself, asked names, talked, listened, began to get-to-know; things were going so well, my confidence was recovering from a state of near-wreckage, my sense of mission gaining ground. Next I would lay out what we were going to do this term, what it was for and *why*—the favour I had always craved from my teachers and was never granted —but as I began to speak I froze, filled suddenly with all of

251

night's cold. How had I not seen her before, that girl—sitting towards the back but standing out, tall enough to touch the stars, Angela Crane reborn, exactly as she had been twenty years or so before. Forget any new-age Tilly Pease, here was a true visitation from the past, the one to destroy my new career, end it in chaos, silly arguments and mocking laughter.

Fizzmonger

'It was funny about the painting—eh?' Wayman's 'Eh?' was, as ever, a teacher's tetchy demand, not a question.

'I suppose it was.' You can insert a sigh there: it was not the first time we had had this conversation. 'Funny. Yes.' Another sigh—rueful? Well, it was complicated...

Glyn Capstone

I didn't have a career; it was more of a careen. I never had any direction, it was all just hurtling around, bouncing about and the impetus was never mine, my momentum always the result of being dragged in the wake of some attractive body or other, or blasted out of the way and sent spinning out of all control (my control anyway) by some irresistible force, something, more usually a someone, who was barely aware that I was even there.

They gave us Careers lessons at the school—not at the secmod, they maintained an embarrassed silence there, *shhhhh now!* Even at the Wayman-school the lessons weren't up to much; we were ushered into this big room where a teacher whose name I can't recall talked vaguely about 'industry' and not much else. But just as in the secmod, the majority of us already knew our choices—pits for the boys, factories for the girls and it was no one's fault that there were plans already afoot to close most of 'em before we were even ready to beg for a job there. There would be the cleverest who'd go to university, there would be oddities like Rosin who would do well no matter what 'cos he was talented and it showed no matter how much anyone else tried to mask it, deny or stop it, and like Species Grogan who was not far off from working out a way of curing all known illnesses and producing a comprehensive theory explaining the mysterious process of how girls think. The odd one or two graduated into extinction, like Stitch Witcherson, who should never have been allowed a hamster-wheel, never mind the one on a car; he oblivionised himself and three mates on the m-way, before the ink on his license was dry.

Most of the time we were left with a long table arrayed with boxfiles, all supposedly chockfull of careers goodies. 'Take a look at some of the bumph, see what you can find,' the teacher would mumble, before following the smell of coffee from the staff room and leaving us to the rows of files full of ageing leaflets packed with not-much. Not that we looked that hard. I had this woolly thought that maybe it was a sort of lucky dip; if you put your hand inside the right box, out you came with the golden ticket, The Job, and off you went to make money doing… whatever. That's all any of us ever said, that we wanted to 'make money,' with the more ambitious and optimistic upping the ante to 'tons of.' Not many of us did. None, to be precise.

What we didn't figure was that the boxes had been pre-raided and the good and golden stuff was gone already. Alan Brotherton, his type I mean, the Brothertons, had got there and struck dead-lucky first dip. The type was always to be there in the future too; I always had the impression that job adverts, applications, shortlists and interviews were a sham, because the powers-that-were knew ahead which Brotherton would get the post, someone who, male or female, bore the glittering stamp of "winner". I never stood a chance; I'm a blankspace, remember, and if anyone manages to spot me on a clear day, the first thing they see is *my* stamp—'Secmod boy, ran off from the biggest exam of them all: Loser. He will fail and fail again until his heart finally fails *him.*'

I'd like to blame the exam, the last big exam, I'd like to pin the blame on Wayman and Fastlane and Wash-Hands, the whole lot of 'em, but in the end there's no point; I'd only be dodging that it was all me. I figured I just wanted, before I got into the books all serious-like, one more damn good doss. But I dossed on, dossed too much and let the world blink and forget me, as I forgot to work or revise. I never did sit the exams; I ran and barely anyone noticed. So much for Wayman's late developer. Blankspaced again, but it was my own doing.

Charles Durant Tobol

Wayman and Lawton may have considered themselves rescuers (and saviours, Old Wash-Hands may have said, 'intended, intended' and his bitterness would be justified, for the Professor and his understrapper succeeded in a way, whereas the old man did not, not ever). And I suppose on the whole they did no harm, making the occasional dimwit feel for a fleeting moment he held the keys to the city of knowledge: it was a waste of time, but benign at least. Wayman's interference with the portrait painter, however, was no flash in the pan, it was decisive, drawn-out and had lasting consequences. It destroyed once and for all a talent, a unique, poisonous talent.

I have retained a small number of his paintings, to remind myself of what he was when he was skilled. He planted, *im*planted, plague spores and worms in warm tones of flesh and comely body-shapes, and his gift was that although these blights would be visible right away to the discerning viewer, no matter how many times that viewer returned to the picture, fresh worms, new spores emerged, spreading, crawling, wriggling; they were not just flesh-worms but soul-worms, which the painter knew well lay just beneath human appearances: the corruption, the tawdry evils. He knew not just how to depict their existence, but to foretell their development, their maturing, their decay.

A curse on every rescuer, every interventionist and every ham-fisted do-gooder who believes a few token gestures will change the world. Instead, they offend nature, they fill that world with lame ducks, the worthless, the pointless, all dressed with false hope, false confidence that they are of some account and that one day their time will come. Lawton, Wayman, Faslane too of late, they are the guilty in this indictment, they are as deluded as pathetic Old Wash-Hands, who believed he could build a Pilatic paradise upon a mentality of slow surrender. Every 'rescued' educational cripple should constitute a scar on Wayman's conscience; none more so than the portrait painter. It was quite unworthy of Wayman, what was he doing, encouraging light and dispelling darkness? The painter had at least eked out a living from his verminous canvases and along came heavens-sent Wayman to eliminate what small talent was ever there to be seen. Eternal cloud-cover, denial of the stars would have been the appropriate punishment for the interfering teacher and the only way to salvation for the miserable painter.

Wayman destroyed one of the finest, if unknowing, crusaders for the cause of anti-art; worse, he turned him from art-destroyer, destroyer by means of art, to (I shudder) *artist,* who readopted all his long-ignored art-school lessons, drew and painted what he had been taught, a brush-plying automaton, time after endless time.

Glyn The Pin

She was a beanpole, a cornstalk, a length o' string or a stream o' piss, depending on who was calling her names and whether she was anywhere near at the time. She was tall and beautiful and you can add a 'very' to each. So was her mum, in fact she was even better looking though a bit crinkle-eyed in the wrong light. Yeah, she was beautiful, the girl, beautiful and... oh work out the rest yourself, can't you? I got close to her, worked with her, just for a brief time; so closely that other kids began to whisper, I loved those whispers and I grieved at their eventual, inevitable dying away to silence. Even when something can't be, you sometimes still want to hear the story and give anything for it to be true.

She believed that the world really was going to end, I mean the mum even more than the girl; she encouraged us in what we were doing and was so serious about it that on the day itself she kept her girl at home, which I suppose is understandable, but it took her from my side. It didn't help me one bit because she was so important to my strike; people wondered where she was and on that score alone several looked like they were going to give up and trail into school. My name had gone out, but she had been the face and voice, the tall mast, the transmitter. She was supposed to be my assistant, a sort of secretary, but in the end I realised she'd become the real leader. She should've been too bloody thin to eclipse or blot out anything, anyone, but I came to understand that this was what she'd done to me; to use a good Waymanist term, she had occulted me. She'd stolen my stolen light, snuffed me out.

I ended following her around for a while after it was done and over, but other than a mild irritation when she spotted me hanging around, she never even gave an indication she even I was there. I was blankspaced again: *feh.*

Old Wash-Hands

My star is fading. That is the saying, is it not?

I am a star, a fading star, guttering, dying; this candle of the night is burnt-out. I know it and I shall not resist. I will not look back over the life that is draining away, for I see no positive purpose in so doing. One has to know when to let go. There is little dignity otherwise. I refer you to my items of philosophy.

Rumour has it that Lawton's little wife persuaded him to quit before he ended up apoplectic and in an iron lung for the remainder of his days. It is surely fortunate that the Secretary of State never paid a zealous, reforming visit to our school, or Lawton would fain have ended his career at the assizes; he would surely have regarded the sacrifice worthwhile. Perhaps I should follow the Professor into retirement; perhaps some smidgeon of, what, shame, conscience, may drag his underling with me? But no, my hopes outstrip reality, but it is my own ideal of a worthwhile sacrifice. My retirement shall be, as indeed it should be, the peaceable laying-down of arms, an admission I have done all in my power and that the forces opposing me (time being not the least of them) mean I must bow to the inevitable without regret or rage. But I suppose I do have regrets, chiefly that so few would give me a hearing, that my philosophy and values never really took root. But I cannot force people to accept, I can merely advocate to the best of my humble ability and bow to the majority if they demur. It is, amongst other matters, a question of dignity.

The man Pilate is portrayed four times over in the Gospels (Apocrypha and downright forgeries left aside, I am tired) and he is different each time, his image and attitudes changed and distorted, viewed through the light-bending eyes of each writer. Which of these pen-portraits is history, which is truth? If I hold to my avowed faith, I must maintain that they all are.

A man can hold justice in his heart, know it perfectly and defend its integrity against those who would call en masse for that which is expedient but wrong. But that man must also know when he, and justice, cannot hold out against an irresistible force: the will of the people. Such a man is a balancer of the scales, not an equivocator, and were his example followed, true and perfect justice would be regnant and at last perhaps our sorry kind would know —what is truth. This man can set himself apart from the crude crowd's calling, can know when the mob's empty voices are not to be heard, but even when he is able to do this he must also divine (intended, intended) when a greater but subtler voice underscores and animates the latter.

'A timid, time-serving man with just conscience enough to make himself uncomfortable and just integrity enough to ruin the best of causes.' Thus runs, in part, one evangelical excoriation of Pontius Pilate: I do my reading. As a summing of the figure of Pilate, I reject it; and yet, hauntingly, it seems a prefiguring (intended, intended) one hundred years before my becoming, of nobody but myself.

I take comfort, however, in the words of another evangelist, our late beloved Professor Lawton; life is not some wretched competition, one's success may only truly be measured against one's stated ideals and the less badly compromised they are, the better one has done. By that measure I have perhaps done modestly well. Besides, I cannot change anything now—*quod scripsi, scripsi*. I believe that I have led a good life—perhaps not an effective life, but a good one. I had in my heart a faith and in my mind a philosophy and I was true to both, sought converts but not followers, sought to do good, even though by means of stealth, and I remain convinced that the world would be a better place if more believed and acted as I do, if so many did not fight a hopeless cause and ever harder still once they know all hope is gone, if they could but see the grander scheme and settle to their allotted place therein. I do not regret my quiet crusade, but rue its failure. The noisy mountebanks have won the day, calling the all-too-easily distracted to heed their gaudy show.

Glyn Capstone
Careen, careen: another pointless interview for another faceless company and once again the light conspired against me; they all looked away from me as if they had strong sun in their eyes. Need I add that I was not the source of the light? They shared the haunting almost-belief that perhaps there was no one really *there*, all ready to yell 'Next!' so that

the void could be filled. He was there among them; I knew him but he did not know me. Advantage or disadvantage? I couldn't venture to say. By the way they treated him, he was pretty senior for one still so young (I considered myself still-young, so he must have been too); how did he get so high, so far? That electricity, that power, the flow of light, it must have returned to him. A brush of his fingers no longer incandesced a small glass bulb, but now he directed his power to settling other people's destinies. *What if he remembers,* I wondered, *what if it all comes back? What will he remember—our boyish bond, the dossing, the adventure in the Hole, or just a fight and the end of friendship?*

Christ, I thought, I am back in the power of Alan Brotherton.

Charles Durant Tobol

So now it is laid before you, the true reason I set the portrait painter onto my chosen target. It is because he is a leech, no, a hookworm, a parasite that enters into people and hollows them out from within. His filthy work is usually complete, his victim scooped-out even before the paint is dry on their treacherous portrait and they have to thank him and pay him and walk away wanting to be sick but with nothing left they can retch out. He is capable of slower destruction, too; I have heard of this chiefly in the case of women, although this anti-talent of his reputedly deserted him some time ago, along with another he treasured, and although he continued to attempt portraits they were just pictures, faces, lifeless, stiff, desultory efforts, no longer faces smeared with the subject's inner poisons and hidden secrets. In either phase of his career, only a dunderhead would have paid him to ply his brush, but there is, was and shall ever be a plentiful supply of dunderheads, so the painter thrived.

I brought him in to reawaken his parasitic talents so that he could open up Wayman, open him up and empty him out. The slowness of his work irritated me at first, but then I became encouraged that perhaps his gut sucking was to be as thorough as any from his palmier days. In the end he never rendered the evisceration I had desired. Instead, he turned out to be another, the last, of Wayman's little projects, the very last late developer to be schooled by the master. I regard the painter as little short of, in fact the precise definition of, a betrayer.

Fizzmonger

The white building by the bend in the water: it was a mill, a memory. We were all happy there, so I thought, so I recall, unless my recall is poisoned or distorted. Wayman says everyone's is, that's what history is all about. We were all artists; painters, sculptors, a glass-blower with near-magical skills, a potter too quiet and modest to claim magical skills, but who saw mysticism deep-laid in every thread of the universe and whose symbol, a five-pointed star, appeared somewhere on every one of her works (I sometimes amuse myself by wondering how Wayman would lecture her for perpetuating infantile misrepresentations), a blacksmith who filled the air with clatter as she nursed the embers of fading crafts and even a wordsmith, a poet, with a sweet voice and disdain for formal rhyme or structure: and then there was me, painting faces and exploring bodies. Also there was one Charles Durant Tobol.

The river ran by so placidly, the water and the air and the peaceful fields around were all there was, all there needed to be, although there was a busy town less than a mile away and its hiss and roar carried on every breeze, we could lay claim to isolation and as our poet put it, in borrowed words or not I never knew, find in art an unworldly bliss. I would often pause in my work and watch the silvery progress of the gentle water from the window of my light-blessed studio. I knew that some of the others would do precisely the same and sometimes a knot of us would gather outside on the shallow river bank, downing tools (of whatever sort) and stopping to draw breath, inspiration, from the gentle interplay and overlap of water and beams of pure, warming sun. Some would meditate; we would all attempt to empty our minds so that we could return to our work, renewed.

Some, however, would brood; Tobol did not join us, not ever. Tobol could see the silver sheen, but called it a slug-trail. He warned us not to empty our minds too much, after all there wasn't much to spare and what if we went into overdraft? We assumed that every peaceful haven needed a dissenter (or every Eden a serpent, Old Wash-Hands would doubtless have said); I think we knew that his biting words were the sound of his limitless, frustrated ambition pacing restlessly within its cage, but we could neither confront nor belittle it, in my opinion, because all of us felt that same stirring, to some greater or lesser extent we knew its power and fought it. The blacksmith punished hers with every stroke on the anvil; the potter drowned hers in unctuous spirituality; the poet fended hers off with desperate, churning floods of words. There were successes, fitfully at least, exhibitions and prizes and respectable sales and we cherished the success of each as our own. With one exception. Tobol worked, exhibited, tried hard, burned with desire for easy recognition and when it didn't materialise, bitterness followed.

I found my reward in the secret messages I encoded within the portraits, by confronting convention with its antithesis disguised as simpering compliance. I found that bodies as well as faces were my study and there were so many; I found a worldly bliss and thought no more of spirit. I came to grief when I encountered the one that I could not paint.

Charles Durant Tobol

Entry was easy for him, the painter, the parasite, all he needed was the smallest space, a nick of a wound, the slightest vulnerability and he was in. Corruption followed, he was its cause and catalyst and finally he would take what he wanted and depart, leaving his mark. It must be plain why I thought of him for Wayman. His powers were in abeyance, I knew that too, but I thought that a suitable subject, plus an innocent such as Faslane to tempt his lust, would re-conjure his powers in all their dark sublimity.

So after that build-up, my astonishment and disappointment at the outcome is understandable. Not one of Wayman's secrets was unearthed; no corruption was even hinted at, there was no cruel satire, no mockery. Not of Wayman.

Glyn The Pin

It was funny what happened. There was no goodbye do for Mr Tobol, though word went round of a 'good riddance' drink, all the teachers getting them in up the pub. Except him, of course. The teachers were even happier than when Doghead left. We said we'd rather have Tobol than

Doghead. Tobol may have taken it out on us sometimes, but it wasn't us he hated, not really. Doghead had it in for kids, he went off to take it out on new kids in a new town, but Tobol had it in not for kids but for art, for artists. Funny, then, how he went off to join them. Old Wash-Hands muttered that every man has his price.

Wayman wasn't keen on being famous, I mean on his face being famous. He wouldn't talk about it; we could usually get him to sidetrack and talk about anything, but not that. Fastlane neither: protecting Wayman, that's what we reckoned. So word started round again that they were... at it. It was the only thing that made sense.

Fizzmonger

Tobol protested that I had tricked him, but I note with a hefty *nb* that he never parted with any of the financial reward, the pelf, even though he virtuously labelled it *dirty money*. Perhaps he regarded it as compensation for being so thoroughly duped. I had 'tricked' him into the fulfilment of his ambition, hoisted him to the summit of his hopes, however artificially. It was also a test of his purity—and he failed it.

He always was a curiosity—he came to rail and rage against art, but out of all of us, the small gathering at the bend in the river, he was the one who was the most deeply immured, steeped, in *art*, that thing he purported to loathe. He was knowledgeable in techniques and art history, knew *how* to operate in each medium he essayed; it was inspiration and originality that evaded him. He peppered his conversation with throwaways that made it clear he had done his reading in literature, drama, philosophy and poetry; he knew music, too, although possibly only as a list of great names to be lauded, no better than a bad historian who can list kings and queens, dates, battles and revolutions and yet is baffled by the need for the whats and whys that make the subject alive and meaningful. He was, what can I call him, a nihilist-connoisseur, although he would never, I think, have made a good forger; he left his own mark upon his work, idiosyncratic but still that of a pale imitator, the man who can only work with ideas someone else has already emptied of novelty and significance.

He became a sideline man, a heckler and his catcalls echoed as the drowning cries of his ambition. No one ever came forward with the garlands he considered his entitlement and so his encyclopaedic knowledge of art became his yoke, his burden, which he attempted to relieve in the art-room of a sinking school, working hard to crush artistic interest or talent wherever it cropped up.

I suppose the logic that makes Tobol a poor forger makes me one too, but a good one—effective anyway.

Charles Durant Tobol

So his career hit a shoal; he met the one he could not paint —for that, read 'could not corrupt.' It wasn't that he could see no flaws, faults, points of entry in her, those things are always there. The crux of the matter was that he *would not* see these things. The result was an emetic portrait of an insipid angel, a bland pretty-beauty that denied individuality, character and soul. All it lacked was a scattering of glitter and rows of icky kisses to crown the painter's shame.

Fizzmonger

Tobol put his work up for prizes, did so with a confident flourish—arrogant, let's be honest—and spent his abundant alone time composing acceptance speeches in his mind and allotting prize monies to one whimsical project or another. Now this is no worse than the behaviour of your average non-artist dreaming his way out of the rat-race with a fantasy lottery win, but the problem lay not in the dreaming but in Tobol's deep-set feeling of entitlement and his reaction to his string of non-appearances in the laurels, short-list or long-list. He raged, a man nursing a bellyful of seething snakes: how had he not won, *how,* what conspiracy of dunces had assailed his profound genius, were good sense, good taste and good judgement all of the past? And then he moved on, he would find a new medium, a new form, a new middling-piddling idea which led him to believe yet again in his ground-breaking talents, to dream of plaudits and to recommence the dismal tail-in-mouth cycle.

Tobol indulged in the perfectly valid method of total absorption—have an idea, revel in it, believe it the first, best, most astonishing that was ever conceived, that you are the finest, greatest artist that ever scribbled, chiselled or drew—self-belief is not just appropriate but essential—and on a totalitarian scale, but when the piece is finished, that's an end to that phase and you should rearrange yourself, view your work with the eyes of your enemies and of the bitterest, most vicious, most pernickety critics, anticipate their moves as if trying to outdo then at chess and defeat them mentally before submitting to their judgement. But Tobol never reached that phase, with all his work he remained absorbed, a steel-clad self-believer.

When his hunger for victory and praise, merited or not, was finally satisfied, he said nothing and simply took what he decided was his, working quietly and privately on the motives for my actions, my gift to him. I got him the very thing he had always wanted, was that not benevolent of me?

Charles Durant Tobol

The poet noticed, the smith too. They both knew how he treated his women and were keen to see him fall. And fall he did—as an artist, that is: he discovered the dreary truth that, like fluffy bears and candy-floss, insipid angels sold, shifted units as the cynical say. He lost his ability with faces, with bodies too, and he became a picture-factory, found the best in everyone, every subject flawless and serenely beautiful; he became a negation of himself and painted out the fungus-spores and worms.

I attempted to rescue him from that path, to invite him back to where his true talents lay; his gift in return was treachery.

Jilly Holdenbridge

I thought of Mr Wayman, I thought of blasting through the door and assailing my astonished audience with a headlong charge and a loud roar of 'nuuuuumber onnnne!' setting them a shock-quiz, questions written up with a manic clack-clack-clack of chalked-up words. The idea made me smile; it helped to distract my nerves, if only for a moment. I could never match his energy, his bombast. I thought too, of course, of Faslane, of Miss, of how I would have liked her to be there to see the success of her work, the Shuffler standing straight and taking confident strides. My mind went out to my family, out there in the Love Cloud, and how my breaking free had not led to my utter destruction, hadn't led to me loving them less and yet outside the Cloud I was, and there had to remain; anything else was impossible.

Impossibility, however, was no barrier to my dad. He was there, ready to watch and listen, cushioned in shadow at the top of the raked room. He sat up there to avoid putting me off and so I could not see how much he shared my nerves. Nothing could stop him being there: nothing at all.

The Clouds

Fizzmonger

'As a matter of fact,' Wayman remarked, as ever not looking at me but aloft, 'you will find that your friend disagrees with you about the stars.'

'My friend?' I was nonplussed.

'Mr Van Gogh, he of the starry night! Did we not establish that you are an aficionado?'

'Wayman, I believe that conversation, such as it was, took place years ago… and it was *you* who mentioned him, not me.'

'Not *I*, you mean, of course. *Hmph*; ah. But nonetheless, as closely as memory allows, he referred in his letters to sparkling stars, green, yellow, pink even, and called them "gemlike", opals, emeralds, rubies in an ultramarine sky… and don't try to get out of it by telling me that he was mad.'

He had just read all that, surely; this was no drawing on the memory of years. I decided not to charge him with it; he had become yet more cantankerous, it was not worth provoking him.

'Lapis Lazuli, sapphires, citron-yellow, blue forget-me-not brilliance, that's what he said. Sky was clearer in those days, 'f course, cleaner, no stray light or poisonous soot. "Putting little white dots on a blue-black surface is not enough," yes, that's right, his words. Perhaps it was that dolt Tobol, perhaps it was him I told that.' grumbled the old man. 'Yes, probably Tobol. He saw nothing worthwhile in the sky. He needed putting in his place. Can't Do…' he muttered to himself a little longer; he enjoyed reliving old arguments, especially the ones he believed he had won handsomely.

The sky covered up with hastily-gathered clouds, as if its modesty were at stake, or it was protesting at our continued and sustained intrusions into its secrets. It had happened so quickly I was oblivious to the threat, still sketching the delicacy of the ashen light on the curved limb of a crescent Venus—a light so fragile it was almost impossible to distinguish from illusion, as plenty before me had seen things there-not-there in those unbreakable, light-repelling cloud tops—when the field of the telescope closed eye-like, overcome by a rolling blankness.

'That's it for the night,' I said dolefully, 'I think I'll pack up. You?'

In effect, slightly abashed, I was asking Sir if I may leave, please. The tagged-on question was otiose, a futility, a conversational observance for the sake of form.

'I think not. I believe that the apposite cliché is "the night is young". The pesky things may roll away again.' Wayman was perfectly affable, but he was scolding my lack of devotion to the cause—after all, the sun was only three hours gone. I may have been longing for rest and warmth and soft electric light, but Wayman was set firmly, keeping his hard-won night-eyes, just in case. He was not about to surrender the night and would spy on isolated stars through jagged cracks in the overcast if need be. I sometimes wondered if he was afraid that if he failed to tend them, the stars would be snuffed out.

Wayman was calm and philosophical about clouds, surprisingly so for someone usually so easily provoked into shows of theatrical volcanism: his enemies, his nemesis, all too often the clouds, would gather in malicious assembly and deprive him of his night's prizes, but of this he was phlegmatic; to him they were just as much a part of nature as the worshipful stars, even if they happened to be as maddening and obstructive as a schoolroom full of impenetrable minds, or a headteacher perhaps.

Sabina Faslane

I have no accusations to make against my parents, other than that I felt that they were rather too content to let me vanish into the growing darkness of the falling night. From as early as I could wangle one, I would carry a door-key with me to assuage the vaguely-nagging fear that one night they would simply lock up and go to bed, leaving me out there, marooned. Occasionally, however, their salutary neglect would lapse and, if anything, that was worse.

One night, one velvet-dark, star-clouded night, I stood outside, feeling the heat being pulled out of the earth, of me, and dragged towards the bitter cold of the upper sky, a sacrifice to the coming winter. I had worked my way into a good position where no earthly light could intrude, tucked behind the garage for shelter against our curtainless, light-polluting neighbours and with the bushes and trees as screens against the stains of streetlights, as secure against unwanted light as anyone could ever be in a suburban garden. I let myself be drawn upwards too, to the gentle glow of the stars.

At first it seemed there was almost nothing there, nothing but the brightest of stars, but so-slowly the blackness around them deepened and became populated with tiny dots of light, pinpricks and flickers, and by degrees that darkening, deepening sky became dusted, decorated with sprays of stars. The thin veil of what had seemed cloud stretching from one horizon to its opposite via the very roof of the sky became bolder, brighter, and I knew it was no cloud, but Milky Way, our galaxy, which is normally driven out of sight by our obsession with creating light, spilling it carelessly and thus burning-out the darkness and everything that lies nestled within its fragility. The bright stars were even brighter, but they were no longer marooned in an empty sky, but almost struggling for space. I had yet to put a lens to my eye and yet the heavens were almost over-populated. My night-eyes were ready, fully developed; my pupils were probably like tunnel-mouths, wide and dark, saucers full of starlight. There was almost no sound; there were faint noises of aeroplanes overhead, traffic from the streets around, voices carrying ridiculously far, even the whispering rumble of trains as they passed on tracks miles away, but around me, close by, silence, a soundlessness that made me feel cushioned and secure, alone with the stars.

I am no screamer, I never have been, but the noise I made the next moment must have carried like a spear through the still air, terrifying the whole night with its shrillness. My mum's voice shuddered as she stood there, steam curling around the mouth of a mug, which she still half-held in her shaking hand. Her other hand was shaking too, the one that held the little torch whose beam had brushed my eyes with its piffling pifco power, feeble but sufficient to destroy my eyes and turn me into a shrieking harridan, pursuing my mother back into the house so I could berate her for her crimes of light.

'For God's sake child,' she said the next day when shame had overtaken and silenced me, 'I was only bringing you a cup of coffee to warm you up!'

Fizzmonger

What colour were they, those night-watching eyes? What is the ideal colour for a stargazer's iris? Which is the most sensitive to the task of welcoming and harvesting ancient, distant, lights, faint and exhausted from their million-year, travelling? There is no one recorded by history who has gazed into those eyes for any length of time—rumours concerning Miss Gaptooth notwithstanding—and so I should be the only one who could know—yet I confess, I don't. They were more often than not turned away from me; we all know in what direction. But I haven't much time for eyes in any case.

This may seem the ultimate ingratitude; after all, I am disparaging one of the essential tools of my trade, but my loathing comes truly. I rely on my eyes, of course, but the old light-catchers are not good friends to me, nor anybody, since everything optical is an illusion and the coming of blindness should be welcomed as the arrival of an overdue truth. Wayman would always clank on about how the sky was full of illusions, things forced into place by our hoping, our credulity, not to mention cruel and naked greed—we all know of his scorn for those who would mine the skies for false promises and answers—but the illusions and delusions begin in the eye, as it greedily seizes and twists light.

I have always been disbelieving of my eyes; what is more unreliable, after all, than an eyewitness? People talk about tricks of the light, but there's no such thing, the trickery is the work of the eye, the way it falsifies light, capturing it and stripping it of its truth and then disguising it in layers of lies. We do not 'see,' we are cheated; a beam of light is hijacked and sent on a mangling journey of misdirection in which it is lensed, bent, filtered through vile jelly, to nerves that face away from the light—yes, *away*, what a failure of design—and even then the mystery-tour is not over. This stolen beam, losing its power, fading, is adulterated by the overspill from fantasies and dreams, intrusions from the ghosts that howl inside the head: and only then do we 'see.' What can be real and true at the end of that? Not for nothing do the songwriters rhyme 'eyes' and 'lies.'

The trouble doesn't end there; it isn't just the falsification of light, but its limitations too. The visible spectrum is just a pitiful segment, a tiny slice of an overwhelmingly greater whole. Wayman's pet stars are not just white, red, blue, pale orange, not even old Vincent's lapis lazuli marks their limits, they are alive with the invisible, burning with energy that mocks our failing eyes. What we would call the faintest of them, deceived as we are by distance and our weak vision, would stand blazing, dazzling if we could see a better rainbow. When I paint, to escape the eye-lies I bring in to service my version of that broader palette, an unshackled spectrum, call it a sixth sense, and more, if you have no better words or imagination. I paint what I *know* is there, hidden from the common gaze though it may be. By that gift and with that skill I possessed people, by which I intend both haunting and ownership. Sometimes within an instant, usually one sitting, sometimes a longer and more intensive period, I scanned, analysed and *knew* them in a way that would take even the most perceptive of them a lifetime of tedious and embarrassing self-discovery.

True artists are capable of such feats if they are prepared to suffer the pain that is consequent to plundering their deepest-lying resources, but even among the best there

274

are few who possess both the vision and courage to do so; most do not even appreciate what is available to them and never attempt to draw on this elemental power. Tobol, long ago when at his best, touched on it, but he mistook it for simple confirmation of his intimations of superiority, the corrosive inward-looking misanthropy that already gripped him; he never perceived anything worth incorporating into his work, even though the weakness and ugliness he saw but never translated could have lent to his sterile creativity what so many said it lacked; honesty and human truthfulness, or in the usage on which the critics insisted, *soul*. Oh, there was ugliness aplenty in Tobolia, but it all came from behind the artist's eyes, a fact that showed itself too easily. The potter at the old mill, she perceived the gift too, but mistook it for and mixed it up with the mysticism she saw everywhere, like Tobol she became hopelessly mired in the unrealities that existed only within the deluded spaces of her fragile skull. They both had a chance to perfect their art, but instead were confused by falsehood, by their tiny-minded errors.

As I was to discover, heightened perception may be satisfying but never sells well. But that was easily-enough fixed; just a few disguising strokes was all it took, a patina of prettiness, then all were delighted to be deceived into the belief that they had been depicted in the best of lights and I could claim both my inner satisfaction and hard currency to boot. This is the measure of what I lost, what I found so hard to forgive, why it took so long. Wayman taught me to use my eyes in a different way, a better one. I dissolved my anger in the stars.

Glyn Capstone

Maybe the problem is not with me—perhaps it's the light? I'm just a victim of the light. Light does whatever I don't want it to and always has. What if it's alive, thinking and malicious too—at least toward me? Or what if it's enslaved, helplessly doing the bidding of my enemies, the lucky, powerful, got-it-easy types, the Alan Brothertons? On-off it goes at their command, it flips and bends and turns corners, breaks up, fans out into pretty coloured strips for their amusement and diversion, then refolds itself, concentrates into a remorseless search light when I'm vulnerable, darkens into a bleak cloak more obscure than Wayman's darkest midnight when I want to be noticed. And it's no accident, the Brothertons can command their performing poodle to do these and any other tricks any time they want; that's power, *real* power. Light itself may not be my enemy, but it's a friend of my enemy. No wonder I never stood a bloody chance.

Sabina Faslane

It began with the floating-thing. Just one little speck, amoeba-like, unfocused, drifting, making a slow transit across the eye. It moved slowly, languid and borne as if on a smooth sea or cushioned on gentle currents of oil. It was not always there, didn't make a faithful, remorseless orbit and for a time remained that way, irregular and alone in its passage. But in time it grew greater, a gathering storm and made its transit with increasing frequency, leaving a wake of specks that remained trailing after it had passed. The fragments then accumulated, accrued and became a cloud, and clouds always attract and gather more clouds, a looming threat of heartbreak for the dedicated stargazer.

Old Wash-Hands

For Wayman, no fate could have been crueller than to lose his sight, to know that slowly he was degenerating, being shut off from the stars. Galileo went blind and so did Milton, his poetic visitor who saw the stars as few men of his time had, through that famous telescope. Much later there was a politician called Edward Grey—the man who saw the lamps going out over Europe as war came to rage —who lost his sight and his tragedy, aside from that war, was that he could no longer see his favourite star. I wonder which one? It was the kind of thing Wayman would know.

Sabina Faslane

He tried to keep the failing of his vision secret; it was the last and worst confession he could make. An admission of vulnerability, but also of the coming of darkness, of a wrongful, unwelcome darkness, the coming of a night of which he had good cause to be afraid, the night that could never be penetrated by starlight.

For a time, all that anyone knew was that his temper had become even more brittle. In the classroom, he grew stiller, more sedentary, his dynamic whirl of limbs tamed, more cautious, gradually stilled. He could no longer flurry among the rows of desks without the risk of a trip, fall, crash, injury—and loss of face. He consulted books less and less, holding forth from memory (which was still prodigious) and some old hands sniffed and said he was simply seeking to ape "his hero Lawton". Old Wash-Hands muttered darkly about 'a visitation, a punishment,' but no friend of Wayman's heard any of this until Wash-Hands, no longer able to outwait Alfred, had collected his good-luck trinkets and washed his hands of us all one last time.

Evelyn Lawton

Alfred brought the bottle himself. I was delighted to see him, of course, but simply to drop in was most unlike him. There was a figure at the door, distorted by the glass, but I knew who it was and called out to him to wait; he knew I couldn't make much speed by then, damned hip. I wondered if he had started on the bottle before he arrived —and I realised I'd also heard a vehicle, a taxi, departing from outside my gate, his car, that absurd car, was left safely at home—as he really wasn't making a great deal of sense, not to begin with. But the bottle was fresh, he was sober; to begin with, that is.

'Glen Alford' he said, handing it over. It was wrapped in tissue.

Old Wash-Hands

To reach too greedily for the stars, was that not to tempt— invite, rather—divine punishment? *Adoratis sideribus*—in terror-stained memory of my quondam Latin master I hope I have recalled that correctly; did the Romans not perform such prayers? And in his way, did Wayman not do so too? If one accepts gods (even if one may not name them as such) does not one *also* accept their justice? Does one not submit? And if one happens to be worshipping the wrong god in full view of the correct one?

Charles Durant Tobol
Clouds, *blight his sky!*

Evelyn Lawton

'He flatters me, Eve, flatters me. He brackets me with Galileo. What do you make of that then?'

Not a great deal, I assured him. The liquid level in the bottle had sunk swiftly, I had only made small inroads into it; Alfred spoke as a sober man, but trembled visibly like a drunk.

'I—we—dared to look upon the heavens, that's the tale, the narrative; I tried to displace the gods and so comes the punishment for hubris... it's all nonsense, of course. People also tongued it that Galileo had looked at the sun, through his,' (he gestured, pulling his hands apart), 'through his telescope. Galileo would never have been such a fool. But he brackets me with Galileo. There's an achievement now.'

'Alfred...'

'One moment he says I'm an apostate under celestial justice, the next I'm a just man suffering under tyrannical excess. He can't come to a conclusion. Bern always did refer to him as the Dithering Tribunal, The Wobbling Prefect. Not Galileo. The other.'

I told him I knew who; just not *what*.

He took a gulp of air that came as a far deeper, more dizzying draught than his worryings at the whisky.

'I'm going blind, Eve. It's progressing—or regressing, depending on your point of view—and there's no stopping it. Once I'd given up denying it, you can make book that I got *that* checked; I've ransacked doctors for opinions. There's no knife, no drug and there's certainly no fucking magic healing word,' (the whisky and that gasp of air were well at work now), 'that will halt it. To be without sight of sky. The curse has come upon me.'

'You said it wasn't a...'

'Poetry.'

'I know. But don't give an inch to Wash-Hands and his ilk. Not even in fun.'

'I'm not having much fun, Eve.'

If I had thought it allowable, I would have put my arms around him and held him; I am truly unsure anyone had done that in thirty, forty years or more. But knowing that such mothering was impermissible, what could I do but take his glass and tip the bottle.

'Glen Alford.' I said, flat-toned, helpless.

Jilly Holdenbridge

Why go on knowing, why go on trying to know; what good does it do? You've done so well and we're proud of you, but we worry. Why go on with this knowing, why try to know more, ever more? This was the last gambit of the Love Cloud; knowledge has its limits, stop now before it gets dangerous, stop *please*, you can only get hurt if you persist, shouldn't this be someone else's to do?

My family would agree, eagerly and vigorously, that who dares wins: however, that would always be provided that the daring and winning was all over and had taken place while they were looking elsewhere—and that the daring winner was not a component of the Love Cloud. They would also agree, equally eagerly and vigorously, that pride comes before a fall—and that is precisely what would be said to the daring winner should she be caught out during the daring and prior to the winning. Indeed, it would be taken as read that the winning was, as a next step, an impossibility, and that the daring an act of arrogance deserving thunderbolt-standard punishment. The darer would be invited to return to the Love Cloud, pointedly, plaintively, to readopt an accepting, silent, shuffling timidity forevermore.

Old Wash-Hands

Time for some nice, relaxing malicious gossip: having exhausted his luck with one kind of heavenly body, it appears, the portrait painter took his chances with another (intended, intended, that was a sitter I simply could not miss).

Who, you may ask, was my informant in this rather salacious and ill-starred (intended, intended) matter? Why, none other than my teaching colleague and the painter's one-time fellow-artist, the somewhat grotesque Mr Tobol. It was not in any way a confidence—I do not break confidences, I respect the sanctity of the confessional—for Mr Tobol became at one stage more than somewhat loquacious; prior to that I had dubbed him Tacitus, which afforded me some microscopic satisfaction. This befell when the portrait of the great Mr Wayman was plainly not what poor Tobol had been expecting (although quite what he *was* expecting was not clear, nor quite how his dear old pal had let him down, though let him down he plainly had) and the enraged art master peppered the air of the Staff Room with exceedingly bitter and extremely enjoyable reminiscences from the days when they wore smocks and floppy berets, had ideals in common and lived, as far as I can make out, in some quite hideous commune, poisoning a passing meander with paint and, what's worse, poetry.

So now our artist has utterly abandoned faces and bodies and charts the stars with Wayman at his elbow, teacher as ever, guiding his hand. Rumour has it that the painter has become some sort of amanuensis to old Alfie

Wayman; he acts as another man's eyes, spending many a night in Wayman's hilltop redoubt painting pretty pictures to make the old man happy. Rumour has nothing much else to say about the matter, which is distinctly unusual for Rumour.

I suppose I must dredge up a little sympathy at this point; Wayman may have irritated and galled me at times, but what he is suffering seems a punishment too far. Try as I might, I cannot reconcile his fate to the mind and actions of a good and loving god—to justice. Perhaps the Olympians are still in business in some residual manner, this is somehow more redolent of their work. But in the end I do not know; if, whoever ye may be, this is your way of punishing Wayman's sins, I cannot in my heart find it just, but I am powerless to interfere. See ye to it.

Fizzmonger
People spoke of her, wonderingly, as 'effulgent'—it sounded like a dirty word to me, and still does. Just move the letters or sounds around and unfailingly you come up with something foul, something reeking, many things even worse; I always hated it. My bemusement was added to by the fact that whenever *I* looked at her or thought of her, there was not the least flicker of luminescence, not from within, nor from without, no glimpse of anything from any spectrum, even from the components my own enriched vision. Oh, she was not invisible, there was a body, a face, but it was to me as if she were unreal, unbelievable, almost dimensionless, a figure rendered on a flat board in sing-a-rainbow colours so simple they were infantile. I was supposed to create her portrait, but to achieve *that* I knew that I would first be obliged to invent her, give her depth

282

and reality, believability; in short, to conjure up something out of next to nothing—but I am an interpreter of light, not its creator.

It came as no surprise to me that I saw something different to everyone else, but what astonished me was that this time I saw less than they, so much less. All I could tell was that light fell into her and that this was no natural phenomenon, it was an act of theft, of voracious, greedy and uncaring consumption. There may have been occasional flashes, lightning-stems crackling erratically around her, which is how she came to be seen at all, but these were simply the last hopeless, dying maydays of the light-pulses that she dragged into herself, breathing them in, feeding on them, negating them. She was a light-canceller, every wavelength whether seen or unseen was swallowed, gorged and yet she was never satisfied.

I made efforts to recover that purloined light by painting her, painting her, a desperate attempted replevin that she defeated without effort no matter how I tried, what I tried. It was a contest and she enjoyed exercising the power of unending victory. I may as well have been painting bowls of fruit, the half-death of still-life; all light, all inspiration drawn out of me; perhaps it would be more accurate to say sucked, vampirically. You could say that she made me money and yet put me out of business. It is not an irony I have ever appreciated. I became prolific, but only in the same way a photocopier is prolific, and possessed of as much intrinsic art—and of all things that is what I found I could not forgive. This is also where Wayman came, however inadvertently, to my rescue: I regarded it as the crisis of my life, which could only be resolved by the restoration of my powers and privileges—he, however, framed it as a problem the solution to which was to satisfy my aching need to be educated.

Charles Durant Tobol

There is pleasure and relief in cutting a long story short. I only heard the painter's desperate distortions through the double-distortion of the accounts of others, but however tortured the facts may have been, the self-pity at the very least came in his genuine tone. The insipid angel was his ruin; he couldn't tempt her, could not corrupt her, could not make her image. He weakened, fell in love with her and at the same time went colour-blind, face-blind. All else is excuses, a smoke screen.

I wonder if the painter ever tried his version of events on Wayman? It's sometimes irresistible, the urge to justify yourself; even to someone who may neither listen nor care. But maybe the old man would care, after all falsification of history is one of the—admittedly many—things that is bound to infuriate him. If it happened, very likely the painter's words sailed aloft to the cold, clear sky, unheard. Too small, too petty a violation of history—luckily for him.

Share The Stars

Sabina Faslane

A great comet is coming. They say that it will be visible in broad daylight and that at night it will shame the Moon. At the moment it can't be seen without a very, very good telescope, but already the rumours—that it's coming straight at us, our little Earth to be smashed to smithereens, or that the comet is a super-snowball that will snuff out the Sun, or has a poison tail that will end the world with its cyanide sting. I'm working hard to explain the truth and kill the doomsday talk, but as ever children and adults love the lies and clasp them close. History is repeating itself as twaddle: how Mr Wayman would roar, eh?

Evelyn Lawton

He didn't claim sole ownership of the sky—some of us just assumed that of him. The truth is, he was always trying to get us to look upward. But to do it *properly*. His drive was to share the stars, as far as he could; he proselytised and it sank in secretly, and to a far greater extent, than one thought. I remember standing before an enraptured group of small children who had cast aside play, gossip, without even any sideways looks or tiny mischiefs going on, as I told them about my friend who knew about the stars, how he had shown me a bright reddish twinkling star called Beetlejuice (I silently sought forgiveness for the simplification; I reminded Alfred, in absentia, that these were six-year-olds and a little simplification was required) that anyone could see if they looked out one of these nights after dark.

All the children were spellbound by star-magic, but the most fascinating, fascinated face was that of little Jilly Why-Why; her mouth had bunched into a tight 'o' which heralded the coming of many questions, but for the moment she was as silent as her classmates, all of them imagining themselves out there in the dark, not with the moon shining bright as day but the flickering red light of Beetlejuice in their keen eyes. The spell, I knew, would pass from most of the children even before they had passed the school gate, but I would have bet my next payday on the scene that would follow as darkness fell that night, little Jilly dragging her father out into the cold night and demanding he find that star, that special star alone, and no other would do. It was a tiny triumph for me as a teacher, another gain, too, for Alfred.

Sabina Faslane
The last time there was a comet of note, I had this conversation with Alfred Wayman.

'They've got the comet. Well, they're going to get it.'

He sounded like a jealous child—sulky too. The promised spectacle had not lived up to its pre-publicity, 'Daylight Comet. Brightest Stellar Show In Centuries' and similar; in truth, it had not proved much more than a grey-white misty puffball as it crawled lethargically almost across our sky, so even the newspapers and doomsayers had slunk away in disappointment after an exhausting orgy of prediction and misinformation, but we knew by now that once it had tucked itself well away from our sight and was only visible to those living south of the equator, it really was going to become a streamer of brilliance, not-quite visible during the daytime but dazzling. In short, a phenomenon.

'It's always the same—"best seen from the Tropics; to best advantage from too-far degrees south and further…".' He really did sound like a little boy whose friends had run away with his kiddy-cars.

I was moving—pardon the expression, *not* intended—heaven and earth to arrange a short-notice holiday so I could witness just a little of this glorious flare-up, despite the fact I didn't fancy my chances. When I suggested that Alfred do the same, he looked at me as if I had proposed elopement. He was annoyed and embarrassed, so much that he attempted neither excuses nor a straight "no", but coloured deeply and quite alarmingly the words jammed in his throat. I knew that he had the same excitement coursing through his veins that animated, agitated, me and set me making calls, begging leave, seeking bookings, but he was not going to chase this comet, it had let him down and on his home territory he would remain.

Evelyn Lawton

Some soft old fools have asked me if I am "waiting to join him". Bernard, they meant, of course. Romantics; fluff-heads. I had to restrain a splenetic, vituperative outburst against "twaddle" that would have left Alfred Wayman in the shade. All this from their gentle old friend Evelyn, who decided to protect them from herself: but all that infuriated energy had to go somewhere. I decided to show 'em all, "waiting to join him", indeed!

I could make things "happen", I suppose; show a kick of life and reassure the other faction, the people who want me to "get on with it" that I'm getting on with it, if not exactly getting over it—but could I sustain the act, continue to convince everyone that needs it that I'm fine-just-fine? But I need events to do my bidding, I need to contain them, make them move at a pace of my choosing, to my comfort. I have no intention of giving up and dying, I may be forgiven for considering that there has been quite enough of *that* going on. I get myself out, try to get back to some kind of normal, but after the going-out there is always the coming home, the realisation that there is no light on, no cheery voice or cooking-smells to greet me, never mind a decent glass of wine awaiting my embrace; no sense of shared space, comfortably, companionably, lovingly filled.

When Bea Chitting left her husband she stripped the house of everything she owned, all she had touched, anything bearing any tang or trace of her; she left empty cupboards, swept-clean sideboards, photo-albums pock-marked with empty frames, vacant wardrobes, shoe-racks, coat hooks, blank spaces everywhere for the poor man to discover and gape at in disbelief. She let it be known that she had acted out of mercy, that it would help him, this violent voiding, it would mean he would not wallow in pointless memory, touching and smelling her abandoned clothes and holding their fabric to his skin, the last remnants of her presence. Let's give her the benefit of the doubt and assume her good intentions, that she sought to soften an unavoidable blow by removing herself in totality and at one strike, so that he could adjust quickly to his new reality—" cruel to be kind" comes to mind—but of course all she did was compound the damage, for he was left with a home that reeked of her absence, but which was scoured of even a token of her presence. He was led to wonder if all his memories, their long years together, had been a phantasm, that his poor lonely mind had long ago been overpowered, deceived by fond, mad imaginings.

I have the opposite problem; I have an over-supply of memories as well as physical tokens, every type of reminder, sweet and painful. Bernard didn't magic anything away, he wasn't planning any departure, of course not, and so I have a home that is just as it was, prepared for and accustomed to his occupation, ready for his return, and yet with his occupation over, his return an impossibility. I swing wildly and unpredictably between the desire to undertake a huge clear-out, a purge, as if this will kick-start some refreshed future in which I shall cope alone, while at the opposite point of this orbit I become a hoarder, a keeper of grave-goods, a relic-worshipper.

I have decided what I shall do, I shall teach myself the shapes of the constellations, the places and names of the stars. And I shall do it quite alone. Alone under the sky. I shan't trouble Alfred with the matter, glad though he would be to teach me. No, I shall do it alone: alone now. I shall ask of Alfred only that he allow someone else to share possession of the night.

Jilly Holdenbridge

I've always been something of a morning creature. As soon as it reaches four or five a.m., I'm ready, not always wide awake but not far from it, with the application of a little will-power and a little water. I would certainly rather make an early start than drag an evening out; past nine p.m. I'm no company at all, I want my bed, my bed. I used to drive my poor dad to distraction as I whizzed around as if powered by twizzed-up rubber bands while he tried to rub the sleep out of his eyes and pulled at his first half-awake half-light breath. I don't run round like that anymore, but of course, but very early on my eyes are open and my day begun. I am there to see the stars displaced by the dawn on all but the longest of the summer days. I see them off, content that they will return with the evening to come. I am no enemy of the stars, but always glad to know that a new sun is here and all is safe. Perhaps a childish part of me is relieved of its lingering fear of the end of the world.

Sabina Faslane

I can forget under the canopy of the stars; I can rest, relax, empty my mind. I feel in touch with the world, the sky, and whenever my confidence has failed me again and I feel small, I can look out at that expanse, that vastness and reassure myself that yes, I *am* small and so for that matter is absolutely everyone else. I sit alone in the night, but always with the comfort of the knowledge that close by there is someone warm and loving and most of all mine. Sometimes he joins me here under the stars, but he is their unashamed fair weather friend. I'm so lucky to have someone who understands, who never feels abandoned when left to himself indoors, or when he puts out a hand on the darkness of a late night and finds the other half of the bed is—still—empty. For a feeling of completeness in life there is nothing like it. I think I shall feel yet more complete when my girls take an interest in the night sky; as yet they cleave to warm home and glowing screen, they can't face "that cold", but I shall bide my time, follow the patient example of Alfred Wayman. *What*, I hear a querulous voice, *patience? Wayman?* Ah yes. I uphold and share his inexhaustible faith in the late developer.

Sometimes I nurse strange notions out here, odd night-thoughts. Just lately it has occurred to me I'd quite like to have my portrait done. I am changing, ageing, my skin has started to tighten in places, loosen in others; I think I've just started to show some real character in my face, whereas before I feared I was a nothing, just-another-pretty. I may be less 'paintable' than once I was (or whatever other words were used of me at the time) and I am surely glad of it. Come, lines of age, and make me *someone*. I don't think, however, that I shall renew my acquaintance with Alfred's painter; he always gave me the shudders and I was never sure that Alfred's great mission to civilise him met with success.

Old Wash-Hands

I could never make any sense of Wayman's dynamic-duetting with the portrait painter (although one may perforce recall the rumours surrounding the infamous comic-book duo; add *that* to the stock of maybes that make up Wayman's very apocryphal story, if you please), but nevertheless I could perceive a beneficial outcome. Loath as I am to lend the least of ears to Tobol, vile as he is, and more reluctant still to lend his cruel whispering credence, I became aware of the very-much realised potential of the painter to inflict harm both physical and spiritual: his destructive force. Diverting a menace, a nuisance, was Wayman's greatest, perhaps one and only, service to his fellow man (or woman, chiefly, as I understand the shabby history).

Fizzmonger

I have learned two things, two final things, about Alfred Wayman. The first is that he never needed me and the second is that he did have a secret mistress after all.

Glyn Capstone

Night is nothing, that's what I say: shut it out, ignore it, pretend it isn't there, wrap it in a curtain and drown it in man-made glare. Night never brought me anything good. Neither did the light, of course.

In a nightfall garden stood Lana Carver, tall, curvy and exuding a miasma of sweet perfume that battled with a foul haze of tobacco fumes; how I wanted her. There were party-sounds and party-lights behind us, a dark winter sky before us; Lana Carver was in the garden because she wanted another fag and I was there because she was there. She was backlit and beautiful and filaments of light snaked through her tumbling auburn hair, weaving a halo glow. I faced an enemy and had a worse one at my back.

Lana Carver stepped away from me and bent over in the final throes of the twilight, as if worshipping. The party-light fell on her backside as her black jeans tightened against her buttocks like sails in a freshening breeze. I was desperate, desperate, desperate for something to say. I grabbed at, 'Are you okay?' She straightened and her half-light half-dark face wore lines of bored contempt.

'I was stubbing my ciggie out. That alright with y'?'

Why was I bothering, why did I care, why did I *want* her so much? Why was I prepared to do or say anything, no matter how humiliating? I stiffened with unexpected joy when she came to stand at my shoulder, leaned close and pointed out into the cold, clear sky, at some vague arrangement of lights she said was her zodiac sign.

'Do you believe they can control our destinies?' she asked, touching me on the arm, her warm breath tickling my ear. *Say yes, say yes, say yes* came a voice within my head, *Say yes, here's your chance, you may get what you desire!* I thought about how old Wayman would have blasted her and her ciggies to the other side of the zodiac. I said yes.

'That's Gemini, the twins.' she confided erotically.

'I can see just two stars.'

'Give it a minute, let your eyes get used to the dark.'

I decided I'd try anything once. Giving it a minute kept me near to Lana Carver.

'I can see other stars nearby.'

'And what shape do you see, what picture?'

I knew I was supposed to see twins, two boys, but all I could see was bright stars and dim stars in the shape of a box, a narrow one. A coffin, that was all I could see; I never was much of a one for pictures, especially in the sky. I suppose it wouldn't have done to call it the sign of The Coffin; it wouldn't have been good for business, I suppose.

There was a metallic click and a flutter of light. I had waited too long to reply, the moment was over and Lana Carver had lit up again.

'Wait a minute,' I said, desperate, desperate, desperate, 'Maybe I'll see better if we go further down the garden.' Into the dark. A spinning red flicker left sparks in its wake; she had pinged her ciggie over into the next garden. She had lost patience with me, I'd failed again and she turned back towards the party, to find the smug, self-entitled Brotherton who would take her home tonight. She said something, but without breaking step or turning her head. It was probably *'feh.'*

Evelyn Lawton

I bought a book; it was old, second-second hand, but that didn't matter, after all, the stars hardly change in fifty years, do they? Its spine was weak and it had all been stickytaped, but really quite efficiently and there was no danger of pages drifting away and leaving me with an incomplete sky. Weighing the book in my hand, I was haunted by a short-lived notion to search the fly leaf for a name, a dedication, a "This Book Belongs To", but that was silly, for he would never have given up such a book, never in this world, it would have remained close to him forever.

Only just over palm-sized, too thick to pocket comfortably, it had a series of sky-maps (season by season), a very handy glossary ("syzygy", anyone?) but most of all an alphabetical treatment of each constellation, giving the name and brightness of each major star and noting up objects of interest; nebulae, star-clusters, galaxies; there was even a little précis of how each star-group had come by its name over the years. I had to de-rust my Greek letters as I mastered how the comparative brightness of stars was measured, learned a little Arabic as the star-names became familiar and gradually put together a coherent picture of the sky that had always been with me but which I had treated with salutary neglect, believing faintly it was somebody else's territory and that it would be impolite to pry. As I came to grasp what could be seen and when, the changing vantage points of the progressing year, I came to the realization of how much I already knew, albeit in an uncoordinated, scattered manner, courtesy of little time-to-time lectures over a period of years.

I found Alfred's "thirteenth sign", the one with the unpronounceable name, with which he had berated many a hapless horrorscoper. I also came to an appreciation of what could *not* be seen, the sights denied us by our fixed and limiting horizons. The book offered a colour-code; the name of each constellation was set in white lettering, on a red background if it was a northern constellation, black if it was mid-way, equatorial and yellow if it only rose in the southern hemisphere. I felt a quick, biting loss at the thought of what could never, never be seen if we planted ourselves at home and refused to move.

'That's the problem with horizons,' Alfred once admitted to me, a little sheepishly, 'once the blasted things are fixed it's hard to breach them.' Had he lived, I would never have told him about my trip to the southern sky, I would have let him, just like the others, believe me a sun-worshipper and nothing more. He was definitely not to know that I made the trip partly in his name—his honour, that is, not an identity heist—and that I thought about him as I saw the sting of the Scorpion, the end of the great sky-river, the Centaur and the Southern Cross. Alfred could have named them on first sight, the False Cross or other deceptions would not have fooled him, whereas I could only navigate those unfamiliar skyways with patience, map in hand.

I suppose it could be seen as my rebellion, or even a form of one-upmanship, that I decided to break Alfred's horizons, go beyond his strange self-imposed limits and see for myself the stars that had never been under his guardianship. 'Pack your sun-cream!' people joked, their voices filled with bemusement, concern, jealousy even as I flew off for far horizons. Some must have thought I was on an old widow's holiday, seeking sun and late-life thrills, but they didn't know my true purpose. Sun cream, who needs it? You can't get night-burn can you, eh? Eh? Eh?

Sabina Faslane

I sometimes wondered why Alfred would never uproot, not even for a couple or a few weeks, and see for himself the treasury of sky that always denied us. I wondered, I did not ask; no answer, no polite answer at least, would have followed. I have never been able to shake the feeling that in his refusal to break his patterns, Mr Wayman, for all his bluff and mystery, was showing that even he could be eaten away by lack of confidence and forced to cling desperately, fanatically to what he knew.

Fizzmonger

'Fix your eyes on that star—that one, orange-red, just breasting the horizon, seemingly all alone.'

'Antares.'

'You're learning. Well done.' (I swear he almost added 'boy' to that.) 'Now travel towards it, but stay on the ground, understand? We're using the imagination but not playing at space flight. Now let's say you've travelled as far as... Greece, where all the wisdom came from; where is that star now?'

'Higher in the sky, noticeably higher.'

'And what else do you notice?'

'There are more stars below it, I can see the sting.'

'What about the stars you already know?'

'I can recognise them all—but they're all in odd places, they've been moved... up the sky, I suppose you would call it. Things are nearly overhead that never make it up there at home.'

'Now travel further; South Africa suit you? Well now. Where is that star now?'

'Practically overhead.'

'And beneath it?'

'Dazzling objects I have never seen—star-clouds, brilliance...'

'Some damn dull, barren patches though?'

'True enough.'

'Where are our stars, the home stars?'

'Behind me, shoved up a few more notches. They look odd, takes a moment to recognise them—they're upside-down.'

'Now move on; Australia's your destination. Look up again.'

'It's a whole new sky, I don't know where I am.'

'You'll settle to it. And the home stars?'

'Gone, so many of them, gone, buried below the...'

'Don't panic; you know they're *there*, of course, and there's just something in the way?'

'Well of course I do.'

'And that is why I don't need to bother myself with all that travelling. But if you go visiting, do give them my love.'

Evelyn Lawton

Naturally I tracked down Bernard's star. I felt stabs of anger at my naiveté, at how I had been taken for a fool; even Alfred would have struggled to locate the feeble thing, so faint it didn't even qualify for a Greek letter, a no-name-just-a-number star that never climbed far enough over the lip of our horizon to make it worthy of attention.

My battered little star-atlas also offered little gobbets of information about the names of the constellations, how they were pictured and named by different peoples over the span of human time. Some names were ancient and almost universal, rusted into place never to be shifted, but others came much later, especially as travellers from this horizon spied out stars that the ancients had never seen and had drawn up atlases of these new skies they promptly filled with names that spoke of their world and what they knew, exporting their vanities and grandiosities. But these sky-names were more fragile, the new sky more fluid, and soon enough along came others who jumped their claims, broke up or scrapped their pet star-patterns and imposed the works of their own imagination, claiming the heavens in their honour and disregarding all that had come before. This undignified cosmic scramble brought me to thinking, however, that in spite of my (never mind Alfred's) qualms, it was no crime to take and name a corner of the sky for my lost love, my beautiful husband, in fact; should I dare to do so I had as much right as anyone to strip even the brightest and best-known of the stars of their accustomed titles, re-map and rename the entire visible cosmos if I so chose, without any need to apologise to any one, and certainly no cause to pay over my money to some grubby, greedy earthbounds who claimed rights not theirs and leeched on my grief. I could recast the whole sky for him, Bernard Lawton, The Professor, My Bernard: but I would also reserve a prominent space for another name well worthy of commemoration, something commanding and visible every night as soon as the darkness takes hold, something that would never set from the vantage-point of that hilltop of his; in keeping with tradition it would be his transport for his unending journey across the sky, I think I would call it Wayman's Wain.

I still see Sabina occasionally, but I am more limited in my travels these days and she has a growing family and burgeoning career, now some distance away. Her head, I am pleased to say, remains firmly among the stars. I invited her over to share the story of my conquest of the southern heavens: well, we all need an audience from time to time and I admit I was flattered by her admiration. She checks on me from time to time, ensuring I am maintaining my hard-won independence, but she knows that on that matter I shall give no ground. Somewhere in her head, I think, she is convinced that my late blossoming is a reaction to a life of marital servitude, but of course it is not. I have shaken off some chains, but had Bernard still been here he would have understood and applauded.

Sabina Faslane
He defies blindness; he has the stars mapped behind his eyes, he can see them still and makes that claim with stubborn ferocity. The same stars rise and set, time and again with absolute predictability. Give or take the odd exciting intruder such as a nova, a comet, there are no risks, no real surprises. How is that for playing safe? The only enemy is the coming of the light. I think I have just mulled out one of Alfred's secrets.

Evelyn Lawton
The stars are not fixed, not over the aeons of endless, unfolding time at any rate. There is only one actual fixed,

unmoving astral point and that is the little wild garden where sat, where sits, Alfred Wayman, his eyes upon the sky.

Sabina Faslane

The great comet made its appearance and what's more lived up to the predictions of its brightness—well, the scientific ones; well, within reason anyway, surprisingly. Also surprising was the way in which it defied Wayman's law of astronomical grumbling—wait, let's call it *one of* his laws of grumbling—and flared into brilliance just as it crept over the Northern horizons, rather than just after it became invisible from up-here, and what's more dusted our skies with its long, fine tail for an impressive time. Only those who wilfully hid their heads from all traces of the night could have missed it. An impressive number of the customarily night-blind turned out to see it and a satisfying sliver of that number kept on looking upwards even after it had gone.

The fabulists soon got to work, claiming it had come for Wayman and that having sighted it once he departed in its wake. Stories require balance and so a prequel was swiftly tacked on, to the effect that the comet had previously appeared when he was born—the tale's been told before, of others; the fabulists are rarely original. What's more, when this bright beauty breached the horizon, Alfred Wayman had been dead for more than a week. It was all *twaddle*.

The Triumph of the Light

Fizzmonger

He never needed me. I served as his eyes, for a time, sat with him under cold skies and described the stars for him, though they were as familiar to him as any loved but no-longer-seen face. It was as if he needed to be reassured that they were still there. He wasn't yet ready to go back indoors and surrender the comfort of their light. But he never needed me. What had I ever been there for?

Glyn The Pin

When someone dies you want to reach out and touch them, even if that wasn't the way things were when they were still touchable. You want to call their name as if that will drag them back, to say sorry for all that you said or did, or failed or refused to say or do. You want to mend those old wounds, take back all the bad stuff you said, usually when they weren't there, and make everything better. Sounds silly, but you go through much the same as when you drop and break a glass, seeing it fall in time-lapse, then shatter and scatter, powdered, not coming back, no. Yeh, it's the same feeling, but broken glass is all done, swept and gotten over in quick-time prepared to how you feel about a person. With a person you just keep on regretting, even if you never knew them or liked them much. I suppose there are exceptions: Stitch Witcherson, I haven't a regret for him. Alan Brotherton too, but his kind's probably immune to death.

Fizzmonger

What have I come here for? I'm no comforter, no face-mopper. What can I do, I mean as an artist? Create a death mask? That would be new—for me. I so hate not having something to do, not having a function. I'm not a damn sitter and yet I sit with Wayman, in a closed room where neither of us see the stars. I could leave, I could. There is no light here, no artist's light. I'm not here to paint anyway, and I'm no nurse. There's one of those here, quite a tasty one; given a different light, I... She represents life, Wayman does not; he's not even still life. He's in shadow, that night-creature; when the shadow lifts then his time is up. His face, his face! The shadow softens it, suits it; a good face for nighttime, he always said so, I'm not a coward inflicting insults on the helpless. The curtains are closed, but when his eyes flicker open, though sightless they see through those curtains, beyond them. He doesn't even notice me, nor the rather paintable nurse (who, well, you never know, perhaps later when I'm less busy...). He sees all the way up, all the way up there. You know where.

Glyn The Pin

The picture is finished, the ugly picture of the ugly man; it was done with a while ago and yet the word is that the painter still goes to Wayman's at night. What for? Black masses, some say, witchy stuff, but I don't think two people makes a mass somehow. Spies, that's what they are, goes another whisper, shining lights to guide enemy planes, but when you ask what it's all for the whisperers don't really know, they're not even sure who the enemy is. Sex parties with Fastlane are another idea and if that's it good luck to them. Stitch Witcherson thinks it's sex too, 'Bumboys,' he says. 'You can tell 'em a mile off.' Mind you, Stitch thinks everyone's a bumboy, it gives him a reason for hitting them. He always likes to have a bit of a reason. But it's not any of that. I know what it is. Aliens is what it is. Wayman was snatched up by space aliens years ago and they took him on a rocket-ride then dumped him back. Now he sits out there every night raking the sky with his eyes, waiting for them to come back, because he doesn't wanna be stuck here anymore, what they showed him on that ride turned his wits, he thinks space is *better*. He could be right. Well, there's not much to be said for down here, is there?

Charles Durant Tobol
There had to be *something* that drove that relentless scouring of the sky. Wash-Hands, after characteristic dithering, decided that Wayman sought some form of fame. He was looking for a new object, a cold ice-rock trailing through the dark, he wanted to sight it, claim it, tag his name to it forever, to aggrandise and immortalise himself. That was the reason he kept on the painter to keep up the search when his own eyes failed him. 'Perhaps, for him, such tenebrous immortality would be entirely appropriate.' mused Old Wash-Hands.

Fizzmonger
It was my usual way—habit and instinct—to obtain something from each of my sitters, something rather more than just a fee and occasional rather fleeting gratitude; the satisfactions of knowing them more intimately than they had intended, that and other comforts. The one I could not paint, she put an end to that, turned me into something new I did not understand and for a while I

303

thought Wayman had turned me into something yet newer, though what that was I didn't know either. I certainly came to feel I had been serving some sort of penance under his tutelage, as what else would explain all those nights shivering devotedly at the eyepiece? Old habit-instinct revived itself when Wayman became helpless; I couldn't keep myself from visiting, hoping that he would be back there at the telescope, dogged, cantankerous and sky-minded as ever, but I was hoping not against hope but fact. I knew, and so did he, that he had gone indoors to die. Even as his sight faded he still turned his face to the night's dome until his night betrayed him, that ice-cold crystal fist that had previously hammered me while he brushed it aside carelessly, laid a crushing blow on him; it stole his breath and only parcelled it back grudgingly in increasingly painful little rasps as it filled his lungs with metallic cold.

No comforter, no face-mopper, but there present anyway, I cast about. I had never been much of a giver; admittedly, I granted Tobol his dearest wish and sat back to watch as he struggled with the consequences of his wishing and my giving. I was not about to treat Wayman like that, but now I wanted to profit from my investment in some way.

I found the reward for my patient devotion to the stars in a trunk, a plain pine trunk, long enough to lay a man inside, deep enough for two, inlaid with open drawers that lifted out in layers; unlike the house and even the books, it was more akin to the well-loved and kept observatory; order amongst chaos, maintained with the neatness and precision Wayman rarely espoused otherwise.

Layer by layer:

- a drawing board mounted with a bulldog clip and small bulb (with fresh, working battery mounted behind the clip) covered by red translucent paper
- a hoard of 2B and 4b pencils, India-rubber on a string, carbon pencils, coloured pencils, ink-pens, ink-bottles, brushes, paints
- stencils of the outlines of Jupiter and Saturn, the former carefully flattened at the poles, the latter providing for all orientations of the magnificent rings
- and in the lower depths, flat and preserved like beloved family albums, Wayman's sketch-books, filled with loving drawings of his sky with North-South orientation carefully indicated, the time of observation in Universal Time, the seeing conditions rated 1-5 on the Antonadi scale

All executed with almost prissy boy-scoutiness, the technocratic perfection that his beloved first-edition of *Practical Amateur Astronomy* would doubtless have demanded.

Perhaps I had made the mistake of listening too closely—indeed at all—to Tobol, who scorned Wayman's tossed-off caricatures as 'sub-adolescent,' and led me to believe he possessed no skill, co-ordination, mastery of the pencil-stroke, ink-nib or fine brush; his paintings of the heavens, said Tobol, made them look a more 'dull and uninviting place than they were already.' Interesting there had once been sufficient intimacy between them to allow Wayman to share his work, and, presumably, for him to grow wary of Tobol, coming to realise the man's true, contemptible nature. Wayman's little satires may have been chaotic schoolboy amateurism, but by contrast, these pages were masterpieces of loving care: the brush, the ink-pen, the pencil, plied with impeccable skill, delicacy and technique; it spoke of unwavering concentration and inexhaustible patience from preliminary sketch through to finished work: how Tobol must have seethed.

The drawings themselves were intended as coolly scientific, but achieved artistry; Wayman's Venus was given a background sky of indigo blue to denote its usual habitat of not-quite-night, the fleeting ashen light rendered as a reality and yet shimmering like a mirage even on the page, captured in a way I could not hope to achieve. Some of his carefully-prepared night backdrops were a beauteous wash of blue-black writing ink—every drop confiscated from delinquent schoolboys, I like to think—waiting for stars and planets to be couched in them as jewels in midnight velvet. The surface of his Mars had its polar caps rendered stark, clean, alien white, while the 'red' of the planet was a living, complex light-dark blend rendered in painstaking layers of coloured pencil. Jupiter, too, was a masterpiece of blended colours with the ingenious suggestion of animation in its swirling stormclouds, soapy-white spots in chains and multihued cloudlets like bubbles in a churning ocean. You can almost see the wild clouds surge and change as he pencils them, frantically keeping up with the giant planet's fast, dizzying spin. Saturn was rendered moodily, with the shadow of Titan cast harshly on its mysterious disc.

His stars were many and resplendent—single and bright, close patterns, burgeoning clusters of newborns trailing the vapours of their becoming, or swarming, inseparable stellar hives, double stars, triple stars, blue and yellow, white, purple, green, all a rebuke to my complaints about the dearth of cosmic colour. Wayman achieved things believed alien to him; subtlety and delicacy, wispy galaxies and gossamer filaments of nebula showed the fragility of their light to our weak, easily-dunned eyes, and yet something in the drawings brought realization of the true blazing power of these bodies, hidden by unimaginable distance.

Finally, it was in this collection of hidden, hoarded skies, I found confirmation not only of Wayman's ability to deceive and conceal but the existence of his secret mistress: here was her portrait painted time after time and always with the most loving and attentive of uxorious care. So he had fallen for the seductress, the Moon he affected so loudly to disdain. Pen-and-ink line drawings over a pencil base, initial sketches built on, toned and tinted and then filled out with colour, until they grew into studies of mood and shadow, the face of one deeply beloved, her beauty and blemishes, crags and depressions, the shadows of her peaks and ramparts rendered with cold precision: and yet in Wayman's hands this dead globe came alive, became precious metal, a jewel to desire, forever fascinating and alluring, so close and yet frustratingly unreachable. Wayman's lunar sketches included none of the full Moon: perhaps on those nights when it spilled its glare and overpowered his delicate sky, he really did sleep a full, deep eight hours—night-creature Wayman driven away by the power of the light.

But it was not just the technical merit of his work, nor the careful choice and use of materials. Wayman's earthbound sky-mission may have seemed romantically redundant in modern days of giant telescopes, space probes and computer-precision mapping of the heavens, but that is to underestimate what he brought. These were immediate, eye-of-the-beholder drawings; they put their viewer into the night's cold and at the telescope lens, there was no false feeling of flying through space to land on mysterious alien shores, you knew you were a small creature from a small place gazing in wonder at light that had travelled sometimes more than a hundred or a million human lifetimes. They were full of true perspective; they came the closest I had ever seen in any human work to discarding the illusions and delusions of the mind and eye, approaching that impossibility, truth. They conveyed an unselfish and uncynical love, filled you with an awed desire to see more, further, deeper, to extend the night without limit and resist the coming sun: at the very last they made the viewer into the artist. They made you, Wayman.

Glyn The Pin
Wayman didn't give up on people easy, even if they were total gits or hopeless cases (that's me, here I am—ta-da!). He'd try to get them interested in something, get them to realise it was worth learning, that things could be better if they did; he tried his rescue-mission on loads of us, only occasionally did he throw it in. He gave up on Stitch Witcherson, eventually and after a lot of sweat. It was probably when Stitch asked him in his usual aggressive growl-whine why Old Wash-Hands was 'always on about ponciest pilots' that Wayman ended up branding him Ignoramus Rex and letting him sink into that ol' morass of ignorance where he was at least happy; mad with frustration was Wayman at the way Stitch just cast off learning, remaining unteachably dense, as if afraid knowledge would damp down the churning mush of violence and hate in his

reinforced concrete noddle. There was no point trying to civilise, Romanise—or especially Waymanise—Stitch Witcherson.

Stitch's only talent was the ability to spot the teacher from far off and yell 'Youuuuuuu!' in a not-bad Wayman impression. But that was it, ability-wise. One day he was at Wayman's classroom and yelled it, 'Youuuuuu!' into the open doorway, bouncing it off all the walls, as Wayman was getting us all in. We waited for an explosion of rage from the madman, but he just tutted, shook his head sadly and muttered, 'Bah. Scum of the earth...' and then set off teaching at wild speed before we had even scattered to our seats. The only interesting thing that Stitch ever said, closest that he ever got to a thought of his own, was about Wayman. 'Jew,' said Stitch, whispering, serious and a bit afraid, 'E's a Jew.' This was all because Wayman ripped up the cover of his exercise book.

Okay, Stitch had one other talent, a bit of a one, he could draw a little, although Mr Tobol basically told him that he couldn't and to forget it. What Stitch liked to draw was that angry kick-legs thing, lashing in all directions, the Hitler-sign, you know. He liked drawing those and putting them in neat white circles (he had to use his compasses for something other than sticking into people) and then shading and filling-in carefully, giving the vicious kick-stick legs some real sharp edges as if he wanted them to razor people. His drawings looked quite good, in a sort of hard-metal way. That thing seemed to be all that was in Stitch's mind, though for myself I was amazed it was big enough even for that. Anyway, point is that Stitch was just finishing a 'specially fine version of his pet thing, presuming that Wayman was busy making us all laugh about how 'The

Duke of Monmouth was illegitimate—in other words a bassss-tarrrrd!' but under cover of the laughter and Stitch's concentration on his 'work' Wayman padded (imagine that if you can—but he did) up to Stitch's desk—back row right against the wall so no one could sneak up behind him, he had good basic cunning had Stitch—and by the time the teacher was on him, Stitch hadn't twigged, was still eyes down on his book, pen twitching, little tongue poking out the side of his mouth making him look stupid.

He looked even stupider as the book was snatched away and held high. He tried to paw at it to get it back, but Wayman shoved him back in his seat, shoved him hard: there was murder in Stitch's face, but shock and fear too. The back of his book, with its lovingly-created steely-pencilled drawing, was torn violently from its stapled spine, shredded by surprisingly fast-moving hands and hurled into the bin. The subject of the lesson got shredded too, moved away from the bassss-tard and replaced with a long tirade about "that thing!" A symbol, said the raging madman, of 'mass-death, murder of innocents of an organised clipboard, book-keeping factory sort, racial slaughter, hate as a plague, an infection dinned into children, war on an unprecedented scale and all by the filth who came up with your stupid little cave-drawing!' and, Wayman added, 'all led off by a monotesticled lunatic, an inadequate, a failure at everything, author of a *very* boring book, and who as a soldier only fired one worthwhile bullet in his miserable little life!'

Got that, Witcherson, eh? Eh? Eh?

All of this didn't stop Stitch carrying on drawing them on desks, books, walls, but he never again did it anywhere near Wayman and he wasn't so keen on doing his youuuuu shouts neither.

'But it's proof,' muttered Stitch, 'he must of come here running like they did—bluddy ref-you-gee, he's a fuckin' Jew. Got to be. Who else would be so bothered?'

Glyn Capstone

It's a funny feeling when you hear that an old teacher has died. Admittedly the feeling I got was not the same as Jon Mealing's when he heard that Gordon Harley the PE master had died; Jon searched far and wide to find the old man's grave to dance on it: he had issues, Jon. No, the feeling I got was the same as—similar to, anyway—the catch you get in your mind when you recall something far, far off away in time, which comes before your eyes (behind your eyes maybe) again just for a brief moment until it's gone and you know you'll probably never get it back. Yes, that feeling, with a flavour of regret, a wish to see that teacher again, to talk as adults, equals and maybe, as in my case, give some backdated apologies.

I was just a few years into my inglorious careen, long enough to know it for what it was, when I walked into a pub, a casual visit just for a mouth-washer on a hot day, and there they were, four of them, round one table, chatting merrily. It must have been one of their much-storied elbows-up sessions of a Friday. There were many tales of booze-fuelled lunches and beer-stinking teachers weaving and incoherent before crammed classrooms, although oddly enough the person telling the story had never seen it himself, it was always someone else, but someone who had no reason to lie.

For once invisibility didn't betray me, I clocked them but they didn't see me and, well, I kept out of their sight, praying for the blessing of bending light to remain with me: *that* feeling took me back to school, especially the workshop where I mangled wood and metal and tried to hide my "work" from all eyes. There was another bar on the other side of the pub, so I got myself nicely positioned where I could take sneaky looks like a naturalist in a hide; I was curious and curiously nervous—I'd realised something after the initial shock of seeing them all in a gang like that: I wasn't their enemy, nor were any of them mine—not any longer, anyway. They weren't to be run or hid from, they weren't idiots or monsters or annoying distorting-mirrors of all that's wrong with parents (or Auntypoos, in my case), they were… well, you know. I got halfway down my drink when I felt the pull, so strong: *go and say something, you've heard that teachers like to be recognised years later, just avoid saying something prattish like, 'Hey, didn't you use to be Mr Wayman?' and everything will be alright.*

He was there, unchanged far as I could see, Miss Fastlane too, Mrs Whatevershewas by then, a little mumsy, a teeny chinny maybe, but still va-va-voom, still with the hair and the dimples and the gap-tooth thing going on. I'd still —you know—even though the sweaters were gone and she wore baggier stuff that lost her shape, plus there were a few lines I didn't remember her having. The shiny-circle interruption on her finger was the final sign she'd gone respectable. Mr Careers too, looking as if his own was well beyond its proper end; he'd aged a hundred years: fagged-out, terminally disappointed. Little Weisel sat with them, grey and frazzled-looking, he was, an un-still life of tics and twitches, some of which I recognised from the old days (neck stretching back and forth, making his hands into a tent over and over) and some that had come on (jutting out his lower jaw and baring his teeth out in, out in, holding a hand before his face, watching it tremble uncontrollably, dropping it again—god, I thought, we probably caused some of this). Notably not there was Old Wash-Hands; typical he kept away from them, he probably had a holy-holy disapproval of drink; he disapproved of most fun, he did, as I recall him. Or maybe he wasn't there because he was dead. I had to get used to the idea teachers could die. I hadn't been free from school all that long and the concept was still a newie to me, that teachers live human and die human, that they're *us*. I had also come to the uncomfortable conclusion I was sort-of on their side, and always had been (though that could have been me back-filling history, like people do; you couldn't have told me that at age eleven, nor thirteen nor probably even sixteen-seventeen). That realization, if that's what it was, had arrived too bloody late to be any good to me, which was typical of life in general really.

It was Wayman who defeated my cover of light and spotted me; I had grown too confident and curious maybe, I'd betrayed myself. He waved, then beckoned, echoing his old "c'mere boy!" gesture, the one that got me Romanised. Then came a gesture I had not seen before—from him anyway—arm up, hand around an invisible glass, tilt-tilt, question-mark. Well; in schoolday-talk, I bricked it. Oh sure I felt the pull, the fascination of spending just a little time with those people, as equals, grownups, humans. But I got scared; I made a panicky excuse and fled. I had my chance and failed. Again.

I add this to my life's long list of what-ifs and should-have-dones. We're all ruled by them, forever. I try to think of how that encounter would have turned out had I possessed the least courage. I could have sat with them, if only for a little while, as an adult among adults, as... their friend? Stupid, I know, but the thought comes to me and keeps on coming, it's like, it's hard to describe, it falls somewhere between a worn-out old movie and recurring dream. It's a lucid dream, if so, because I add bits, dock others, I keep trying out new angles, I even draft in extra people, ones who had no business being there, whose presence was barred by simple impossibility. Sometimes new scenes, new people, add themselves; whether it's a film or dream; I'm not completely in control, sometimes not at all.

Wayman waves me to a chair; it should be friendly but feels like an interview, an interrogation. Wayman and Fastlane are in front of me, Weisel on my right, Mr Careers on my left. All others who pass by are intruders, ghosts.

'So,' says a cheery Wayman, 'Mr Capstone. Glyn. Tell us what a brilliant success you made of your life. Help us to feel that we weren't just wasting our time, lavishing our care, plus all that fantastic, shiny education, on you.'

Old Wash Hands, who has no business to do so, pops up like a spectre: 'Stop encouraging him, Alfie. Shame on you for trying to turn back the waves yet again! He's a secmod boy. You should have let him slither back into it, that morass whence he came, now leave it be!'

He turns to me. 'You disappointed him, boy, but you confirmed my opinion of you. Thank you for proving me right—but, most of all, for proving *him* wrong.' And then the old man vanishes, ghosted.

Mr Careers nods in grim concurrence. 'From what I hear, this young man has been in the best of offices and the biggest of boardrooms! Cleaning the desks, mainly. Huh, the career-track of a pinball. It's your own fault boy. You dawdled. You dossed. You let others raid the boxes and take the good stuff. You never knew which boxes to look in; that was the secret, knowing the best boxes.'

Wayman looks at me sadly. 'How could you let it go so wrong—all that promise, that potential?'

Fastlane pats his hand to shut him up, it's a wifely gesture I think. 'It's confidence; lack of self-confidence, that's what always lets people down. That is the real enemy.'

'It was really other people's lack of confidence in me. It's hard to be confident in someone's ability when you're not really sure they even exist.'

They don't look remotely impressed at my self-defence. I'm not doing well.

Little Weisel is up next: he has the sad face of the eternal victim, the vengeful eye of an accuser. 'It was *him*, him and his accursed classmates, them and their constant noise, singing and chanting in class, never listening to a word I said, even fighting one another, right in front of me! They caused my breakdown, the first one. I prided myself —*prided* myself—that I had never sworn in my life, no matter the pain, no matter the provocation—it was far more to me than just honour. They knew, they *knew* I was coming back to work after *they* had broken my health, but did they relent, did they show mercy, a shred of human feeling? No! The chanting, the dissonant adolescent singing, it returned with more intent, more venom than ever. "*We are eeeee-villl, we will killllll yoooooou, Mr Weaselllllllll!*". His eyes are full of tears. Fastlane's too. Wayman looks ready to kill:

to kill *me*. I remembered all that chanting, the thrill of being part of the howling gang. I used to think it was so funny, that we were all so big and hard, with that little man standing before us, shaking with impotent rage, raging impotence.

'How my fury grew! I tried one last act of self-restraint, I gave them ten seconds to sit and be quiet; as one creature (which is very much what they were) they fell silent, they took a long and cunning beat, sufficient to make me believe for a split second I had finally tamed them, and then; *"We are eeeee-villl, we will killllll yoooooou, Mr Weeeeaselllllllll"* it was soft at first, then built to a crescendo, to climax; there was nothing in my world but their cruel young voices. I bellowed above their din, 'By… *jingo* I'm really *livid* now!' It was a last-ditch, desperate measure, intended to terrify, and one doomed to fail; I was white-faced, on the verge of cardiac arrest, surely they would take me seriously? But ah no, they laughed, viciously, loudly, freely and cruelly, and then the devil took the floor, and me also; the voice that emerged from my mouth was not me, not mine.

'All right, you fucking want *trouble?* I'll give you little bastards *trouble!'* and with that I deliberately flung myself at the biggest, toughest, nastiest character, grabbed him by his needle-points of short bully's hair and hauled him up; I saw his bulging, watering eyes, his gaping mouth, no longer mocking and felt I could fling him bodily over my head and through the window. In an instant I became aware of my capacity for murder, my relish for the idea. I have never forgiven myself for learning that I harboured such a capability, such base animal bloodlust.'

'The room, seconds before in the throes of riot, went shockingly quiet and a savage glee grew within me: I had done it, had done it! I dropped the boy back down, realizing how heavy a lump he was. He glared his brutish spite at me, but then, a miracle, he broke, he burst into childish tears. At that point the laughter returned, the cold, vicious boy-child mockery, and with shame I realised they were no longer laughing at me, it was now their classmate who was the target of their peevish shrieks. I had bought fleeting respect from that feral pack, but at the price of my soul.'

'God, I remember it all. We didn't respect you for that— sir—you were a fucking hero. Nobody ever in the world had made Stitch Witcherson cry.' We never got a chance to laugh at Stitch again, he made sure of that.

'My second breakdown followed,' says Weisel mournfully. 'And my third when you all goaded me unmercifully to get me to do the same thing again.'

'Sorry sir.'

Fastlane tries to smooth things a little, but it doesn't go well.

'What became of that tall girl, your partner in crime?'

Wayman growls. 'Crime indeed, your stupid star-struck "strike!" And you never even looked up at the true stars...'

Fastlane pats his hand again, more sharply, so wifely she is, surely they're an item. 'Hush, Alfred dear. You were head over heels in love with her weren't you, Glyn? We all knew it. Also, you could never have managed that strike without her; if she'd not been there to egg you on you could never have done it at all. Now, did you ever gather the courage to ask her?'

'I meant to, always mean to. It didn't happen. But she barely noticed me, I never found a situation where the light favoured me... then I found out she'd got a boyfriend anyway, he'd moved to a private school a while before, clever bastard he was, dead-lucky too. Creep by the name of Brotherton.'

'Who?'

'Never mind.'

'Did you finally beat your, er, light-wave problem? Did you meet a nice young lady, did you settle down?'

'I met a few, Miss, hovered round them waiting for them to notice me, but usually it went no further than that. I got lucky once, got seen, got married, it was okay for a while but eventually even her gaze slipped off me and fairly quickly lit on someone else. Another Brotherton.'

Wayman keeps up the pressure. 'You didn't become an historian; you couldn't even manage that? Little Jilly Holdenbridge did, just as I predicted. *Doctor* Holdenbridge she is now, University of Reading, no less.'

'Sorry sir. Somehow that never came about for me. To be honest not much came about. But I've learned why the losers never write histories—even if they survive, they're too busy getting on with it, surviving I mean, just hanging on. Plus they're too embarrassed to admit the truth.'

Careers addresses his glass, 'Looked in the wrong boxes, just like I said.'

'You shouldn't have fled in the face of those exams. Knowledge is power.' pontificates Wayman.

'And money,' adds Careers.

'But it's no good just knowing things sir, it's no good having the certificates, they're just paper.'

'Tell that to *Doctor* Holdenbridge. You never got any decent qualifications at all, did you? It helps if you don't run out on the exams, the ones that matter, the ones that could help get you somewhere, make you someone.'

'But it still isn't enough, sir. They find other ways to stop you. Species Grogan could out-science anyone in the country but he freaked out at uni and nearly quit because he didn't know how to hold a fork properly. They made him miserable for that—just for that, nothing to do with his sciencing. He wanted to be a top prof, but they said how can you be a top prof when you don't know how to hold a fork? Doesn't make any bloody sense—sir.'

'It's tough at the top,' chips in Careers, harshly. I ignore him, pleading direct to Wayman and Fastlane.

'I didn't just need papers, I needed a little flash of cash behind me and within me I needed…'

'Confidence.' Fastlane caps me, as if she's selling the stuff. And I bet she finishes her husband's sentences for him too.

'Well yeah, but also something else, the ability, the power to… to make little bulbs flare bright using just your fingers and look like you're not even trying.'

'Eh?' expresses all their faces.

'Never mind. I mean something that I never had, something even you couldn't give.'

Wayman sighs. 'You disappointed my hopes, ruined my record for rescues of the hopeless. Dammit, I even tamed that crazy painter. I have only two major failures blotting my record—you and Ignoramus Rex. That's not good company to be in, son.'

'Sorry sirs; Miss.'

All: *'Jeh.'*

Fizzmonger

Now, allow me to be a little romantic: where I mentioned the 'technical merit' of those sketch books awash with

319

stars, read 'beauty' instead, deep, startling beauty. On seeing Wayman's work, I encountered an unfamiliar sensation , though I suspect it was a daily dish for the likes of Tobol. As an artist, I felt overawed, outclassed, envious. I had attempted the same subjects, offered my work to Wayman like an eager pupil and he, benign, comfortable in his easy superiority, had nodded his approval and said nothing. And now let me be myself, satisfying my habit and instinct. The drawings were not signed, after all they were never intended to be seen and admired, but I always could place a value on beauty and although never meant for sale by their creator, they could certainly be made so by his accidental beneficiary. I was able to add a signature to each piece, doing for myself, in a way, what I did for Tobol. How Wayman would have raged at the marketeering of his stars, but I deserved my reward: after all, had I not put in the hard work? Very well, it shows my own capacity to deceive, but it was a minor and harmless deception, victimless; the beauty of the work remained unsullied even by my appropriation and monetisation of that which Wayman regarded beyond price.

Evelyn Lawton

I hadn't seen Sabina in a long time, but her arrival at my door was appropriate and unsurprising. We said little; what words were available to us? We sat for a long time and I held her hand—or she mine, does it matter?—and then she took her leave, to return to her family. I returned to the task that my visitor had interrupted, packing my bags ready for another journey, to visit stars Alfred never saw.

Wayman was restless, incoherent. At one point he seemed awake, demanding peevishly, 'Who let them in here?' Both the nurse and I were taken aback.

'Who let them in?' snapped Wayman again, 'Tobol and Old Wash-Hands, parading by my bed like spectres, what did they want?' He wouldn't hear of it that they had never been there, he had seen them plainly, 'In future keep 'em out. I've nothing to say to them. But if the boy comes back, tell him I want to see him. I've something to say.' Gently, I asked him who was this boy, but he had already relapsed into semi-coma.

I tried repeatedly to think of an excuse to get up and leave; to be true to my nature and fair to myself I should have left, taken advantage of his state of unknowing and walked away, taking my prizes. And yet I remained. He was struggling, struggling for something—against something? It was as the dawn light crept in I came to understand: he could not see the stars and yet would not surrender until the night was done. Now that darkness was abolished, the struggle could end, and he could close his eyes.

It was the final triumph of the light.

LEAF BY LEAF